EVERYBODY NEEDS A HERO

KC LUCK

1

Catching her reflection in the glass for a moment, Tess Landish didn't like what she saw—an aging actress without any makeup and too much gray in her long, golden-blonde hair. The appointment scheduled for later in the day with Raul, her fabulous hairstylist, would take care of the latter. There was nothing to be done about the former. At forty-six, Tess knew she was pushing the outermost edge of the celebrity envelope for desirable leading roles. Only her stunning track record of box office hits kept her in the running at all, but over eighteen months had passed since her last job, and she had started to worry. No matter how many promises her longtime manager made that she had a lot of years in front of the movie cameras ahead of her, Tess didn't believe him. Until the last offer cropped up out of practically nowhere, because of another actress literally breaking a leg, the horizon looked bleak. *But no longer*, she thought. Tomorrow morning, Tess was back to work—day one of principal filming on a movie Hollywood critics were already buzzing about.

Learning the one hundred and twenty-seven-page script

in such a rush had been a daunting effort, but her experience in the entertainment industry memorizing lines served her well. Seventy-two hours of mad cramming, and she would be able to get by with few or no prompts. The director was an old friend too, which would help her acclimate to the movie's cast and crew quickly. She had no idea other than the name of her co-lead and a few other supporting cast as to who was making the magic happen, but it was no matter. After over two decades in Hollywood, she was familiar with pretty much all the major talent. Not that it truly mattered who was who. Tess was thankful to have the job as a lead on a big-budget feature. She wasn't ready to be relegated to "mom" roles or other supporting characters. Not yet.

"Chai tea latte, skim, extra vanilla, and not too hot," Tess's daughter said as she slid open the patio doors to join her mother outside. She set a white ceramic mug on the large teak patio table. "Just the way you like it."

Tess looked at the beautiful, blonde-haired young woman who was the light of her life—Ashley Landish, her twenty-eight-year-old daughter. Even though Tess had been barely eighteen and nothing but a starstruck, aspiring actress when a one-night stand with a married casting agent got her pregnant, she never regretted her decision to have Ashley. Of course, her own agent had dropped her as a prospect the minute she announced she was keeping the baby, and the casting agent father refused to acknowledge he had ever even met her. That had been a scary time for Tess, and it looked like all her hopes of being a big-name movie star were over. Yet, fortune shined on her, and through a friend of a friend, she landed a job as a commercial voiceover actress. The hours were long, and the pay wasn't much, but it covered the rent of the shabby studio in Inglewood and kept her in the business. Looking back on all the priceless memories with her baby girl, as difficult as life was at the time, Tess wouldn't change a thing. The challenges made her appreciate her later success and even more gave her the wonderment of raising an exceptional child.

"Thank you, sweetheart," Tess said as Ashley slipped into the padded patio chair at the table. "You are so talented at that espresso machine."

Ashley laughed. "I would hope so," she said with a smile. "I've been running my own coffee shop for three years now."

Tess smiled in return. What she said was true. Her daughter wanted nothing to do with show business. Even though she was stunningly attractive like her mother and charismatic in a way that made her coffee shop customers adore her, Ashley had turned her back on the entertainment industry. Scouts had circled promising all kinds of roles, but Tess shooed them away. She insisted her daughter follow her own path as a businesswoman. Ashley's first venture, Landish Coffee, did extremely well as a shop along the famous Venice Beach boardwalk, and Tess could not be prouder of all she had accomplished.

FINGERING her own mug of chai latte, Ashley regarded her mom over the patio table. She loved seeing the spark back in her famous blue eyes. The last year and a half had been rough to watch as no real jobs materialized for the once highly sought-after actress Tess Landish. Talking and texting multiple times every day, Ashley was very aware of how much her mom struggled with growing older. At only twenty-eight, she couldn't quite comprehend the fear of being cast aside for younger actors, but she remained ever reassuring. "Something will come along," Ashley said to her mom like a mantra. "It always does. You are Tess Landish. Everyone loves you."

And she had been right. A spectacular opportunity landed

right in her mother's lap. Even though Tess appeared to have no clue about the book the movie was based on, Ashley had read the novel and loved it. The author, Drew Andersen, seemed to come out of nowhere to write a runaway hit and rule the New York Times bestseller list for months. What the critics called the book of the century was a heart-wrenching love story between a cynical, alcoholic nurse and a legendary actor fighting to hide his onsetting dementia. Ashley only hoped the book's adaptation and her mother in the challenging role of the nurse would do it justice.

"How are you feeling?" Ashley asked. "You holed up here in your house memorizing that script for three days. We hardly had any contact, and I was beginning to worry you'd fallen off the face of the Earth."

Tess put her hand over Ashley's. "I know," she said with a smile that lit up her face. "I missed you. But thank you for providing me caffeine nonstop. Having your staff run over here all the way from Venice Beach to keep me fortified was an absolute lifesaver. You have no idea."

Ashley smiled back, and their faces flashed such a resemblance that people never missed guessing they were related. Even though she almost always wore her long hair up in a messy bun and toned down any makeup, at least once a day, a customer noticed Ashley and asked if it was possible she was Tess's daughter. Occasionally, the fact irritated Ashley, particularly when she was in the middle of running her coffee shop, because there would be a million questions about her famous mom. Still, she never hid who she was because, in the end, she loved being Tess Landish's child. Her mom was a fantastic woman, and Ashley was proud of her. Not only talented and a huge success, but warm, caring, and always there for her.

Especially when it came to heartbreak over another of Ashley's failed relationships. One downside of looking gorgeous like her mother was finding a partner who wanted her for something more than her looks. Or her supposed contacts with the entertainment industry—something that didn't exist. Besides, Ashley had never brought a woman home to meet her mother. No one had yet come close to meeting that standard. Her mom was everything to her, and she would never expose Tess to some starstruck fan with their amateur movie script hidden under their coat.

"You know I'm super excited for you to have the role," Ashley said. "I wish you'd had time to read the amazing book, though. Even at almost seven hundred pages, the story was worth every minute."

Tess picked up her latte. "That's not always a good strategy. It might put an idea in my head of how the role should be played," she said before taking a sip and licking her lips. "And it might not align with what the director wants."

"I suppose that's true," Ashley admitted but furrowed her brow. "But it really is an amazing love story."

"I'm sure it is," Tess said with a twinkle in her eye. "All the more reason I'm thrilled to be the one playing the role. We might be up for a run at awards season after this."

Picking up her own latte, Ashley held it up as a toast. "Then, let's drink to that," she said as her mom laughed but touched their mugs together.

"It's not champagne, but why not?" Tess said. "Hopefully, there will be plenty of bubbly in the near future."

ON HER THIRTIETH BIRTHDAY, Bryce stood at the edge of the dirt and noticed grass was starting to take hold in places. Considering the unusually high temperatures, especially for March, she considered it a good sign. Watered every day by the rotary sprinklers she heard working in the distance helped. Before long, the patch would be another indistinct grave in the vast green lawn of Bakersfield's Hillcrest Memorial Cemetery. Only the marble headstone she picked out would mark the spot where her dad, Donald Cooper rested. Looking at it, Bryce read the simple text she picked to etch onto the stone. 'Donald Allen Cooper. A Good Man Taken Too Soon.' Underneath were the dates of his birth and his death. He had been fifty-three, and the once hearty and healthy man Bryce remembered withered to nothing from liver cancer.

Wiping away a bead of sweat that trickled down her temple, Bryce didn't cry. In fact, she'd only cried once in a long, ugly, middle-of-the-night bout of pure anguish. That was all. Every other moment from when she returned home three months ago to start taking care of him until they put him in the ground, she was solid. No one was surprised that she didn't shed a tear. Bryce was a United States Marine, trained to withstand any kind of pain, even emotional. That didn't mean she was emotionless, though, and her eyes lingered over the three words—taken too soon. They reemphasized something Bryce had already started to figure out after her first mission in the Marine Corps. Life was short and death was unpredictable.

"Goodbye, Dad," she said, not sure when she would be back to visit his gravesite again. There were some things she needed to take care of a hundred miles away in Los Angeles and resolving them might take a while. Or at least she hoped they would. And then there was the state of things with the Marines, and she had to consider what happened next in her career. She was due for reenlistment, and the Marine Corps was considerate enough to let her use extra leave to care for her dad. Their expectation was she would be back, especially after training her to be a reconnaissance specialist, but Bryce was no longer sure what she wanted to do with her life. With her dad gone, no brothers or sisters, and her mom long since remarried to a man Bryce didn't get along with, the military was the only family she had left. It seemed an easy decision for her to reenlist tomorrow and continue to work her way up the chain of command.

Only one thing made her hesitate to pull out her phone and tell her captain to start the official paperwork. It was something with an outcome that would most likely amount to nothing. Still, she was too tempted to deny how she felt. All it required was getting in her dad's old Ford pickup and making a quick trip to Los Angeles to visit a particular coffee shop. Although Bryce had never been there, she knew where the place was after googling the owner one lonely night in the middle of some Godforsaken country—Venice Beach.

Reading of the business owner's success had not surprised her. The woman who ran the shop was brilliant, and when they were in college together, showed she had a head for business. When they worked as a team on class projects, starting a coffee shop in a popular tourist location was always the woman's plan. For some reason she could not seem to deny, Bryce wanted to see the result. But the desire was more than that. She also needed to see the owner one more time and maybe, just maybe, find the courage to tell Ashley Landish how she felt.

2

Standing on the carpet in front of the oversized mahogany desk in the movie producer's plush office, Drew Andersen's head spun from what she heard coming out of the man's mouth. She had to be in the middle of her worst nightmare, because what he said was nothing short of absurd.

"I know you're upset," the producer said with his beefy hands held in a manner apparently meant to pacify Drew. "But there was absolutely nothing I could do. We are already over budget, and shooting can't delay any longer."

When Drew didn't respond, his lips pressed into a tight line, and she could almost read his mind. *Why are writers always so damn difficult?* His opinion wasn't fair though, because Drew had done her best from the start to be flexible with the film adaptation while keeping the core of her book's story intact. But she was only willing to go so far. Enough was enough.

Crossing her arms, Drew stood up to her full five-foot-two height and prepared for battle. "And if I say no to your crazy change?" she asked, eyes narrowed. "Then what happens to the movie?"

The producer sighed as he pinched the bridge of his nose with his thumb and forefinger. "Then I reach into my drawer, pull out the contract you signed four months ago, and explain you don't have a real choice," he answered. "In case you didn't read the fine print, the final say as to who is cast in the role is mine."

Feeling her face start to flush from anger, Drew lifted her chin. "You're really going to do this to me?" she asked, trying to hold her temper in check a little longer. As much as she wanted to blast the man for pulling a fast one on her, letting go of her emotions wouldn't help her case. "There's got to be someone else. Anybody."

Shaking his head, the producer pulled a glossy headshot off a pile of tattered scripts on his desk and held it up for her to see. The face looking back at Drew was of a startlingly beautiful woman who was immediately recognizable. "I don't understand why you are so upset," he said, giving the picture a shake. "Tess Landish is an A-list actress, and her name alone will help ticket sales."

Drew didn't care about ticket sales or how many millions the thing made at the box office. *This can't be happening*, she thought, working to keep her breathing even though she was ready to scream. All she wanted was for the movie to be quality. "We searched for three months and held a hundred auditions to cast the two lead actors," she said through clenched teeth. "Having that actress as the nurse will change the entire feel of the movie. Can you see her as a gritty nurse facing an impossible situation?" She shook her head. "Because I sure can't. This is a huge mistake, and you know it."

With an exhale of clear exasperation, the producer dropped the picture back on his desk and met Drew's eye.

The frustration in his look was unmistakable. "No, I don't know it. In fact, I completely disagree," he said. "Trust me. Tess is a pro. You'll see in the morning."

Without another word, Drew stormed out of the office, slamming the door behind her. If that was the hand dealt to her, she would find a way to make it work. If she was anything, she was resourceful. Twenty years as an emergency room nurse in Los Angeles was no joke. *Tess Landish doesn't know what she signed up for*, she thought, marching down the hallway. Drew planned to push the woman to the limit of her skills no matter what the producer or the director might say. Slapping the elevator button to go back to her car, she resolved to squeeze the true heart of the role out of the actress. If it meant being in Tess Landish's face every second, Drew was willing to do it. Anything to protect the story that took her ten years to write. Her heart was in that story. The book was her baby, and the message on the pages needed to be shared. Blasting through the skyrise's lobby, past the security guard, and out the revolving door, Drew squared her shoulders. She sure as hell wouldn't let some diva ruin it.

"HAVE A GOOD NIGHT, KIM," Ashley called from the doorway as she waved to the barista at the espresso machine behind the high, wooden counter. "Text me if anything comes up."

Kim smiled in her direction, but her hands were busy making a latte for a waiting customer. "No problem, boss," she said over the hiss of steam. "Thanks for coming in at the last minute to cover for Elle. I hated to call on Sunday."

"Not a problem. I hope she's okay," Ashley said before slipping out the glass door onto the sidewalk and stretching her legs. A nice long run along the beach path was exactly what she needed to work out her tight muscles. Four hours of making ice coffees and other hot or cold beverages for the nonstop tourist crowd might make some people want to get off their feet, but that was never the case with her. Ashley loved to be in motion and attributed part of her success with the coffee shop to her ability to go long hours on her feet. When she first started the business, it was her and only her behind the counter. Twelve-hour days, seven days a week for the first six months. Even though the work was exhausting, seeing her dream come true made it easy to keep going. Three years later, she had a staff of four and most weekends off.

Starting a light jog to warm up, Ashley passed the other businesses along the Venice Beach boardwalk. There was an eclectic mix of stores of all shapes and sizes. Souvenir shops selling t-shirts with every imaginable saying on them. A famous tattoo parlor. A thirty-three flavors ice cream shop. She felt energized by the mixture and smiled when a man in a turban and white pantsuit playing an electric guitar rollerbladed past her. As she kept going, she noticed the different street artists along the path were packing up their supplies. A couple, who often came to her shop for coffee, waved to her, and she returned it before coming to the famous Muscle Beach outdoor gym. As the sun would set soon, only a few bodybuilders remained lifting remarkable numbers of metal plates on bars with what appeared to be ease.

Ashley slowed and started jogging in place. "Hey, Lou," she called to the muscle-bound man closest to the metal railing surrounding the space. "The protein powder you wanted came in. Come by tomorrow and take one of our new smoothy recipes for a test spin."

Lou grinned, his white teeth seeming to glow against the deep, dark tan of his face. "Can't wait," he said. "Strawberry?"

"Yes, just like you asked for. Strawberry," Ashley confirmed as she picked up her pace again. The cement path widened before her, leaving space for bicycles on one side and runners or walkers on the other. She only had one more person to check in with before the three-mile run north to Santa Monica. Up ahead, a woman wrapped in pieces of a red and white checked blanket over a gray sweatshirt and dirty jeans sat in a mishmash of belongings at the edge of the route. A ratty, LA Dodgers, blue baseball cap covered greasy hair pulled back into a ponytail, and a tattered cardboard sign asked for donations to feed her dog. By Ashley's estimate over the last few months, the black and white pooch who sat patiently beside the woman had to be one of the best fed in Los Angeles. Slowing as she approached them, Ashley held out a small white paper sack. "Hi, Bev. Hi, Floyd."

The woman gave Ashley a wide smile with only a few teeth missing among her stained ones. "Hi, honey," Bev replied as she reached to take the offering. "You're too good to us."

Ashley winked. "Good karma," she said, knowing the freshly made banana nut muffin for Bev and the pumpkin dog biscuits for Floyd would make their evening a little nicer.

"You'll have plenty as far as I can tell," Bev called after Ashley as she lengthened her stride. Although her life was great, she didn't mind the sound of that.

Staying in the slow lane, Bryce nursed her dad's old pickup truck up the long hill that separated the Los Angeles Valley from cities to the north. Six miles of steep incline known as the Grapevine, notorious for bringing truckers to a slow crawl and indiscriminately overheating engines. As the sun started to go down, Bryce tried hard to avoid the latter, although the temp gauge on the dash flirted with disaster. As she passed yet another sedan on the side of the highway with steam billowing out from under the hood, she checked the odometer to see how many miles were left. Only one more. Then she would be over the top and cruising down into the valley. Forcing herself to relax her hands on the wheel, she made herself focus on what she would say to Ashley when she finally saw her again after all that time. After years of replaying it, Bryce had the scene set in her mind. Going by the coffee shop, ordering something simple off the menu, and hoping against hope Ashley recognized her. If the woman didn't, that would be that.

Although she trained in the Marine Corps to always have a Plan B, in this case there wasn't one. Bryce needed Ashley to at least remember her enough to say hello if they ran into each other on the street. Hoping for a romantic spark seemed a bit farfetched, but there had to be at least something there for Bryce to run with. Of course, there was no reason she couldn't be the one to initiate a recollection. Yet in her heart, she knew that if their time in college together didn't make enough of a lasting impression on Ashley for her to recognize Bryce when brought face to face, then any hope for more was unlikely. Instead, Bryce would slip away with her coffee and go back to her life in the military. Ashley would never be the wiser, and maybe Bryce would finally be able to move on. Maybe be able to put away the fantasy they made a connection during all those long, late-night homework sessions together.

Only once had Bryce ever tried to broach the subject of how she felt about Ashley. They had celebrated the end of a term with other classmates in a bar near the college campus. It was a bittersweet gathering for Bryce, because the next day she was driving to Bakersfield to see her dad before leaving to start Marine Corps basic training. Due to circumstances outside of his control, her father explained to her the college money had run out and finishing even one more term was out of the question.

After several tequila shots with beer chasers, Bryce had felt fortified with liquid courage. When Ashley declared it was time for her to go, Bryce made a point of leaving at the same time and walked the woman to her car. Standing in the parking lot with only the glow of a single blue security light nearby, Bryce tried to find the right words to tell Ashley how much she meant to her. The words didn't come. As if sensing her struggle, Ashley smiled as she ran a hand up Bryce's arm. "You're amazing, Bryce," she said. "I don't know how I will get along without you."

Bryce nodded, desperate not to let the moment pass before she told Ashley what was in her heart. "So are you," was all she came up with, and then Ashley was kissing her on the cheek and climbing into her car.

"Be safe," Ashley said before driving away leaving Bryce standing alone in the near dark wondering how she let Ashley get away.

Taking a slow, deep breath, Bryce steered around a creeping eighteen-wheeler and was thankful for the green Tejon Pass road exit sign ahead. Her truck had made the challenging climb, and she shifted through the gears as the vehicle picked up speed to make the long run downhill. She considered it a good sign to have surpassed that first obstacle on her quest. In another thirty minutes she would be at her motel. Being on a tight budget, it wasn't much in the way of luxury, but at least it was on the west side of the city. That put her not too far from the Venice Beach boardwalk and the place she needed to visit. In the morning, she would go to the Landish Coffee shop and roll the dice.

3

Tess took a deep breath, lifted her chin, and focused on the woman with short brown hair sitting in a chair across the parking lot from her. She sat near where the film crew worked to set up the movie's first shot. Thankfully, Tess didn't think she looked at all intimidating in her khaki shorts, green tennis shirt, and black hoodie. Her attention concentrated on a large open binder on her lap, which made sense. After all, the woman was not only the author of the book the script came from, but also the screenwriter, and so she would be interested in the upcoming scene. *The talented Drew Andersen,* Tess thought. *Who apparently already doesn't like me.* As soon as Tess arrived, the movie producer advised her that Drew was not a fan of her work. That had come as a bit of an ambush when she had only been on the set five minutes. Not that she expected the cast and crew to look to her as a hero for stepping in to help the production, but outright hostility from the writer could be a real problem. So, she planned to fix it.

Starting to walk across the parking lot, ready to turn on every ounce of her charm, Tess was about to call out a hello when the movie's director intercepted her. "Tess," he said, walking toward her with a warm smile crossing his face. "It's terrific to see you." Turning to return the director's greeting, out of the corner of her eye, Tess saw Drew's head whip up and a scowl settle on her face.

With a sigh at the unlucky turn, Tess looked at the director. "Hello," she said. "I'm glad to be here."

"Thank you for being flexible and bailing us out," the director said. "But shouldn't you be headed to hair and makeup? We can catch up later."

"In a second," Tess said, looking in Drew's direction. "I wanted to introduce myself to the brilliant author whose book the movie is based on." If the woman heard the compliment, it didn't register on her face. Even though she had refocused on the binder, the scowl was still in place.

"Well, let me introduce you," the director said, walking with Tess as they approached where the author sat. As they did, Drew's brown eyes lifted, holding a cold stare that didn't waver, but Tess didn't drop her eyes. As much as she wanted to be friends with the woman, she wouldn't be intimidated. She had too many years of experience in the industry to succumb to that. The director held out a hand to point at the author. "Tess, this is Drew Andersen." He waited for a beat, and when neither woman spoke, he cleared his throat and nodded toward Tess. "And this is—"

"I know who she is," Drew snapped, her tone surprising Tess even after the cold stare. "Most of the world knows who she is, and that's the problem I keep trying to explain to everyone."

Eyebrows raised, Tess didn't immediately know how to respond, especially in the face of Drew's brown-eyed glare. *Intense and beautiful eyes actually*, Tess thought for a moment. *But she sure has it in for me.* "Why exactly is that a problem?"

she finally asked, working to stay as pleasant as possible, but Drew snorted a laugh.

"Really?" she said. "People know you and will never buy you in the role of the bitter nurse."

Tess narrowed her eyes. The desire to remain pleasant starting to fade. "I disagree," she said. "I can play any role."

Shaking her head, Drew refocused on the script in her lap. "Not a chance."

What the hell? She's not even willing to give me a try, Tess thought. "Listen," she said, having enough of her insults. "You don't know me, but I have what it takes to bring the role to life."

Drew's head whipped up, and her eyes bored into Tess. "Oh yeah," she growled. "How much time have you spent in the Emergency Department at LA General Hospital? Not as a patient, but as the nurse thrown into one crisis after another." The venom in Drew's words was nearly enough to make Tess step back, but she wasn't done. "How about dealing with gunshot wounds? Abused babies? Drug overdoses? Seeing the worst part of humanity night after night." The author looked so angry Tess thought she might spit at her. "So, let's not pretend you have what it takes to make that come to life on the screen. Because you don't."

SINGING along under her breath to the classic indie song on the coffee shop's playlist, Ashley pulled the hot milk from the steaming espresso machine before mixing in the chocolate. After a quick stir and pour into the pink mug, she made a perfect heart with the foam. The little girl eagerly watching her every movement clapped her hands. "You make it so pretty," she said with a slight lisp. "And the best tasting hot chocolate anywhere. I tell everybody."

Ashley laughed, loving the enthusiasm, as she leaned on the counter to be eye-to-eye with the girl. "Well, Kelly, not too many customers want our hot chocolate in March, especially since it's been so warm," she said. "But thank you. I'm glad you think so."

"Thank you, Ashley," the girl's mom said, holding out a credit card. Once Kelly had scooped up the mug in her stubby fingers and started walking carefully toward a booth in the corner, the mom leaned closer. "She really does tell everyone about your hot chocolate. Thank you for always being so patient with her."

Letting her eyes follow the child, Ashley couldn't imagine anyone being anything but patient with the little girl. And it wasn't because Kelly had Down Syndrome. For Ashley, that had nothing to do with it. The girl's smile and cheerful attitude were infectious. She was happy to have the pair among her many regulars.

Moving on to the next called in order, Ashley heard the bell over the shop's door chime and glanced up. A man she didn't recognize wandered in, looking a little disoriented. Licking his lips while his eyes jerked left and then right, he shuffled his way toward the counter. Body odor rolled off him, nearly enough to make Ashley take a step back when he reached her. But she didn't, knowing from experience it would be best to take his order, serve him a coffee, and usher him out. "What can I make for you?" she asked, plastering a smile on her face. "Maybe a cold brew? I hear it's already getting warm out there."

The stranger stared at her but didn't answer. Ashley's unease only grew stronger, and she was about to call her coworker, who was on break in the back, to come out. Even though Kim wasn't more than five-foot four, there was strength in numbers. Before she could make a sound, the man mumbled something to himself a second before pulling a long, slender, kitchen knife from his hoodie pocket. "Money," he barked. "Give it to me."

An instant later, Kelly squealed from the table in the corner. "He has a knife," she yelled at the top of her lungs while her mother pulled her onto her lap. As if spurred on by the noise, the stranger lunged for Ashley, grabbing her by the wrist and pointing the knife within an inch of her face. Ashley froze but couldn't miss the crazy in his eyes. Maybe from drugs or insanity, she couldn't tell. Fear made her heart race, and everything seemed to speed up as her brain tried to comprehend the real danger she was in. Then, in the mix of the man yelling in her face for money and Kelly screaming in the corner, the bell over the door rang again. Not sure if the new arrival would make things better or worse, Ashley was surprised when she heard three quick steps, and then the stranger yanked backward away from her.

The force was enough to break the man's grasp on her wrist but not before his dirty fingernails clawed into her skin. Crying out in pain and surprise, it took a minute for Ashley's overly excited brain to comprehend that someone else indeed was in the coffee shop with them. Someone who came to her rescue. A person who had grabbed her attacker from behind by the hood of his sweatshirt and swung him across the room. With the stranger's back to the counter, Ashley couldn't see the face of the woman with long dark hair, but she could see the man with the knife clearly, and he was furious.

RESTING GENTLY on the balls of her feet, Bryce waited to see what the crazy man would do next. His face flushed red, and his unfocused eyes darted everywhere. She had no doubt he was a drug addict. *Hoping to steal a few bucks from some shop owner to buy his next fix,* she thought with frustration. People died all the time in altercations like that, and Bryce's throat tightened at the thought of what could have happened to Ashley. If the man had done anything to her, Bryce would have snapped the man's neck in a second. That wasn't the case though, and instead, she needed to subdue him without anyone getting hurt. She turned her head just enough to keep her eyes on the addict but still able to talk to Ashley. "Call 9-1-1," she said. "Tell them we have a man armed with a knife threatening people here."

"Okay," Ashley replied with a clarity in her voice Bryce appreciated. The fact the woman kept a level head helped. While Ashley dialed, Bryce used her peripheral vision to take in what was happening in the corner. Thankfully, the coffee shop was nearly empty. A girl whimpered in the arms of who Bryce guessed was her mother. It wasn't much noise, but Bryce didn't like the way the man's eyes kept creeping in that direction. The last thing she wanted was for him to try to take anyone hostage.

"And you two in the corner," Bryce said to the mother and daughter, keeping her tone gentle but authoritative. "I want you to hurry to get with Ashley behind the counter, okay?"

As the two scrambled from the booth and rushed toward Ashley, it was clear the man did not like how Bryce had taken control of the situation. He started to fidget, shifting the knife from one hand to the other. "I should stab you," he muttered. "I have the knife."

Bryce didn't answer while waiting for the woman and the child to get behind her with Ashley. When the others were out of harm's way, Bryce prepared to talk the guy into putting down the knife or at least stall him long enough for the cops to arrive. *No one has to get hurt today,* she thought. *I only need to keep him calm.*

Before she said a word, a door near the back of the coffee shop opened, and a young woman dressed in a red apron that said Landish Coffee walked out. "Hey, I was on the phone with Christopher, and I thought I heard a scream—" she said, and before Bryce could call out a warning, the crazy man grabbed her by the arm. Thankfully, the woman struggled to break free, giving Bryce the few seconds she needed to close the distance between her and the attacker. Noticing her coming, the man tried to lunge with the knife, but he was too slow. Using her Marine Corps training, Bryce gripped his wrist with her strong hands and, with a practiced twist, felt the man's hand open in reflex to the pain.

The knife clattered to the floor while the man wailed in agony. "You hurt me," he cried as Bryce kicked the weapon out of reach and then guided the crying man to the ground.

"Down on your stomach," she said, thankful to hear a police siren in the distance. Soon the whole wild scene would be over, and she could go back to her original plan— simply ordering a cup of hot coffee from Ashley and hoping to be recognized. Releasing the man, she knew he was no longer a threat. The fight had gone out of him when she sprained his wrist. Bryce wished he hadn't forced her to do it, but there was no other choice. People's safety was at stake.

As she ran a hand through her dark hair, hoping it wasn't a mess from the commotion, she felt someone come up beside her. Looking, she found herself staring into the face of the beautiful young woman she hadn't stopped thinking about for six years. "Bryce?" Ashley asked, and when their eyes met, the woman covered her mouth with her hands. "Oh my God. It is you. You came back."

4

Sitting in a director's chair outside a corner grocery store cordoned off for shooting in downtown Los Angeles, Drew watched the camera monitor the crew set up for her. She could follow the scene unfolding inside the building through the same lens as the cameraman. The movie director stood watching over her shoulder to see how the final scene of the first day would play out. They were on the fifth take, and everyone involved was ready to nail it so they could wrap for the day.

Much to Drew's surprise, the problem wasn't Tess but rather her male costar flubbing his line. If Drew was being honest, Tess's acting had been impressive all day. A person who didn't know any better would never believe she came to the script cold. She had none of the preliminary read-thru with the cast and minimal staging in advance. Virtually zero of the usual preplanning prep, yet the actress knew her lines and brought the right emotion and demeanor to the role. Not that all those things were enough for Drew to start singing praises. Aside from the last scene they struggled through at the moment, the first day of shooting focused on relatively easy setups with Tess playing the part of being a cynical bitch. Most people could channel that, especially herself. Thinking of being a bitch, a twang of guilt made Drew shift in her chair. She was aware her verbal attack at the start of the day wasn't fair to Tess. The fact the actress was there at all wasn't Tess's fault. The producer offered the woman a role, particularly a powerful one, and she wisely accepted.

What Drew needed to do was apologize for being rude while explaining in a more levelheaded approach why Tess couldn't play the part. *Talent or no talent, the chemistry necessary for the role wasn't going to work*, she thought. The problem for Drew was how the woman looked. Even with no makeup and her hair an unkempt mess, barely pinned back with barrettes, she was gorgeous. Not the plain Jane Drew envisioned when she wrote the character. There were no hard frown lines dug into Tess Landish's face. Hers was a mouth made to smile and melt hearts. Looking at her, it certainly did for Drew, a fact she tried hard to ignore. *That makes it worse actually*, she thought and resolved to find Tess after shooting wrapped and talk to her. If she had to, she would go to the actress's assigned trailer and make her understand it wasn't personal.

Refocusing on the camera viewer, Drew held her breath as the line the costar kept screwing up was next. It was a simple enough statement, so she didn't understand what the problem was with him. The scene was the first meeting of the two characters. Tess buying cigarettes when the costar would interrupt and tell her cigarettes would kill her. The comment would mount a pivotal moment between them. The annoyance and disdain Tess generated for her character all day played well on screen, but the scene would require her to dig deeper. Assuming the costar could deliver his line.

"You don't even know me," Tess said as she whirled on

her costar's character. Her voice was tight, and her eyes narrowed while she pinned him with a glare. Drew held her breath as she waited for the response. The next line was crucial to the scene and needed to be delivered with a mixture of insult and pity.

"Why would anyone want to?" the man said, and Tess's character's eyes widened, furious, but also with a glimmer of vulnerability and pain in them. Without a reply, she fled the store.

"Cut," the director yelled. "Perfect. That was what I was looking for." He looked at Drew. "Didn't I tell you she was good?" Drew clenched her teeth, loving how the scene went but hating to be so wrong about Tess. The emotion on Tess's face had been spot on, but it didn't change things on the grander scale. When it was clear Drew had nothing to say, the director went to intercept Tess before she left the set as Drew watched. "Excellent work today," Drew heard him say. "We should have cast you from the start."

THERE WAS ABSOLUTELY no other way to put it—Tess was on cloud nine. Pulling from her decades of experience and pushing her acting skills to the limit, in her mind, the day went perfectly as she nailed scene after scene. Even better, the director said he was thrilled. Add in that the angry writer kept her mouth shut as she sulked in her chair, and things couldn't have gone better. Digging her phone out of her purse where she had flung it on the trailer's sofa at the start of the day, Tess couldn't wait to tell her daughter everything. Ashley would be excited for her. Although she never came out and said so, Tess knew she was a little worried about the sudden gig. To be honest, so was Tess after the altercation with the writer that morning. The woman had struck a nerve, but if Drew had meant to knock Tess off her game, the insult did the opposite. Tess hadn't been so dialed into a role since she first started in the business.

The phone suddenly buzzed in her hand and looking at it, she smiled to see it was her daughter Ashley. That happened all the time—where one of them was about to call the other and then the phone rang. She loved their connection and believed the bond went beyond the normal mother-daughter instinct. Since day one, the two simply operated on the same wavelength. "Oh my God, it went so great," Tess answered without even a hello, unable to keep the excitement from bubbling up in her voice. She started to pace the large, plush trailer. "Can we meet for a late dinner? Are you free? I have so much to tell you."

"Yes," Ashley exclaimed through the phone. "I have stuff to share too. My day was crazy." She gave a small laugh filled with disbelief. "Someone tried to rob the coffee shop this morning."

Pausing mid-step, Tess's heart jumped into her throat at the idea Ashley might have been hurt. "Are you okay?" she asked, all other things she wanted to share immediately losing importance. "Did anyone get hurt? Did the robber get away? When did it happen?"

"Whoa, Mom. I'm okay. Everyone is okay," Ashley answered. "I promise."

Tess shook her head, trying to get her mind wrapped around what her daughter was telling her. "So, what happened?"

"It was amazing," Ashley said. "Everyone is okay, thanks to an old college friend of mine. She was incredible. I thought stuff like that only happened in the movies."

Tess furrowed her brow. *An old college friend?* she thought. Something in her daughter's tone made the friend sound like someone special. While Ashley was in college, she talked about her projects and assignments but rarely shared about her friends. Tess had never met anyone her daughter showed interest in.

Before she could ask more about the friend, Ashley rushed on. "I'll explain everything tonight. But get back to telling me about your day!"

For a second, Tess considered pressing Ashley for more details of the robbery but then let it go. Her daughter would tell her if there were anything to worry about. Starting to dive into how wonderful her day went, Tess didn't get a word out before there was a hard knock at her trailer's door. "One sec, Ashley," she said, moving to the door and opening it a crack to peek outside. Of all the people Tess might have expected to see, it was Drew Andersen standing at the bottom of the steps, shifting her feet, and looking very uncomfortable. "Well, hi. Is everything okay?"

Drew cleared her throat. "I was hoping we could talk," the woman said, not making eye contact. "About this morning especially."

Based on how the writer acted standing there at the bottom of her steps, Tess guessed the talk would include an apology. She had to hide her smile of satisfaction. "Give me one minute," she said to Drew before telling Ashley she would see her later at their usual restaurant in West Holly-wood. Refocusing on Drew, Tess opened the door wider. "Do you want to come in?"

.

SWALLOWING HARD, Drew wasn't sure what to do with Tess's invitation. When she planned her approach around how to talk to the actress, somehow it didn't involve being inside Tess's trailer. That would put her in the other woman's territory, giving her an advantage when Drew tried to explain the situation. Still, there was no obvious reason other than being outright rude that she could provide for not joining the actress in her trailer. Knowing she was stuck, Drew nodded. "Okay," she said, moving to the stairs, and Tess gave her a warm smile before going back inside. Working hard not to be dazzled in the wake of the famous smile, Drew followed her.

Tess was already at the trailer's full-sized fridge, moving things around. "I always have my trailer stocked with foods I like on hand, but also, always champagne," she said before grabbing a bottle and closing the door. Holding the thing out for Drew to read the label, the writer wasn't sure what to do. *Why are we having champagne?* she wondered, not seeing any reason to celebrate. Clearly realizing Drew's confusion, Tess laughed. It was a sweet, carefree sound that was one of the things that made the woman world famous. Unable to help herself, Drew smiled. That was the effect the woman had on a person, *which is the problem.* She needed to keep reminding herself of that fact and not get caught up in any nonsense to do with champagne.

Squaring her shoulders, Drew put on a serious face. "Now listen—" she started, but Tess waved her off as she walked past her to the counter.

"Not before we toast," she said and opened the bottle with a practiced hand. "Check the cupboard. There should be at least a half dozen champagne glasses."

Opening her mouth to protest but seeing the gorgeous woman standing before her with an open champagne bottle, she couldn't seem to bring herself to say no. Instead, she went to the cupboard. *This is ridiculous,* she thought but reached for two flutes anyway. Knowing she was losing complete control of the situation, she tried again as she turned with the glasses.

"Tess, seriously, we need to talk," she said, realizing the actress had moved much closer to pour. Drew sucked in a breath. Even after a long day of filming in the surprisingly warm March heat, Tess smelled good. Soft, a slight hint of flowers, and far too inviting. Not sure where all the unexpected attraction was coming from, Drew suddenly focused hard on Tess filling the glasses. When they were full, Tess lifted hers.

"So, let's talk," she said. "After we toast the amazing start to filming your movie we had today. It's a bit of a tradition with me to celebrate a strong first day."

Not daring to jinx the making of the film, Drew lifted her glass too. Even if Drew got her way and Tess was on her way out, karma was karma. "Fine," she said. "What do you usually toast to?"

"To Thalia and Melpomene, of course," she said. When Drew frowned, having no idea who the two people were, Tess laughed. "The muses of Comedy and Tragedy. Don't worry. Most people outside of acting don't know them. Maybe you've seen their masks?"

Even though she never had an interest in drama growing up, the image of the two masks—one smiling, one frowning —came to mind. "Yes," she said. "Never knew they had names."

Tess sipped. "I actually have a tattoo," she said, setting the glass on the counter and pulling up her blouse to reveal her tight midsection. The small laughing and frowning faces stood out on her hip. "They have had to cover the tattoo with makeup for some of my scenes over the years, but I'm very proud of it." She dropped her shirt back into place. "So, what do you want to talk about?"

After seeing the woman's skin so unexpectedly, Drew had trouble refocusing on what she had wanted to discuss. Again, she was entirely taken off guard by her reactions to Tess. "I'm concerned," she managed to say. "About you as the nurse."

Tess frowned. "Didn't you like how I played the part today?"

That was a good question because Drew liked how she handled the role today, but it didn't fix the long-term problem. "Yes, but there are much grittier scenes," she said, and then a thought came to her. Tilting her head, she regarded the actress. "Have you read the book?"

Blushing, Tess picked up her champagne and took a sip before answering. "No," she admitted. "I didn't have time before shooting started. But I obviously read the script." She lifted her chin. "And there isn't anything in there I can't pull off." Drew didn't know if she should be offended or not. From her book sales, it seemed most of the world had read the novel. Regardless, the fact Tess didn't know the complex layers of the story would hinder her ability to play the role. Even if she wasn't too beautiful for the part.

"I just don't think—" Drew shook her head, trying to explain again when Tess touched Drew's shoulder. Even through her shirt, she felt the warmth of Tess's hand. For some crazy reason, she thought she could get lost in that feeling, even though it was nothing but casual contact.

"Don't give up on me yet," Tess said, with a little more desperation in her voice. "I can do it."

When Drew met the actress's eyes, they pleaded with her. "Okay," Drew heard herself saying. "One more day."

5

With the sun setting in West Los Angeles, Bryce couldn't stop smiling. As she strolled down the walkway at the edge of the parking lot past one orange motel door after another, Bryce's head spun from the day's turn of events. Her plan to see Ashley certainly hadn't gone as she expected. *Not sure it could have gone much differently*, she thought with a shake of her head. When she approached the coffee shop that morning, the last thing she ever anticipated seeing through the glass front door was a man brandishing a knife. When the attacker grabbed Ashley by the wrist, Bryce didn't hesitate. Blowing through the front door, her only focus was on getting the guy away from Ashley before he did her any harm. Then, there had been the mom and daughter cowering in the corner, and finally her nearly having to break his wrist. Although she had worried the cops might give her grief for taking control as she did, they seemed more impressed than anything. "U.S. Marine Corps, huh?" one of the police officers said while taking her statement. "Well, sounds like you were in the right place at the right time to keep things from getting ugly here."

Bryce had shrugged, not comfortable with a lot of praise, but Ashley stood beside her and wouldn't let it end there. "She saved Kim's life. Possibly mine too," she said, and when Bryce raised her eyes, Ashley beamed at her. "Bryce is a hero."

The police officer slapped her leather notebook shut and put it in the back pocket of her uniform pants. "No argument here," she said before smiling at Bryce. "Ever get tired of the military, we could use people like you on the LA Police force."

"Thanks," was all Bryce could think to say, and then the cops were leading the drug addict out of the shop in handcuffs. Not sure what to do next, she shoved her hands into the front pockets of her jeans and waited.

Ashley laughed softly. "Oh, Bryce," she said. "You haven't changed a bit. Marines or no Marines, you're still the humblest person I've ever met."

Bryce shrugged again but liked the thought Ashley found her humble. Her father always expressed how vital modesty was in a person. His motto was 'work hard, stay humble, have honor, and do no harm,' and the words had served her well, although people often mistook her for shy. Bryce disagreed. Unlike some people, she didn't feel the need to comment on everything and often kept her opinions to herself. If she were anything, she would call herself a lone wolf. Yet, as Ashley stood looking at her, Bryce hoped that might be changing. Taking a deep breath to say why she came to the shop in the first place, a tug on her pant leg made her pause. A glance down, and she was looking into the serious, slightly hooded eyes of a young girl. She recognized her as the one in her mother's arms so afraid earlier.

"Are you a superhero?" the girl asked. "Like Batgirl?"

Bryce blushed and, out of the corner of her eye, saw

Ashley hide a smile under her hand. "No," she said, kneeling so they were eye to eye. "Only a regular person like you."

"Oh," the girl said, a thoughtful look on her face. After a beat, she brightened and gave Bryce a wide smile. "Then can we be friends?"

"We can totally be friends," Bryce answered with a smile of her own. "I'm Bryce."

The girl clapped her hands. "I'm Kelly."

"And I'm Elizabeth," the woman behind Kelly said. "Her mom. I don't know how to thank you. If you hadn't come in…"

Her voice caught, her eyes shining with tears. Ashley moved closer and wrapped an arm around the woman. "But she did," she said. "And everyone is okay. How about another hot chocolate?"

"Yes, please," Kelly responded, hopping up and down with glee.

"Well, okay," Elizabeth said. "But only a small one, or you won't want anything to eat later."

Ashley looked at Bryce as she stood. "And for you? Do you like hot chocolate?" she asked, and their look held. Ashley's beautiful blue eyes twinkled, and the spark Bryce drove miles to see was in them.

Feeling her smile widen further, Bryce nodded. "It's my favorite."

STARING at the blinking cursor on the computer screen was not helping her make any progress whatsoever. Even resting her fingers on the keyboard, index fingers on the F and J, did not force words forth from the depths of her brain. Drew dropped her hands into her lap and lowered her chin to her chest with a deep sigh of resignation. There was no way she would meet her word count goal tonight. The sequel to her novel would have to wait. There was too much other stuff on her mind. Tess Landish, for example. "Shit," she said, leaning back in her ridiculously expensive, black leather swivel chair. The thing had been part of her short splurge with the movie advance money. *Maybe it's the problem*, she thought, remembering the ratty old desk chair she used for years. Cracked vinyl seat. One arm loose. Certainly not comfortable by comparison and tended to slowly sink as the hours went on until she hit the lowest setting making her posture horrible. *Maybe I should have kept the thing for posterity.* But the chair was long gone, as was her crappy apartment in El Segundo. When her book hit number one on the New York Time's bestseller list, her brother called from San Antonio and told her it was time to move up in the world. "You're all set, sis. Quit your job and buy yourself a nice little place near the beach," he said, and Drew remembered laughing at him.

"I'm not making that kind of money, thanks," she said, trying to explain how royalties worked. "And it won't be number one forever." In the end, her brother had been right though. The book stayed at number one for thirteen consecutive weeks, was translated into over forty languages, and even she couldn't continue to protest when her agent came to her with the movie studio's offer. After that big chunk of money hit her bank account, she was indeed all set. Probably for life. Turning in her chair, Drew looked out the sliding glass doors that lined one wall of her modest house in the hills above Malibu and saw the start of the day's sunset. Although she couldn't bring herself to spend a fortune on the house itself, she indulged over the view. It was spectacular. *And I almost missed seeing the show tonight*, she thought. *Like so many things in life.*

Drew didn't like to think about how she had turned fifty-three years old a month ago. With so much extra time on her hands after she quit her thirty-year nursing career, there was too much time to reflect on all the things she hadn't done in her life. No marriage. No kids. Not even a pet. Work had consumed every minute of her time, leaving little for a social life. *That was my choice though*, she reminded herself. All the extra shifts she picked up, all the nights spent in the ER, working until she was exhausted and didn't have the energy to do anything but fall into bed when she got home, were by her choosing. Her job had been everything to her for a long time. When she finally realized the toll it was taking, she was too weary to change.

People constantly told her it was admirable work, and they were right. Caring for the broken and beaten bodies that came through the emergency department at the hospital every day made a difference, even if it was unfortunately rarely acknowledged. Looking back over her life, she would like to say she didn't regret giving up perhaps the best years of her life to take care of others, but it would be a lie. Hindsight was twenty-twenty, and she realized too late that life needed balance. There had to be room for happiness, joy... and love. Her life had been fulfilling and meaningful in its own way, but there were so many things she missed out on. *I didn't even take the time to have a little cat*, she thought with an ache of regret in her chest. As she watched the sky's brilliant display of red, yellow, and bright orange, Drew took a deep breath to let out the tension her thoughts had built in her chest. "Please let there still be time," she whispered. "It can't be too late to find someone to love."

FINALLY ABLE TO GET TOGETHER FOR dinner, Ashley held her fork in midair, ready to take a bite but too wound up to stop talking long enough. "And then Bryce twisted his wrist, and he dropped the knife," she said, finally putting the leaf of Arugula and slice of red beet in her mouth and chewing.

Sitting across from her at their favorite table, discreetly hidden from possibly nosey fans in the corner of Café Amici's, Tess's eyes widened. "Literally?" She wasn't sure what she expected from her daughter's harrowing telling of the attempted robbery, but the fact a stranger saved the day wasn't it. *At least no one stabbed anyone*, she thought with some relief. The idea her child was in so much danger earlier in the day made her stomach clench. Although she was flushed from the adventure of it, Ashley seemed to be taking the scary experience in stride.

Nodding while she swallowed, excitement showed in her daughter's eyes. "Literally," she answered. "And in a flash. Like out of a movie."

"It sounds like it," Tess said, shaking her head as she stabbed at her own Gorgonzola salad. "And she is a friend you knew in college?"

Before Ashley answered, one of the waiters checked on them. "Ladies? Can I bring you anything?" he asked. "Perhaps more bread? Another glass of wine?"

Ashley lifted the red cloth napkin on the breadbasket, and Tess saw it was empty but for some breadcrumbs. "Both?" she said with a smile, and Tess loved that Ashley didn't hold back from the enjoyment of good food. In the film industry, everyone, including herself far too often, was on some new diet. Luckily, the latest movie didn't require her to be super-model thin, at least. "Mom? Want more wine?"

Eyeing her nearly empty glass for a moment, Tess thought about the next day's shooting schedule and ended up shaking her head. "Not tonight. Early start in the morning."

Ashley set down her fork, giving her mom her full attention. "You haven't told me anything about filming today," she said as the waiter left. "I've monopolized the entire conversation."

Tess raised a finger. "But I needed to know about what

happened at the coffee shop first," Tess said. "I worried when you mentioned what happened."

"I'm sorry about that," Ashley said, nodding her apology. "Everything was scary for a few minutes, but the whole thing turned out fine." She laughed. "The little girl I told you about, Kelly, asked Bryce if she was a superhero. It was adorable."

Tilting her head, Tess took a moment to look at Ashley's face. She glowed whenever she mentioned her friend. *I've never seen her like this over someone,* she thought, even more confused as to why the woman's name had never come up.

Ashley went back to eating her salad before glancing up meeting Tess's eye. "What?"

Tess shrugged as the fresh bread, and her daughter's glass of wine arrived. Grabbing a piece of the warm bread, she knifed some of the whipped garlic butter. "Honestly? I'm confused about the woman who saved the day. I know what she did was impressive, and I'm grateful she was there, but you can't stop talking about her."

Leaning back in her chair, Ashley wrinkled her brow. "I guess you're right," she said after a beat. "But when the cops finished taking our statements and left, she stayed around, and we talked until the shop got busy again." She tilted her head as she leaned forward, looking Tess in the eye. "You know Mom, I think we could have talked for hours if I didn't have to focus on work." She shook her head, going back to the food. "I really didn't think I would ever see her again."

Tess sipped the last of her wine. "And why not?" she asked. "She sounds special."

Ashley nodded. "Yes," she agreed. "She is. I guess I never let myself go there. You know how I was. Laser-focused on school, and then suddenly she was leaving, and I didn't have a chance."

"And now?" Tess asked with a lifted eyebrow. "Please tell me you asked for her phone number at least."

At that, Ashley smiled, her face lighting up again. "We exchanged them," she said. "And she said she would call me tomorrow."

Touching her daughter's forearm, Tess leaned closer. "Don't wait until tomorrow," she said. She knew from experience special people were hard to find. "Call her tonight."

6

*E*njoying the feel of the warm sun on her face as her feet tread a perfect rhythm on the wide dirt path, Ashley felt terrific. The hills of Runyon Canyon Park were some of her favorites to run, and at seven a.m. the weather was perfect. Best of all though was the sense of companionship she felt from running with the woman beside her. Following her mother's advice, Ashley had called Bryce last night after they finished dinner. What she worried would be an awkward conversation after not seeing each other for so many years didn't exist at all. They fell into a chat, reminiscing about old times at college, and an hour blew by without Ashley noticing. Thrilled to hear Bryce was an avid runner, Ashley invited her on an early morning outing. When she learned Bryce hadn't ever tried the routes in Runyon Canyon, the location was a must to visit. "The views of Los Angeles are stunning," she told her. They reluctantly hung up after setting a time for Bryce to pick Ashley up at her apartment. For the first time in a long time, Ashley had trouble sleeping because she was so excited to see Bryce again.

"You were right. The place is amazing," Bryce said once they were underway at the park.

Ashley smiled at the pleasure on her friend's face. "Wait until we get closer to the top," she said. "The air is clear enough this morning that we will be able to see for miles."

True to her word, she slowed as they came to a broad clearing on the trail. "Are you okay with taking a quick timeout to see the view?" she asked. "I promise the time spent is worth it."

"Of course," Bryce said. "Maybe I'll even take a picture." Together, they stopped at a viewpoint along the path. A pair of wooden benches faced the city for those who wanted to rest awhile, and a trashcan for litter helped keep the trail clean.

Ashley spread her arms wide, taking in the vast expanse. "Well, what do you think?" she asked, and when Bryce didn't comment at first, she glanced over. The woman wasn't looking at the cityscape but at her. A tenderness in her brown eyes made Bryce look even more beautiful than usual, and Ashley felt her heart skip a beat.

Then, caught looking, Bryce blushed. "Sorry," she murmured, looking away in the direction of LA's skyline. "But so far, all the views have been beautiful today." After a beat, she let out a long whistle and shook her head. "Wow, that's a lot of houses all jammed together." Still a little flustered from the comment, Ashley took a moment to register what Bryce said. Then, she turned to the view too. Although she never really noticed, Bryce was right. House after house sprawled across the valley floor, along the canyons, and up into the hills. In the distance, skyscrapers towered over downtown. "It is impressive," Bryce added. "But I'm not sure I could live so crammed in there."

"Yes," Ashley said, letting her eyes scan for miles. She wasn't sure but thought she read somewhere that Los

Angeles had twelve million people living in the metro area. Even if you counted four people to a house, that was a lot of buildings. *If something ever happened and people had to evacuate...* she thought. *It would be chaos.* "I guess that's the word for it. You can't say it's beautiful necessarily, but definitely impressive."

Turning away from the suddenly unsettling view, Ashley saw Bryce fishing her phone out of her running shorts' pocket. "I want a picture though," she said, glancing at Ashley. "Will you take a selfie with me?"

Ashley smiled. "If you promise to text it to me," she said as she stepped closer. For a moment, Bryce didn't move as if undecided what to do, but then she put her arm around Ashley's shoulders to pull her closer, so their faces were together in the shot. Unable to help herself, Ashley sucked in a breath at the contact. Something about the woman's touch made her stomach flutter. *This is crazy. Why am I having such a strong reaction to her?* she wondered a moment before Bryce asked if she was ready.

"Yes," was all Ashley managed to say in response.

Then, Bryce held the phone up to frame their faces with the city behind them. "Smile," she said, and Ashley didn't have to because she was already.

"The dailies look great," the director said with a smug look on his face. "You can't deny that, Drew. Tess wasn't only good, she was great." Drew frowned as she sat looking at the last shot from yesterday. The hurt face of Tess Landish as the nurse stared back at her. The film froze on the closeup of her reaction in the grocery store. Pain showed in her eyes. *No,* Drew thought. *That's deep-felt anguish.* She couldn't help but wonder where the actress could channel so much pain from.

She shook her head. "One great scene doesn't mean she

can carry the character through the entire film," she said. "Put her amid the chaos when a flood of crushed bodies come in after a multicar crash on the freeway, and then let's see. I can't believe it will work."

The director crossed his arms and leaned back in his chair. "I can see your point," he said with a frown. "Emotions are one thing a quality actress can evoke, but maybe she's too... delicate for the disaster stuff?" Before Drew could agree, there was a soft knock at the trailer door. The director clapped his hands together, starting to stand. "I do believe that's our cue to get on set and start filming for the day."

Not done with the conversation about the film's lead, Drew stayed seated. "Wait," she said with a wave at the screen still showing Tess's face. "What are we going to do about this?"

With a sigh, the director settled back in the chair and looked Drew in the eye. "We don't have a choice," he said. "The producers are very clear on the topic. Tess is it. Or this film may never be made at all." Drew's mouth fell open. She couldn't believe what the man had said. *Not make the movie?* she thought. *But that's impossible.* With a shrug, the director rose to answer the door. "And you don't want that."

What the man said was an understatement. Drew didn't only want the movie to happen. She needed it. Standing, she was in a daze, and it took her a minute to comprehend who was at the door. Instead of one of the second assistant directors like she expected, Tess stood on the steps. In her hands was a hardcover copy of Drew's book. "Sorry to interrupt, but I wanted to catch you before we were all on set," Tess said, fixing Drew with her million-dollar smile. "So, you can autograph my book." She held up the novel. "I read it last night. Cover to cover, and let me tell you, makeup wasn't happy with the sleepy bags under my eyes." She laughed. "Worth the scolding though."

Looking at the familiar book cover, Drew shook her head. "You read my story?" Drew said, not able to stop the pleasure from filling her chest. "The whole thing?"

Tess nodded, stepping into the trailer past the director and moving closer to Drew. "And now I understand why you're worried," she said. "But Drew Andersen, I can play the part. You'll simply need to coach me."

"Coach you?"

"Yes," she answered. "Because this is you, isn't it." The words weren't a question. Tess no longer smiled, and her eyes held Drew's. "And I want to do the role." Feeling her chest tighten at the claim she had written about herself, Drew wasn't sure how to react.

The director shifted his feet by the door, clearly uncomfortable with the intensity in the air between the two women. "I'm going to head to the set," he said. "I think you two have some things to work out." With that, he was gone, leaving Tess and Drew.

Alone again, Drew thought, remembering her surprising reactions in Tess's trailer yesterday.

Making her hands into fists, she wasn't going to get flustered. "Parts of the book are like me," Drew said, steel in her tone. "But not all."

Tess sank into the chair beside Drew. "Then tell me which parts. I want to know what's you and what's not."

Surprisingly, Drew found herself wanting to share the private details with the woman. No one had ever asked the question. No one had cared to know. "How I handled the emergency department stuff? That was a mixture of many real moments," she said, then hesitated, and Tess tilted her head.

"And the not real?" she asked, and Drew dropped her eyes to stare at the floor.

It was hard to say what was next, but her soul longed to

share. "The love affair," she whispered. "I've never had one of those."

PARKING her truck on the street a few blocks from Landish Coffee, Bryce wasn't ready for her time with Ashley to be over. While they talked about all kinds of imaginable topics, the run together had made for a perfect morning. Ashley's suggestion for getting together was spot on for keeping things casual while spending quality time getting to know each other better. Unfortunately, it was about to end. *But only for now,* she thought. *I will text her later and see if she wants to hang out again, maybe grab dinner.* Bryce would keep things casual, but there was no way she would let Ashley slip away again.

As if having similar thoughts, Ashley paused before opening the truck's door. "Want to come in and have an iced coffee or something?" she asked, looking at Bryce. "You've earned free drinks for life after what you did for us yesterday."

Bryce felt her cheeks warm a little at the praise. She did what needed to be done in the moment. "I don't expect a reward," she said. "I'm just glad I was there when it happened."

Ashley touched her arm, and her eyes were serious. "You saved us," she said, holding Bryce's look. "And I will never forget it. Come inside." She smiled to soften her words. "Please."

With nowhere else to be and nothing she had to do, plus getting to spend more time near Ashley, the decision was easy. "Since you said please," she said with a grin. "Do you make smoothies? Because I could use a little protein after you made me run up all those hills."

As she opened the car door, Ashley laughed. "Nice try," she said. "You hardly even broke a sweat."

That part was true. Bryce enjoyed the run but compared to the Marine Corps physical training exercises, it was a walk in the park. If she didn't get back into more intense training soon, returning to service would be grueling while she got into shape again. The thought made her pause as she climbed out of the truck and met Ashley on the sidewalk. *Am I going back to the military?* she wondered while feeling the woman's closeness beside her as they walked. *Now that I've connected with Ashley again, do I want to return?* She tightened her jaw. *Well, the decision doesn't have to be made today.* Refocusing on the present, Bryce noticed a woman and her black and white dog sitting along the beach path. From the stained, torn clothing and overall look of her, Bryce guessed she was homeless. As they approached, she wasn't surprised the woman was holding a cardboard sign asking for money.

"Hi, Bev," Ashley said, stopping in front of her. "Hi, Floyd. This is my friend Bryce. She's the one who stopped the robbery yesterday."

Bev's eyes widened. "Ohhh," she said. "The badass Marine. People all over the boardwalk are talking about you. A real hero."

"Well, I don't know about that," Bryce said, trying to ignore the heat rising up her cheeks. It seemed she couldn't stop blushing lately. "But I'm glad—."

Suddenly, Floyd stood and started to pull on his leash, nearly yanking Bev over. "What the hell, Floyd?" Bev said. "Get back over here." The dog obeyed but continued to whine, and Bryce noticed the dog starting to shiver. Not liking what she saw, Bryce turned, scanning their surroundings for any threats. Everything seemed quiet and peaceful in the early morning.

"What is it?" Ashley asked, but Bryce only shook her head.

"I don't know," she said, looking back at Bev again. Floyd stopped whining as Bev petted his neck, and there was no more shivering either. Whatever made the dog upset had passed, but it didn't help lessen Bryce's unease.

"They hear things we can't hear, ya know?" Bev said. "Probably some sort of siren somewhere that upset him."

Bryce slowly nodded. "Maybe," she said, forcing herself to relax. Bev was probably right, and there was nothing to be concerned about. But Bryce would keep an eye out for any sign of trouble.

7

*U*sing the paper straw, Bryce stirred the remains of her second, bright-pink, strawberry and banana smoothie. The drink tasted delicious, but the best part of being at the coffee shop was watching Ashley. Running the business with an easy confidence but also a certain grace, the woman was born to be a success. Add in her natural charisma with regulars and new customers, and Bryce was captivated watching Ashley. Whenever there was a lull in the stream of customers, Ashley would look over at Bryce with a warm smile and tiny wave. Although it was tempting to order a third smoothie so she could stay longer, even to Bryce that seemed like overkill. She didn't want to totally freak Ashley out by sitting there watching her all morning.

I need to ask her out before I go though, Bryce thought, considering their run in the park earlier. As wonderful as it was that didn't have the feel of a first date, but more like a couple of friends meeting to catch up. Bryce wanted them to have a real date. If she had her way, a romantic date. The question was how Ashley would react if Bryce asked so soon after they started talking again. After all, they only met twenty-four hours ago after years apart with no contact. Bryce shook her head having trouble believing it was only yesterday she returned. It seemed like forever ago the addict came in, and Bryce subdued him. Even in that short amount of time, she felt like she knew Ashley well. *But I want to learn so much more about her.*

As Bryce reluctantly slurped the last of her smoothie, the door chimed, and in walked a man with bulging muscles like she had never seen before. Although there were plenty of weightlifters in the Marine Corps and Bryce spent a lot of time in the gym herself, that guy was huge. Barely covered by the tight shorts and a small Gold's Gym tank top, every inch of his tanned body seemed to ripple and flex as he walked across the coffee shop to the counter.

"Hi, Lou," Ashley said with a smile, clearly knowing the bodybuilder well. "I was wondering when you would show up. Ready for that smoothie I promised?"

Lou nodded, but his face was somber. "Ashley, I can't believe what I heard about yesterday," he said, flexing the muscles in his arms and chest. "If I'd have been in here, that guy would be nothing but a puddle on the floor."

"I know," Ashley said, with a glance in Bryce's direction. The admiration in her twinkling eyes was unmistakable, and Bryce couldn't help but feel warm inside. "But everything worked out."

They did indeed, Bryce thought, standing to return the smoothie glass and say goodbye. Asking Ashley out on a date would have to wait with so many people around, but she vowed to do it tonight on the phone. As she neared the counter, the door opened again with a pair of tourists leaving the coffee shop, and Bryce swore she heard a dog barking. The sound was faint, but enough for her to wonder if the dog might be Floyd. *Why is he upset again?*

Before she formed another thought, the floor lurched

under her, nearly knocking her to the ground, but she caught the back of a chair to stay upright. Dropping her smoothy glass, it fell to the tiled floor and shattered. Lou grabbed for the counter but went down in a crash as the entire coffee shop started to shake. Over the loud rumble of the moving earth and the shaking building, Bryce heard the sound of mugs and more glasses breaking. "Ashley," she yelled, ducking under the nearest table. "Get under the counter." Suddenly, the glass in the front door cracked into a hundred pieces before blasting apart. Some sprayed on Lou who had managed to get to his hands and knees to crawl toward cover. He was halfway to a table when Bryce noticed the tall shelves along one wall starting to shake free from their safety moorings and list forward. "Watch out!" was all Bryce could say before one of the cases tipped, dropping its contents, and then fell. Horrified but helpless, Bryce watched as Lou was peppered with decorative mugs and bags of coffee before the entire thing landed on him.

HIDING under the counter beside her coworker Kim, Ashley squeezed her eyes closed and listened to things falling with a crash around her. Bryce yelled something about Lou, but she couldn't make out all the words over the rumbling. The shaking seemed to go on forever, and then…

…it stopped.

As suddenly as it began, the earth no longer moved. As Ashley opened her eyes, there was a beat of silence in the wake of the rumble only to fill with the sound of car alarms and people yelling outside.

"Ashley," Bryce yelled. "I need you to come help me."

Trying to stem the surge of panic that Bryce was hurt, Ashley crawled from under the counter. Sharp shards of ceramic were everywhere along the floor, making her move slowly until she could stand. Scanning the room, Ashley couldn't move, her eyes wide as she took in her coffee shop's destruction. The front door had shattered, and the windows were all cracked. One of the light fixtures had fallen from the ceiling. Furniture thrown everywhere. Then, she saw Bryce on her hands and knees looking under one of the large showcases that had fallen over.

When Bryce called out, "Lou, can you hear me?" Ashley jolted into motion.

"What happened?" she asked as she knelt beside Bryce. Looking under the case, she let out a moan. Her friend was lying flat underneath. "Lou? Please talk to me." The man didn't respond or make any movement.

"He was trying to crawl to hide under a table," Bryce said standing. "Come on. Let's try to lift the case off him enough to move it aside," she said, putting her hands under the edge. As Ashley mimicked her actions, Kim came to help though blood covered half her face from a cut over her eye.

Wicked looking, the wound had to be painful, and Ashley appreciated her worker's willingness to help. "Thank you," she said, and the woman nodded as she gripped the wood.

The women were ready. "On three, okay?" Bryce asked, and the others nodded. "One. Two. Three." Ashley grunted as she helped lift the heavy wooden case up a few inches. Working as a team, they shuffled across the floor until the thing was clear of Lou's unmoving body.

Dropping it with a crash, Ashley watched as Bryce moved to check Lou. He was flat on his chest, and there was no way to see if he was breathing. While Bryce put two fingers to the man's neck, Ashley held her breath. *Please let him be alive*, she thought, and when Bryce let out a breath, Ashley realized the woman had been holding hers too.

"He's alive," Bryce said. "We need to try to call 9-1-1, but I bet the circuits are busy. It depends on how big the earth-quake was."

Suddenly, Ashley felt her heart stop. "My mom," Ashley whispered as she realized she had no idea where the production was filming.

Bryce nodded. "Try to call or text her," she said, already fishing her phone out of her back pocket. "But do it outside on the boardwalk. You can't stay inside this building. Lou might have a broken back, so we can't move him. I'll stay here and start dialing 9-1-1."

Ashley tried not to think about Lou having broken bones and went outside. "What should I do?" Kim asked from beside her, and Ashley realized the woman looked sickly pale under the blood smeared on her face.

Untying her apron, Ashley wadded it up. "Put this on your cut to stop the bleeding, and I'll help you outside," she said, handing it over. "We can sit on the curb while I call my mom and we wait for an ambulance." As Kim pressed the apron to her head, Ashley looked at Bryce. There was a smear of blood on her cheek, and Ashley wondered for a second where it came from but then pushed it away. "I don't like you staying in here. What if there's another one?"

"Then I'll take cover again," Bryce said. "But I want to monitor Lou. If he starts to struggle to breathe, I'll turn him over even if his back is injured." Studying the woman's face for a moment, Ashley could tell there would be no talking her out of staying with the injured man.

Reaching for Bryce's cheek, she wiped at the already drying blood. "Are you always the hero?" she asked softly, and the tender look from that morning at the viewpoint came back into Bryce's eyes. When the woman didn't reply, Ashley knew yes was her answer.

. . .

WHEN THE SLIGHT tremor shook the carpeted floor under Tess's feet, she thought at first someone nearby had slammed a door. As others on the set inside the small apartment in South Los Angeles began to react, she realized they were having an earthquake. It wasn't much, but enough to tip over a paper cup of coffee sitting on a nearby counter and send a handful of papers and pens onto the floor. Before anyone could react, the trembling was over.

"Was that an earthquake?" one of the cameramen asked, clearly as uncertain as Tess was about what happened. Looking around, Tess noticed half a dozen people, including Drew, were already on their phones searching for information. Drew was the first to speak up.

"Channel five is already calling it an earthquake," she said, frowning at what she was reading. "Early estimates are saying it was over a four-point-oh, but something is strange." She looked at Tess. "They think the epicenter is along the coastline."

Tess covered her mouth with her hands. "Oh, God," she said. "I need to call my daughter." Already in motion, she headed for the door. She had to get out of the apartment and find her phone. The thing would be in her purse back at her trailer.

"Use mine," Drew said, holding out her phone as she intercepted her at the door. "While we go get yours."

Tess registered the word 'we' long enough to appreciate having someone for support and then dialed. "Come on, Ashley," she said. "Please pick up." After two rings, a recorded message broke in telling her all circuits were busy. "Shit. The call won't go through."

"Try texting," Drew said while they hurried down the hall together.

Tess shot off a brief "are you okay" but moaned when the phone immediately returned an 'unable to send' message.

Putting a warm hand on Tess's forearm, Drew turned her until they were face to face. There was a calmness in the woman's eyes that helped Tess center herself.

She knew what to do in an emergency. "Keep going back and forth between calling and texting," Drew said. "Lots of people are checking on loved ones, but it will go through eventually. Now, follow me." Drew led her down the rest of the hallway, past the elevator, and to the door marked stairs. Realizing what Drew thought, Tess swallowed hard. If there was one earthquake, there were often aftershocks. Getting trapped in an elevator could be a disaster.

"Thank you for helping me," Tess said as they started down.

"You're welcome," Drew said without looking back. "Hang onto the handrail. I know you're focused on calling your daughter, so I don't want you to trip and fall." Tess did as instructed and using one hand to hit redial and the other to hang on, they descended the four flights.

Frustrated, she still hadn't been able to get through to Ashley even after they gathered her phone from her trailer and returned to the parking lot. "The message keeps saying all the circuits are blocked," Tess said, trying to get through using both phones. "And texts are going nowhere." She knew what she had to do. "I need to go find her." The task wouldn't be easy though. Transportation services provided by the movie studio picked her up every morning to drive her to the set. The town car was nowhere around, and she didn't have a vehicle anywhere nearby. Glancing at Drew, she saw the woman watching her. The author's face was unreadable. Tess sighed, knowing what she wanted was a big favor, maybe even a dangerous one.

Drew nodded before Tess could even ask. "I'll drive you," she said. "Let's go find her."

8

Navigating her white Pathfinder in dense traffic on the ten lane I-105 freeway through South Los Angeles, Drew did everything she could to keep them moving in the direction of the beach. The task was not easy as an unusually bad jam of LA traffic clogged every lane of the most direct route heading west toward the coast. In the passenger seat beside her, Tess continued to dial and text Ashley's number every few seconds. Even with the phone to Tess's ear, Drew heard the recorded voice say over and over that all circuits were busy. "Damnit," Tess said, shaking the phone, exasperation mounting in her voice. "I can't believe what's happening."

Changing lanes again to try to keep them moving, Drew glanced at the woman. She didn't know Tess well enough to know how upset she might be getting, but the last thing she wanted was for the woman to panic. In her years as a nurse in different emergency departments, Drew saw an unfortunately large number of distraught parents and knew how crazy they could get when their child was hurt. "What's your daughter's name?" Drew asked, working to keep Tess calm.

Watching her try again, Drew waited, hoping the call would connect. After a moment, Tess blew out a frustrated breath, and Drew heard the recorded voice again.

Angry, Tess pushed the disconnect button on the phone to silence the irritating operator's repeating voice. "Her name is Ashley," she answered. "She's twenty-eight and owns a coffee shop along the Venice Beach boardwalk." Tess rubbed a hand over her eyes. "There isn't anything between her and the ocean but two hundred yards of sand." She sent another text and started to redial the phone. "I'm scared sick."

"Keep trying," was all Drew could advise as they crawled along. While Tess kept dialing, the radio started broadcasting updated news, and Drew turned the volume up.

"We've been provided with a bulletin on the status of the region most impacted by the earthquake," the announcer said. "As of this update, although there have been injuries, there are no reported deaths. Officials ask people to stay home and not try to reach any of the cities from Santa Monica to Marina Del Rey. Traffic lanes need to remain clear to allow emergency personnel access." As Drew stopped the vehicle in the wake of red taillights, she watched for Tess's reaction.

Biting her lip, the woman turned to Drew with pleading eyes. "I heard what they advise," she said. "But until I can reach Ashley, will you please keep going? I have to know if she's all right."

Considering the situation, Drew wondered what it would be like to care about someone as much as Tess clearly did for her daughter. *How much would I risk to ensure she didn't need help?* she thought. In the ER, she learned early on never to let herself become attached to any patient. For one thing, they rarely stayed in the unit long, and for another, too many of them didn't make it. But the mother-daughter scenario she was witnessing firsthand felt different. Somehow over the miles, she had become invested in making sure everyone involved was okay.

As traffic picked up again, Drew kept going. "Let's see how far we can get." After another few minutes, traffic came to a complete standstill again, and Drew was tempted to take the upcoming exit. There was always the chance the surface streets might be better. *Unless everyone has the same idea*, she thought. *And assuming nothing is blocked from impacts of the shaking*. That seemed unlikely. The earthquake was reported as a four on the Richter scale, which was enough to knock dishes out of cupboards and give everyone a good shake but rarely powerful enough to damage most buildings. Plus, they were miles away from the predicted epicenter. It might be worth taking a chance. She turned to Tess. "What do you think of getting off the freeway?" she asked. "Try our luck using another route?"

Tess furrowed her brow, holding the phone to her ear. "I don't know," she replied. "The freeway is a straight shot to the coast, assuming it moves soon."

Before Drew could decide, she heard Tess's call finally connect. "Mom?" came a young woman's voice loud enough to be heard in the car.

"Oh my God, Ashley," Tess said. Out of the corner of her eye, Drew saw the woman's hands shaking. "Are you okay? Where are you?"

Drew couldn't hear all of Ashley's answer, but it sounded like she was okay. "Do you want to keep going west?" Drew asked, and Tess held up a finger, listening for a moment.

"Come to my house as soon as you can." There was a pause while Ashley talked, and then Tess nodded. "Yes, bring your friend too. Please go straight there, okay?"

Drew guessed Ashley must have said okay by the way Tess sagged back into her seat after hanging up. "Thank you so much for helping me," she said with her eyes closed. "And

I know I'm asking for too much considering we are basically strangers but…"

When Tess didn't finish, Drew raised an eyebrow. "But?"

"But can you drive me home?"

With nothing and no one waiting for her anywhere, Drew nodded as she reached for the Pathfinder's GPS. "What's the address?"

EYES CLOSED and holding the phone to her chest, Ashley could finally take a full breath again. Not knowing where her mom was filming that day had been tearing her up. Hearing her mom's voice, knowing she was safe and headed back to her house, was a huge relief. After repeatedly calling her but not getting through, Ashley no longer had to worry about her. They would meet back home later when things were taken care of at the coffee shop. That information helped Ashley focus on what else was happening around her.

Her coworker Kim sat leaning against the wall outside the coffee shop holding Ashley's apron in her lap. Bloodstains covered part of the white Landish Coffee lettering on the apron, but at least the bleeding above her eye appeared to have stopped. Ashley was no expert, but the ugly gash would probably need stitches. "Can I try and get you anything?" she asked Kim, who shook her head, then winced at the movement.

"Ouch," she said. "That was dumb. But I think I'm okay. Wondering if I should try to drive to the hospital."

Ashley frowned. "I don't think that's a good idea with a head injury," she said. "Bryce is inside calling 9-1-1." She glanced in the direction of the smashed doors but couldn't see her friend. "Maybe wait until the paramedics get here, and they can look at you too."

Leaning her head back, Kim stayed where she was. "That works for me," she said. "Did you get ahold of your mom?"

"I did," Ashley said. "A call finally came through." Then she realized she was being selfish. "Is there someone you want to call? I can go in and get your phone." *And then maybe I could check on Bryce*, she thought, but the woman started to shake her head before catching herself and grimacing.

"Not really," she said. "Maybe my boyfriend, but it can wait. He works construction in the valley, so I'm sure he's fine."

"Okay. Let me know if you change your mind," Ashley said before glancing at the boardwalk. People were milling around the different storefronts, and she recognized some of the neighboring business owners she was friendly with. "I think I'll go down the boardwalk a little bit and see how other people are doing." She refocused on Kim. "Will you tell Bryce where I went if she comes out?"

Kim looked about to answer when Ashley heard Bev calling from the boardwalk. "Ashley," she said, huffing and puffing from her effort to get to the coffee shop. "Did you feel that?" Ashley looked to see the disheveled homeless woman shuffling down the boardwalk with Floyd loyally on his rope leash at her side. A black plastic bag of what looked like would usually be trash but was likely Bev's most trea-sured possessions was slung over her shoulder. "I don't know about you, but I've never been so scared in my life." She shook her head. "I thought a wall was going to tip over and crush me." Panting from the exertion, Bev dropped the bag at her feet as she reached Ashley. "And now those waves are freaking me out."

Furrowing her brow, Ashley wasn't sure what the woman meant. In the chaos, she hadn't been paying attention to anything much beyond the boardwalk. "What do you mean?" she asked while turning her focus on the ocean. Her eyes widened at the sight. There was something weird going on. The usually mild waves that Venice Beach was famous for were surprisingly higher than she was used to and seemed to roll in with more velocity. As she watched, one of the white-capped waves ran clear up the beach to the edge of the children's play area to swirl around the legs of the swing set. In the three years she had been working on Venice Beach, that had never happened. "They are freaking me out too," she murmured to Bev, not sure what to think, but her instincts told her what she saw was bad news.

BRYCE WAITED in the coffee shop for medical help to arrive. Continuing to scroll the internet on her phone, she flipped through report after report emerging about the LA earthquake. Finally, her call to 9-1-1 had gone through, and all they said was all available emergency personnel were already dispatched to the area. *I could have figured that out myself,* she had thought as the call disconnected. All she could do was wait and hope Lou remained stable. She frowned as she read that the earthquake's epicenter was supposed to be a few miles offshore. *Could that trigger a tsunami?* Then Lou groaned, and Bryce let the thought go. Surely, there would be a warning if they should be concerned. "Where am I?" Lou asked, lifting his head to look around. "And what was the number on the bus that hit me?"

"Take it easy," Bryce said as she knelt by his side, putting a hand on his shoulder. "There was an earthquake, and some shelves fell on you."

With a groan, Lou rolled slowly onto his back. "No kidding?" he asked. "I don't remember anything other than getting ready to order a strawberry smoothie."

Bryce nodded. "I think you had a hard blow to your head, and the memory will come back to you. But it might take a little time. How are you feeling otherwise? Anything really painful?"

Rubbing his neck with a beefy hand, Lou flexed one muscular leg, then the other. "My neck hurts, but I don't think anything's broken if that's what you're worried about."

"That's exactly what I was worried about," Bryce said, happy to hear the man wasn't in any extreme pain. "Do you think you can stand up? I'd kind of like to get out of the building, just in case."

Lou winced as he started to move but made progress getting up. "Why? Do you think there's going to be more earthquakes?" he asked standing.

Bryce grabbed his arm when Lou started to weave back and forth. "Maybe aftershocks," she said. "You're sure you are okay to move?"

"I'll live. Let's get outside," Lou said, and the pair moved toward the busted door.

Before they made it outside, Ashley was in the doorway. A look of relief passed over her face when she saw Lou. "You're awake," she said to the bodybuilder. "Are you okay?"

Lou limped past her. "I'll be okay," he said. "But damn my head hurts."

Bryce helped him a few more feet onto the boardwalk and then paused when a wave of water splashed over her feet. *What in the hell?* she thought, looking around. An ocean wave receded across the large expanse of beach, but there were more coming behind it.

"I think we might want to get out of here," Ashley said from behind Bryce. "Because those waves keep getting higher and higher."

Swallowing hard, Bryce was ready to kick herself for not taking her original thought of more danger seriously. An earthquake close to the coastline was bad news. As part of Marine Corps reconnaissance training, they learned about all kinds of catastrophic scenarios. *And one of them was tsunamis*, she thought, moving into action. Unlike what most people believed from watching blockbuster movies, tsunamis weren't necessarily one giant wave of water coming out of nowhere. Instead, they were a series of large waves, each with increasing intensity. The ocean water lapping at Bryce's feet might be as high as the tide would get, and they would be fine. *Or they are the precursor to something bigger.* She wasn't going to risk it. Even a five-foot wave running ashore could do serious flooding and damage. *And drownings.* "Start telling people to move inland. Right now," she said to Ashley. "But meet me at the truck in five minutes. We don't want to be anywhere near here if these waves keep rising."

9

*R*iding in Drew's Pathfinder with the late morning freeway traffic, Tess tried not to be frustrated at the slow-moving progress. All she wanted to do was get home and hug her daughter. When there were signs for another exit, she considered suggesting going down onto the surface streets to see if the going was more accessible. Unfortunately, the line of cars waiting in the exit lane told her a lot of other drivers were going to try the same. As restless as she was, Tess would simply have to be patient. *At least Ashley is safe*, she thought, settling into the leather seat to get more comfortable. At the rate they were moving, they wouldn't be at her house for a while, so she let her thoughts wander. In all the years raising Ashley, Tess couldn't think of a scarier time than that morning. When she didn't know if her daughter was safe, she had found it hard to breathe and not fall apart. *Thank God Drew kept a level head.* She glanced at the woman who drove with her hands at ten and two on the steering wheel. *Calm and cautious. And nicer than she pretends to be.*

"Thank you for helping me this morning," Tess said, keeping her eyes on Drew. "I don't know what I would have done without a car."

Drew shrugged. "Someone else would have helped you," she said without even a glance in Tess's direction.

"Maybe," Tess said. "But you were the one to act first. You instinctively knew what I needed before I even expressed it." She reached to touch Drew's shoulder. "So don't act like it's not a big deal. Because it is to me."

Braking to stop for traffic again, Drew finally looked over. "I've spent my life helping people," she said. "It's a hard habit to break."

Smiling, Tess shook her head. "You're something, Drew Andersen," she said. "And I'm not buying that you don't care about what happened today. You were worried about Ashley too." Tess watched as Drew searched her face, her eyes questioning. *Does she think I'm insincere?* she wondered, trying to think of what to say to convince her, then Drew smiled. It was tentative and small but reached her brown eyes.

Turning to refocus on the traffic which had started to move again, Drew sighed. "Maybe a little bit," she said. "You seem like a good person, and I can't imagine what it must have felt like not to know what happened to your child."

Tess sobered. "It was horrible," she said, not wanting to think about the million scenarios that ran through her head. *Everything is okay*, she reminded herself, but she wouldn't be able to fully believe it until she had her arms around her daughter. They would meet at the house. She hoped they could get there soon.

Clearly sensing her unease, Drew reached across the console to pat Tess's knee and draw her back to the present. "Hey," she said. "It's going to be okay. The GPS says that even with traffic, we'll be in Beverly Hills in thirty minutes."

"You're right." Tess nodded, ready to think about something other than Ashley for the moment. Sitting there worrying the rest of the way wouldn't solve anything. Tilting her head, Tess regarded Drew again. She had a nice profile, and Tess couldn't deny she found her attractive. A fact that made her question what the woman said earlier in the trailer. *Could she truly have never had a love affair?* Tess wondered. *Or did she mean not like the one in the story?* And even if there was never a passionate love affair, that didn't necessarily mean she was always alone. "So, you don't have children?"

Drew's eyebrows shot up. "Me?" she asked. "Oh no. Not even a cat." She shrugged. "For me, it was all about work."

"And don't forget writing," Tess added. "You did that. And very well. The book is incredible."

"True. I did do that too," Drew said, her voice lacking enthusiasm. "But it took me a decade."

Tess pursed her lips, not quite understanding. "But all those years of effort were worth it, right?" she asked. "You've touched millions of readers." When Drew didn't comment, Tess worried she had said the wrong thing. By her thinking, having millions of people read her book was a good thing. "You disagree what you wrote was special?"

For a minute, they rode in silence with only the sounds of the traffic around them. "I don't know," Drew finally said. "Sometimes I think I was only lucky."

DREW HAD no idea why she said those words to Tess. She had never admitted that she felt what happened was simply luck to anyone before. Not her agent. Not even her brother. But there were a lot of times Drew felt she was a fraud. An imposter and not really a good writer. So many nights the words she wrote were simply to purge her anger toward life, let out her frustrations with the world, and far too often, soothe her hurt. When there was an especially bad shift at the hospital, if she witnessed a moment of unnecessary tragedy, the story served as her outlet. Amazingly, ten years and over one hundred thousand words later, there was a book. It would have stayed unpublished and forgotten if not for her brother's unexpected visit one random Thursday morning. He surprised her with coffee and donuts as she finished a double shift. "Work sent me to LA to give a presentation tomorrow," he said with his most charming smile. "I wanted to surprise you." When she frowned, he laughed at her dark expression. Drew was never one for surprises, but he was always the good-natured one in the family. "Now I can see maybe that was a bad idea. But let's enjoy the donuts at least."

Going back to her apartment, Drew hadn't thought about the printed pages of her manuscript sitting on her desk. According to him, when her brother went to grab her rickety old desk chair, something on a page apparently caught his eye. Having gone to her bedroom to change, Drew didn't know he was reading what she wrote until he was three pages in. "What are you doing?" she asked, rushing to grab the sheets from his hand. "This isn't your business."

"Did you write that?" he asked, and Drew didn't know if she should be pleased or offended by how surprised he looked. "It's really good." He shook his head. "No, I take that back. That material is great."

Drew shoved the pages into a drawer and slammed it. "It's not," she said. "Just stuff I write when I can't sleep." Yet, no matter how much she told him to forget the whole thing, he wouldn't let it go. After weeks of badgering her to show some chapters to him, she emailed him the first fifty pages to shut him up. That should have been the end of the discussion, but a literary agent called her out of the blue a month later. It took a while for the man to convince Drew he was even legitimate. The bottom line was—he wanted the rest of the story.

And eighteen months later, the book is being made into a movie. Starring Tess Landish of all people, she thought, still unable to quite grasp everything that happened to her after the book came out. "Do you really think so?" Tess asked, breaking into Drew's memories and bringing her back to the moment. "That all of it was only luck?"

Crawling along in traffic, Drew blinked, trying to refocus on what Tess was saying. "About the book?" she asked. "Yes. A lot of the time, I do."

"No," Tess said. "I don't believe that. You're talented and worked hard." She shook her head. "Trust me, I know from my own career that things might happen by fate, but not blind luck. Everything happens for a reason."

Suddenly the orange gas light glowed on the car's dash. "Like us needing gas, you mean?" Drew said, pointing at the indicator. "You're saying the bad timing is for a reason."

Tess leaned over to check what Drew said. She frowned. "I agree. That seems random and not good news," she said. "But you'd be surprised."

Unable to help herself, Drew rolled her eyes. "Yep," she said, checking the GPS map on the dash for gas station indicators. "I'll be surprised." With a few taps, their path rerouted to take the next exit off the freeway. "At least we aren't going too far out of the way."

COMING DOWN THE BOARDWALK, Bev shuffled her feet as fast as she could while Floyd pulled her along by the leash. If Ashley didn't know better, she would think the dog knew what was happening. *And Floyd wants to get the hell out of here*, she thought, trying to ignore the fear rolling in her stomach.

"A little faster, Bev," Ashley coaxed as they neared where Bryce had backed her truck up onto the curb. Kim and Lou already waited in the truck's bed. Ashley tried not to think about what the ocean might be doing behind her. So far there hadn't been another wave that even reached close to the boardwalk, but she would feel better if she could get Bev and Floyd in the truck. Even if they didn't leave to go further inland immediately, at least they would be ready. Watching her, most of the other shopkeepers along the boardwalk thought she was overreacting.

When she tried to explain the risk, they waved her off. "My store is a mess," a few of her neighbors said. "I need to clean everything up. I can't just leave it." Their arguments were so convincing, Ashley considered telling Bryce to wait a while. After all, her front door was demolished, and if she left now, there would be no way to secure the coffee shop. Anyone could walk in and take whatever they wanted.

Even Kim acted surprised when Ashley approached her. "You're leaving?" she asked, the gash above her eye seeping blood again. "Don't you want to wait for help to get here?" Ashley had bit her lip. The decision was hard to make, but for some reason, her instinct was to trust in Bryce's judgment. *If she says go...* Ashley thought. *For some reason, I believe in her.*

Ashley squatted beside Kim. "Come with us," she said. "We can take you to a hospital." She looked at Lou sitting there too. "And you too. Bryce is in the truck. Let's please go."

Lou groaned. "Seriously? I feel like I was hit by a bus," he said. "Why can't I wait until the paramedics come with some drugs and an ambulance?"

"Because that will probably take hours. And Bryce thinks staying might be dangerous," Ashley said. "And I believe her."

"Dangerous how?" Lou had asked, and Ashley pointed to the turbulent ocean.

"She's worried about that," she answered, watching Lou and Kim study the pattern of waves and decide for themselves. In the end, Ashley convinced them and Bev to come along, but at the rate the homeless woman moved, that last part might have been a mistake. "Nobody else wants a ride?" Bryce said, jogging up beside her. "You told them about what might happen?"

Ashley nodded. "I even used the word tsunami," she said. "But look at the waves. They are almost back to normal." Watching Bryce's face as she looked at the ocean, Ashley hoped the calmer water would be enough to change the woman's mind, and they could stay.

Her dark eyes scanned up and down the shoreline before she shook her head. "I still don't like it." She blew out a frustrated breath. "Damnit. Why are people so stubborn?" After another moment of staring at the ocean, Bryce scooped up Bev and started carrying her to the truck. "Can you grab Floyd's leash? I don't want to wait any longer."

Something in the way the woman said the words resolved all doubt Ashley had about leaving. Waves or no waves, Bryce wanted them to go. Grabbing the twisted rope that served as Floyd's lead, she followed. *At least I have plenty of insurance for the coffee shop*, she thought. *If thieves come and loot the place, I should be okay. Although I could have at least emptied the till.*

Suddenly, Floyd yanked on his leash so hard the rope nearly burned her hand as it slipped through. It was all she could do to keep hanging on at all. "Floyd," she said, trotting to keep up. "Slow down."

As they reached the pickup truck, Bryce was helping Bev into the back to join the others. "Everybody ready to go?" Bryce asked as the woman settled beside Kim with her back against the truck's cab.

"Yep," she said. "Floyd, hop into the back like a good—" Even though Bev didn't finish the sentence, the dog obeyed in a flash. "—oh God." Not sure what was wrong, Ashley followed the woman's stare. She heard Lou swearing or praying or something, and it took her a minute to comprehend what she saw. The water was rushing out like a super low tide, while in the distance, the ocean was swelling.

10

*A*s Bryce slammed the pickup truck's tailgate shut, she heard Ashley say her name. The woman's trembling voice sounded like a mixture of awe and fear. Turning to look, the last sight Bryce wanted to see was happening two hundred feet in front of her. An ocean swell like a monster rising from its depths was forming offshore.

"Ashley, get in the truck," she said, forcing her voice to stay calm but already in motion. "And everybody, grab ahold of something. We are getting out of here in a hurry." She saw Bev grab Floyd by the collar at the same time Bryce threw open the driver's side door to climb in. Suddenly, Floyd started to bark furiously in the direction of the ocean. *Not a good sign,* she thought, knowing when they were all safe again, she would be buying Floyd a huge T-bone steak dinner. As Ashley got in on the other side, Bryce cranked the key. The engine roared to life. *Thank you.* Bryce was grateful they weren't in the middle of some kind of adventure story where the cars never started.

Someone started slapping a hand on the rear window

between the cab and back. "It's coming!" she heard the group behind her all yelling. "Go! Go! Go!"

Not bothering to check for herself, Bryce threw the truck into gear. "Hang on," she said and hit the gas. The tires screeched as the truck shot forward, racing down the block. Glancing at the rearview mirror, Bryce saw the beach beyond the boardwalk. A wave was cresting as it ran toward shore. An already big wave. Everything she learned about tsunamis in her training raced through her mind. The thing would slow down when it hit the sand but rapidly grow taller. What looked to her like a ten-foot wave coming in could easily triple in height in seconds. At over thirty feet, anything less than two stories high would be entirely washed over. Out of the corner of her eye, she noticed Ashley watching out the back window. From her experiences in the military, Bryce's instinct was to tell her not to look, but that was an impossible ask. Turning away from impending disaster was nearly impossible.

Racing in a straight line down Rose Avenue, Bryce estimated they would be at least three blocks away when the wave hit land. It wasn't nearly enough. Moving up to a hundred miles an hour when it crashed into the beach, the water could overtake them. They would have to stay far enough ahead of the water for it to slow and then recede. She pushed the pedal harder into the floorboard, watching the red arrow on the speedometer climb past seventy. In response, the truck began to shudder. "Oh my God," she heard Ashley murmur, and Bryce didn't have to check the mirror to know what was happening. She focused on their sprint through the neighborhood to safety. People on sidewalks who fled their homes after the earthquake turned to look as the truck raced past them. All Bryce could do was lay on the horn to keep them clear and hope it served as a warning about the wave coming. There was no time to slow down and yell at them to run.

Blasting past another intersection and then another, Bryce started to think their head start might be enough. Then, as she blew through a red light at the next intersection of a busier street, the sound of a horn blaring warned her in the nick of time to swerve. The car coming from the cross street narrowly missed them, but the swerve forced the truck to sideswipe a parked vehicle. Stupidly not haven taken time to put on her seatbelt, the impact slammed Bryce's head against the door's window. Momentarily dazed, she struggled to drive. Screams from the truck bed had her thinking the worst. "Bev? Kim?" she yelled. "Are you still there?"

Someone started slapping the window divider again. "We're okay," Lou yelled. "Go!" With a shake of her head, desperate to clear the cobwebs, Bryce hit the gas again only to feel the truck list hard to the left and barely respond. Creeping along at a walking pace, the truck wouldn't go any faster, and she guessed the sidewall had been crushed against the tire. Any minute the thing could blow, and it would be game over.

"What's wrong with the truck?" Ashley asked, a hint of panic in her voice. Bryce looked at her, and tears streamed down the woman's face. A glimmer of something was in her eyes, and Bryce recognized the look from combat. It was dread.

WATCHING the giant ocean wave hit the Venice Beach boardwalk was something Ashley would never forget. *All those people who wouldn't listen*, she thought. *My friends...* She had to stop thinking about it or go crazy, so she focused on what Bryce was telling her. "The tire is stuck," Bryce said, reaching for the door handle. "I'm going to try and pull the metal away from it."

Ashley grabbed for her arm. "No," she said, desperately trying to keep herself together. "Stay inside. Keep driving as long as we can."

Relenting, Bryce pushed on the gas, and the truck did nothing but limp along. "It's no good," the woman said before glancing over her shoulder. "I have to get out... oh shit." Ashley looked too, and the wall of churning water already carrying debris channeled between buildings was gaining fast. "We need to get inside somewhere. Right now!"

Scanning the street, Ashley had no idea what to do. "There's nothing but businesses here," she said. "And it looks like everyone has evacuated." Suddenly, the truck veered, throwing her against the door, and Ashley thought the tire blew. Looking over, she saw it was actually Bryce driving toward a familiar multi-story orange and white building. A Los Angeles Public Storage.

Before she could ask what was happening, the truck hit the black metal gates, which looked to hold at first but then snapped open. Bryce rolled them to a halt beside the main building. "Get out and get ready to run," was all Bryce said before jumping out of the truck.

With no time to argue, Ashley climbed out while Floyd leaped out of the back and spun in a frantic circle at her feet. "What are you doing?" she heard Bev yell, and then Bryce ran around the front of the truck with the woman over her shoulder in a fireman's carry. Kim and Lou were hot on her heels.

"Come on," Bryce said, sprinting toward a pair of glass doors in the front of the concrete and otherwise windowless building. "We need to get in there." Not sure what Bryce was thinking, but knowing they were out of time, Ashley followed everyone into the building with Floyd right behind her. The door opened into a foyer. No one was behind the counter, and aisles ran in every direction, each lined with orange doors for dozens of storage lockers. Apparently not what Bryce wanted, the woman kept moving. "We need to find the emergency stairs and climb higher. They should be in the corner. Everyone, look for an exit sign."

"What?" was all Ashley got out before they were off and running again.

Bouncing around while Bryce ran, Bev seemed as baffled from where she hung upside down on the woman's back. "Exit?" she asked. "Why are we going back outside?"

"We're not," Bryce said, then slowed to point. "There."

Ashley saw the metal door marked STAIRWELL and ran to yank it open. Floyd flew past her, his toenails clattering on the metal stairs, with Bryce and Bev right behind him, then Kim and Lou, and finally Ashley could go.

"Close the door tight," she heard Bryce yell from somewhere already up the stairs.

Acting on nothing but faith, Ashley did and then started to run up the first flight after the others. They were only to the second landing when she heard things hitting the side of the building and the roaring start. The wave had caught up to them.

Suddenly, the lights went out, and Kim let out a scream. "Bryce," Ashley yelled, her heart racing while she forced herself to slow enough to make sure of her footing. Any minute she expected to hear water rushing up the stairs under her.

"Keep coming," Bryce said. "Trust me. The stairwell is high enough it will be pressurized for safety. We are going to be okay."

As the roaring continued, Ashley had to keep from

freezing with fear as she imagined the water going around their building. She couldn't believe she heard Bryce correctly and replayed her words in her mind as she climbed. *We are going to be okay*, she thought, although that seemed impossible. Yet Bryce sounded confident. *Can this building really save us?*

SITTING in the Pathfinder while Drew stood outside pumping their gas, a wave of unexplainable dread rolled over Tess. *Ashley*, she thought, somehow knowing without even a shadow of a doubt her daughter was in trouble. *Terrible trouble.* "Drew," she said, unable to keep the sound of desperation out of her tone as she opened the passenger door to lean out. "We need to go. Please."

"What?" Drew asked as she removed the nozzle from the vehicle and put it back in the cradle. "Did something happen?"

"Yes," Tess said, then shook her head. "Maybe. I don't know. Please hurry. I need to hear the radio."

Thankfully, Drew was quick climbing back into the car. Pressing the ignition button, the radio came back to life. "... substantial flooding from the tsunami," the radio announcer said. "Again, authorities are asking people to stay out of the area until all threats have passed."

Tess moaned, her heart seeming to stop in her chest. "No, this can't be happening," she said, closing her eyes as if she could shut out what she heard. *Had Ashley left the area before the wave hit?* she wondered. The plan was to meet at the house in Beverly Hills, and her daughter could easily be halfway there and well out of harm's way. But the mother-daughter bond they shared convinced Tess she wasn't. She felt it.

"Try and contact her again," Drew said as she turned them

out of the gas station's lot. "Maybe she's already at your place waiting for you." Wanting Drew to be right, she opened her eyes and dialed Ashley's number. Once again, the familiar recorded voice was back—all circuits were busy. In her frustration, Tess wanted to scream.

Never had she felt more helpless. "I don't know what to do." Her instinct was to find Ashley, to save her somehow, but there was no way to know if she was still at the Venice Beach boardwalk. Going there might be futile. *Or worse*, she thought. *It could be horribly dangerous.* The image of streets flooding with walls of water filled her mind. A whimper escaped her throat at the thought her daughter might be caught in the disaster.

Drew's hand grabbed hers. "Hey," she said. "Don't start thinking like that. We need to stay positive. Your daughter? She's resourceful, right?"

"Yes," Tess said, nodding, trying to breathe. "Very levelheaded." Suddenly, an idea came to her. "And she's probably with a U.S. Marine."

"You're serious?"

Tess felt a glimmer of hope. "Yes," she said. "A friend from college. Ashley described her as some kind of hero." Although she didn't dare say it out loud, it seemed the best person to have with her daughter in the middle of everything would be a Marine. She hadn't even met the woman yet, and Tess already liked her.

"Well, then let's get to your house and wait," Drew said, making a turn in the direction of the freeway. Tess hoped things would be moving faster than earlier, but Drew had to stop before they even made it to the onramp.

A long line of vehicles waited to take the freeway. "Shit," Tess said. Sitting in a long traffic jam was the last thing she wanted to deal with.

Relaxing her clenched hands on the steering wheel, Drew

did her best to hide her growing frustration. "Well, this is a problem," she said. "Maybe we should have stayed on the damn thing and tried to get home on what was in the tank." She reached for the GPS and changed the route to surface streets. The time estimate for their arrival at Tess's house doubled.

11

*S*tanding on the top landing of the stairwell, Bryce pressed her ear to the cold metal door she assumed was the roof access. They could not climb any higher. Although she believed they would be safe indefinitely where they were, enough time had passed that she wanted to know if it was dangerous outside. She listened but could only hear the others whispering behind her in the total darkness. "Why did we stop?" Lou asked in a hushed but trembling voice. "Are we high enough?"

"I don't know," Ashley answered. "Maybe we are at the top?" Her questions were followed by a sob that Bryce guessed came from Kim.

Only Bev, who stood beside Bryce with Floyd at her feet, kept quiet. "We're okay. But I need you to quiet down," Bryce said. "Everybody, stop talking and listen. I need to know what's happening outside." The stairwell fell silent, and she put her ear to the door again. Holding her breath to lessen any sounds, there was no more roaring from the wave that initially passed the building. *A faint lapping noise maybe?* Bryce thought, straining to hear over the beating of her own heart echoing in her ears. *We are probably more than high enough, especially since the wave should have started to lose height as it spread.* After another moment, she calculated the risks and decided to move forward. Standing in the dark not knowing what was happening elsewhere would be too hard on the group. "Everyone, wrap your arms around the handrail. Hang on tight, because I'm opening the door to the roof." She didn't want them knocked down the stairs if she was wrong, and water came rushing in.

"Wait a minute," Kim said. "What if we're underwater?"

"We're not," Bryce said, making sure she sounded confident although she wasn't one hundred percent positive. Anything could be happening outside the door. *But the only way to know is to open it and see,* she thought. "Is everyone ready?"

Lou swore under his breath. "As I'll ever be," he said while Bryce grabbed Floyd's collar. Then, taking a deep breath, she slowly turned the handle. Bracing her body against the door just in case, Bryce opened it only a crack, and nothing came in but light, half blinding her. Blinking to focus, Bryce peeked out. The rooftop was not only dry, but two people were standing on it, looking over the edge.

"Oh, thank you, Jesus," the woman in the pair said when she noticed the opening door. Arms outstretched, she rushed in their direction until Bryce stepped through the door in her civilian clothes. The woman stopped with a frown. "You're not a fireman."

Standing aside to let the rest of her group come out, Bryce hated disappointing her. "No, I'm not," she said. "We came up the stairs to get away from the wave."

"Same," the man staying back said. He wore blue coveralls with his name on a patch on the front pocket—Pete. Standing with his hands in his pants pockets, he seemed relatively unphased by what happened. Even with a balding head of gray hair and a bit of a potbelly, Bryce guessed by his confident stance he used to be something other than a handyman. "I was outside having a cigarette across the street, obeying the fifteen feet from the door rule," he said. "Saw the water coming and decided we needed to get on the roof."

Bryce nodded. "That was the right thing to do," she said. "We were lucky."

"Sure were," he said. "I watched the whole scene. Honestly, when the truck stopped moving, I figured you were done for."

"We would be if it weren't for Bryce," Ashley said, coming to stand next to her. Bryce looked at her and their eyes locked. "I owe you my life. We all do." Before Bryce could respond, the young woman took Bryce's face in her hands and kissed her. Surprised, but feeling the flare of heat go all the way to her toes, Bryce instinctively put her hands on Ashley's hips to pull her closer. Even with all the chaos around them, and half surrounded by strangers, she didn't want the kiss to end. It was a fantasy come to life to finally feel Ashley's lips on hers. After another beat, Ashley pulled back but continued to look into her eyes. What Bryce saw could not make her happier. There was much more than a spark.

TRAFFIC on all the major streets across Los Angeles was nearly at a standstill. Only by twisting and turning along alleys and side streets was Drew able to keep them moving at all. The GPS had a fit every time she went off the designated path, continuing to try and reroute her back to a jampacked major artery. Unfortunately, Drew wasn't familiar enough with the part of the city they were in to get by entirely without it. Thankfully, Tess kept quiet as Drew did her best. Glancing at her from time to time, Drew was impressed by how calmly she went about dialing and texting on her phone over and over. Every try resulted in the same disappointing results though.

"Do you have a phone charger?" Tess finally asked when Drew slowed for a stop sign.

One problem with the side routes was constantly stopping and waiting for a break in the cross traffic. Blowing out a frustrated breath at the sight of a long line of cars blocking her, Drew opened the center console. "The plugs are in here," she said. "We should make sure both of our phones get a good charge in case anything else happens."

As she plugged the white cable into her phone, Tess shook her head. "I'm not sure if I can handle much more," she said. "All I want is to get home, hug my daughter, and have a large glass of wine. A very large glass of wine."

"Then that's what we will do," Drew said, pleased to hear Tess stay positive even though she couldn't get any calls to go through. Tapping her finger on the wheel, she continued to watch out the windshield for any chance to cross. Just as it looked like she had an opening, someone knocked on her door's window, making her jump. "What in the hell…"

About ready to give whoever surprised her a piece of her mind, she paused at the wild look of panic on the face of the man beside her car. "Please help me," he said through the window. "It's my wife." He pointed at the vehicle directly behind hers. "In the car."

Drew wasn't ready to lower her window. "What's the problem?"

He grabbed his short dark hair with both hands as if losing his mind. "She's having a baby," he answered. "Please. I don't know what to do."

Glancing at Tess, she was about to explain she had to help when the actress nodded. "Go help them," she said.

Without another moment's hesitation, Drew was out of

the Pathfinder and jogging behind the man to take a look. "I see," she said, staying calm, taking in the scene. The young black woman in the passenger seat looked in severe pain. As if to underline how bad it was, the woman let out a blood curling scream. To make matters worse, a toddler in a car seat in the back wailed too.

"Can you help me?" the father said. "She says the baby is coming, but I can't get through to 9-1-1."

Tess joined Drew beside the man's car. "How can I help?" she asked, and Drew felt a new appreciation for her. Even with all her stress and worry about her own daughter's safety, she wanted to do what she could for the family in crisis.

Taking over the scene, Drew pointed at the crying child in the car. "Get the baby out of the car seat, take her over to the sidewalk, and do what you can to calm her down," she said, then turned to the father. "I'm going to need that car seat out. Your wife needs to move into the backseat to lay as flat as possible. I don't want her to have this baby on the ground, and it's too tight in the front seat."

Tess was already moving, but the man stood in place, his eyes wide. "Is she having the baby right here?"

"Seems likely from the sound of things," Drew said. "I have to look, but first, I need that car seat out." She pointed into the vehicle. "Now, do it."

As if she shocked him with her last barked command, the man sprang into action. Pausing to take in everything around her, Drew took in a deep breath, held it to the count of four, then let it out slowly as she walked to her vehicle. Opening the back, she grabbed her emergency bag and tried to relax. She had helped deliver babies in the emergency room, but so many things could go wrong. *Think positive*, she reminded herself. *It's only one more birth. Nothing different other than the location.*

. . .

GENTLY BOUNCING the baby girl on her hip, Tess cooed into the scrunched-up, tear-streaked little face. "It's going to be okay, sweetheart," she said. "Shhh. You don't need to worry." The tone in Tess's voice seemed to get through to the little girl because her crying slowed. Watching her open her large brown eyes, Tess worried for a moment the child would howl again when she realized a stranger held her. To her surprise, the little girl did the opposite, seeming fascinated to see her. With a final hiccup, the crying stopped altogether. "Well, there you go. See? Nothing to worry about. Your mom is in good hands." Considering how Drew had taken control of the situation from the minute she stepped out of the car, Tess believed her words were true. As she watched them from the sidewalk, under Drew's direction, the father helped her lift the struggling woman out of the passenger seat so she could shuffle around to the cleared backseat.

Tess noticed a blanket was spread out for the mother to lay on, and with a practiced hand, Drew snapped on latex gloves.

"You go get in on the other side and hold her head in your lap," she said to the father. "Let her squeeze the hell out of your hand if she wants to but try to keep her focused."

Tess watched the man do what Drew said, knowing from the look on his face, he was near panicking himself. *I wonder if he knows how lucky he is right now,* she thought. *He could have knocked on a hundred windows and probably not found a woman more qualified to help in the emergency than Drew Andersen.*

While Tess was distracted watching Drew crouch at the open back door, she was surprised to feel the little girl's hand on her face. Turning to look, she realized the child was reaching for Tess's long blonde hair. "Oh, so that's what you're distracted by?" she asked with a smile, letting the child's waving hand feel it. As she did, memories of holding Ashley rushed upon her. In the emergency, she had been able to focus on something other than her worry for her daughter. Her chest clenched with anxiety. *Oh, Ashley, where are you?* she thought. *Please be at home waiting for me.*

When Ashley was not quite a year old and starting to walk everywhere, Tess had been so worried about her daughter falling and getting hurt. Friends and family who visited teased her for all the baby gates she had to corral the curious girl. Still, for all her precautions, Ashley slipped past her defenses, and to her horror, Tess heard a thump, thump, thump coming from the stairs leading to the basement. In a panic, she feared the worst, only to find Ashley tottering around exploring the new world she found with nothing more than a bloody bottom lip. *And like then, I must trust that my girl will bounce back from whatever is happening and be fine.*

Suddenly, the woman in the backseat let out a scream much louder than the others, pulling Tess back to the moment. In response, the little girl started to cry all over again. Fearing for the worst but unable to stay away, Tess crept closer. Drew glanced over. "Stay right here with me," she said. "I want you to hand me that beach towel when I ask for it."

Tess nodded, seeing it on the roof of the car as she pulled the crying child tighter to free her other hand. "I'm ready."

"Okay, everybody, we're going to make this look easy. On three, I want a big push," Drew said. Tess held her breath. "One, two, three." The mother screamed but clearly pushed, because in another moment Drew held a squirming, red-faced baby cradled in her hands.

12

Running gentle fingers along the newborn's forehead, Drew watched the little boy snuggle against his mother and begin to nurse. She loved nothing more than to see the mother-child bonding experience happening in front of her. Of all the sights in the emergency room, watching a baby take to its mother was her favorite. *All things considered, he's off to a great start*, she thought. *And his family will have a hell of a story to tell about the day he arrived.* "Well done," she said. "He's very handsome and looking hearty."

Her eyes filled with tears, the mother reached to take Drew's and held it tight. "Thank you," she said, a sob of happiness in her words. "I don't know what we would have done…"

Smiling, Drew squeezed the woman's hand. "Everything has a way of working out," she said. "I am glad I could be here to help bring your son into the world. And now…" She turned her focus to the father who hovered protectively near her. "I know traffic is horrible, and it will take you a while, but you need to inch your way to the hospital."

His eyes widened. "Is something wrong?" he asked. "Is it the baby? My wife?"

Drew shook her head. "Nothing is wrong. Not at all," she said. "But they both need a thorough check. Routine procedure."

Nodding, the man looked relieved. "Right," he said. "I'll go now." He hesitated. "Can I put my daughter's car seat in the front?"

Drew smiled. "Considering the circumstances, yes," she said. "I imagine you'll be driving more cautiously than anyone could believe possible." She stepped from beside the car so the backdoor could be gently closed. "Let me get my car out of your way." Looking toward the sidewalk, she saw Tess rocking the comforted toddler against her while the little girl held a handful of the woman's long blonde hair. The picture of the two of them was so serene and sweet, Drew took a beat before interrupting to tell Tess it was time for her to give up her charge. Considering how chaotic and stressful the morning had been, the fact Tess could focus only on soothing the child impressed her. *There is no way to know where Ashley is or if she is okay, but she put that all aside to help,* Drew thought. *All the more reason I have to do everything I can to find her daughter.*

As if feeling Drew's eyes on her, Tess glanced over and smiled. "Are you ready for this one?" she asked, moving toward the car. "I think two minutes in her car seat, and she will be fast asleep."

"Thank you," the father said, taking the sleepy little girl from Tess. "Thank you both so very much." As he held the toddler in his arms, he paused. "I'm sorry, I know my question is weird, but are you Tess Landish?" He grinned. "My wife and I are big fans. You were amazing in *Lights at Night.*"

Before Tess could respond, one of the bystanders gathered to watch the drama approached. "I'm a huge fan too," the woman gushed. "Could I get an autograph?" As if the floodgates had opened, more people came forward, telling Tess how much they loved her. Drew had never seen anything like it, and although Tess seemed calm under the onslaught, she sensed the attention wasn't welcome. Especially considering everything else going on with Tess at the moment. They didn't have time to be standing around giving out autographs when they needed to find Ashley.

Banking on Tess wanting rescuing, Drew waded into the forming crowd and took the actress by the elbow. "If you'll excuse us," she said, not hesitating to push people aside. "We're late for an appointment and have to go." While a few protested, Drew led Tess away toward the Pathfinder.

Tess leaned in as they hustled for the vehicle. "Thank you so much for that," she whispered. "I don't know if I could have kept myself together much longer. Soothing that little girl has been tearing my heart out about Ashley."

Holding the door for Tess to climb in, Drew nodded. "Then let's go find her."

STILL A LITTLE IN awe they were all okay, Ashley watched as Kim plopped down on the rooftop. In all the activity, blood had started to seep from the cut over her eye again. "I'm not moving another inch until someone officially comes to tell me it's safe," she said. "My head hurts, and I'm sick of being scared."

Kneeling beside her, Ashley tried to think of something to motivate the woman to keep going. She wasn't ready to stay in one place, at least not that close to the beach. As a group, they had watched from the rooftop as the wave washed back out the way it came. Things Ashley didn't want to recognize were in the water. Bryce's truck was gone entirely. Even with the wave receding, low-lying areas looked flooded. Still, for the most part, the street was clear enough to at least walk. "Kim," she said. "Everything has been scary for me too. But I need to find my mom. I don't want to leave you behind."

"She's fine to stay with us," Pete said from where he stood at the roof's edge, studying the street. "We're safe up here. No wave bigger than that one is coming."

Although Ashley didn't understand how the man knew, Lou was clearly happy to hear that news and settled down beside Kim. "In that case, I'm staying too," he said. "But if you want to go find your mom, I get it. If my mom weren't living in Las Vegas, I'd be worried too."

Ashley looked at Bryce beside her. "What do you think?" she asked. "Is it safe to go back down to the street?" With her brow furrowed, Bryce walked to stand beside Pete, and Ashley watched as she surveyed the street.

Finally, she nodded. "I think we can make a run for it," she said. "But if we are going, I want to do it now. Let's not tempt fate."

Taking Kim's hand, Ashley looked hard into the woman's face. "You're sure you don't want to come with us?" she asked, and Kim nodded.

"Yes," she said before wrapping her arms around Ashley, nearly knocking her off balance. "I owe you my life, Ashley. When I think about what would have happened to me if I didn't listen…" The image of the wave slamming into the boardwalk rose in Ashley's mind. Her heart hurt to think of those people who didn't listen. She would never forgive herself for not trying harder to convince them. *But I had no idea what it would be like*, she thought. *I couldn't quite believe it either.*

Ashley hugged Kim. "We are the lucky ones," she said, her voice wavering a moment with emotion. "And remember to stay thankful for what we have."

She felt Lou's big hand squeeze her shoulder. "Kim's right," he said. "You and Bryce are heroes. Thank you."

Tears threatened, so Ashley broke away and stood. "We will send help when we find someone."

Bryce had come to wait beside her. "Are you ready?" she asked, and Ashley nodded.

"Yes," she said. "Let's go." As the two of them started to walk toward the stairs, Ashley caught sight of Bev and Floyd falling in behind them. "Oh." She wasn't sure what to say. Having Bev and her dog stay with them hadn't crossed her mind.

Bev put her hands on her hips. "You don't think I'm going to let you out of my sight?" she said. "We're only alive because we stuck with you." She waved a hand at Bryce. "I'll follow this badass chick anywhere." For a second, Ashley wondered how long Bev intended to hang out with them. Seeing her hesitation, Bev laughed. "Don't worry. I'm not trying to move in on your girl. Just trying to stay alive."

Looking to Bryce for assistance, she found no help when the woman shrugged. "We can make it work," she said. "Once we get past the flood damage, maybe we can get a ride to Beverly Hills from someone." She moved to rub Floyd behind his ear, making the dog grin with pleasure. "Besides, I kind of like having this guy with us. He's got a sixth sense." At that, Ashley had to agree. She hoped there wouldn't be any more reasons for them to need it.

MOVING with the stop-and-go traffic again, Tess went back to dialing and texting her daughter's number. Repeatedly, the recording was the same frustrating voice or the same undelivered text message. With no means of communicating with her, all she could do was hope Ashley was waiting for her at the house in Beverly Hills when they arrived. Resting the phone in her lap for a break, she watched Drew drive. Back to hands at ten and two, the nurse looked comfortable and confident. *How did I ever get so lucky to have her in my life?* Tess wondered. "You're amazing, you know that?" she said. "I've never met anyone like you."

With raised eyebrows, Drew glanced at her. "Where did that come from?" she asked, and Tess shook her head.

"I watched you deliver a baby in the backseat of a car stuck in traffic," she said. "Like it was something you did all the time." She tilted her head. "Did you help with the delivery of a lot of babies in the emergency room?"

Drew shrugged. "Some," she said. "Bringing babies into the world was one of the high points of the job. All things considered, we were very lucky with that one."

"Lucky?" Tess asked, not sure having a baby in the back-seat of a car was lucky. "How so?"

"No serious complications. The baby boy appeared healthy and strong. Which is truly a good thing," Drew answered. "With this traffic, there would be no way to get paramedics on the scene. Even if there was a pathway through all the mess, I imagine most emergency personnel have responded to the disaster along the coastline..." Her voice trailed off and she glanced over, looking apologetic. Tess guessed she realized what she was implying. There were likely a lot of injuries or worse from the earthquake and the tsunami. Injuries similar to the ones her daughter could have sustained. Drew frowned. "Sorry I said that."

Without responding for fear of acknowledging what Drew said might make it come true, Tess started on her phone again. Expecting the recorded voice as she held it to her ear, when the phone rang normally, she almost didn't know how to react. *Pick up, Ashley,* she begged as it rang and rang. *Come on, honey. Answer the phone.*

Just about when Tess was sure it was going to roll to

voicemail, she heard the word her heart craved. "Mom?" came the sound of her daughter's voice. "Can you hear me?"

Her hand shaking, Tess couldn't hold back the tears. "Yes," she sobbed. "I'm here. Are you okay?"

"We're okay, Mom. Don't cry," Ashley said, although she sounded close to tears herself. "But it was scary. We are in Venice Beach on a rooftop."

A *rooftop*, Tess thought, hating to imagine what the circumstances were that put her daughter there. "Are you trapped?"

There was the muffled sound of Ashley talking to someone else for a moment. Then she was back. "No," she said. "We aren't trapped. Bryce says it's okay to go down and start walking."

A sense of relief washed over Tess. Bryce the U.S. Marine was with her daughter. Still, she didn't like the idea of Ashley on foot. "Walking?" Tess asked, knowing they were miles from her house. Ashley seemed to hesitate. Tess didn't like it. "What?"

"We did have Bryce's truck, but, well, it got washed away," Ashley replied, and Tess felt her heart stop for a second.

"Washed away?" she whispered, not wanting to think about the implications around that statement. She gathered herself. "Okay, so we will come to get you." Tess knew she was asking yet another favor of Drew, but there was no way she would let her daughter walk to Beverly Hills. It was miles through some not-so-great parts of Los Angeles. After everything they'd been through, Tess wouldn't rest until she could put her arms around Ashley and hold her safe. "Where exactly are you?"

13

*A*s they reached the security guard shack at the main gate onto the Sony Pictures Studio lot, Bryce had never been more ready to sit down somewhere and have a long, cold drink of water. Walking the five and a half miles along Venice Boulevard with the stream of displaced people headed east away from the coast wouldn't have been particularly bad normally. But she had ended up carrying Bev while Ashley held Floyd's leash. When they finally saw the signature white walls of the movie lot, Bryce was ready to put Bev down. The woman rode piggyback, and it wasn't so much that she was heavy, but she didn't smell particularly good. A cross between vinegar, old sweat, and wet dog. Plus, she seemed to think giving a nonstop monologue about their harrowing escape from the tsunami was necessary. "I can't believe I'm still alive," Bev said as they reached their destination, and Bryce gently set her down. "When you sideswiped that car and we slowed way down, I thought I was about to punch my timecard."

"That was a close call," Bryce murmured in response. "We were definitely lucky."

Bev patted Bryce's arm. "Lucky? Like hell," she said with a gap-toothed grin of stained teeth. "We made it because you are an A-number one badass. Saved by a Marine. Go figure."

Out of the corner of her eye, Bryce noticed Ashley was covering a smile with her hand. "What?" Bryce asked, starting to grin.

Ashley shook her head. "Nothing," she said. "Just glad Bev reassured me earlier she wasn't trying to steal my girl."

"She's a keeper," Bev chimed in as she took Floyd's leash. "If I was a little younger..."

Bryce appreciated the recommendation, no matter what the circumstances. "Thank you, Bev," she said. "But really, I was only doing what I was trained to do."

Bev waved off the comment. "You're more than only that, hon," she said with a chuckle. "Thanks for the lift. You kids take care of yourself." Bryce raised her eyebrows.

There hadn't been any mention of splitting up. "Are you leaving?" Ashley asked, sounding as surprised as Bryce felt. "We just got here."

"Oh, you know I can't go in a place like that," Bev said with a nod toward the studio lot. "But it's okay. I know some folks who hang out around here." She shrugged. "I'll find something to eat and a place to spend the night."

Ashley shook her head. "No, you wait," she said. "They will let you in with us once I tell them who I am. Don't go yet."

Holding up Floyd's leash, Bev hesitated. "With Floyd too?" she asked, and Bryce was relieved to see Ashley nod.

"Floyd too," she said. "Let me talk to the guard. Maybe Mom is here already." She walked toward the guard at the entrance. The plan Ashley and her mom had come to while Ashley was on the roof of the public storage building was for everyone to meet at the studio. Tess, in Drew's car, would continue to drive west while Bryce, Ashley, Bev, and Floyd walked east. Sony Pictures was a logical point between them where Tess knew they would be welcome. Plus, Ashley knew precisely where it was after spending a fair part of her childhood visiting her mom working there. Tess assured Ashley they would treat them like royalty. It hadn't mattered to Bryce either way. All she wanted was to get out of the immediate area of the Venice Beach boardwalk.

It wasn't that she worried another tsunami might come, but because once the water receded completely, looters would start showing up. In her experience in the Marine Corps, she witnessed the speed at which thugs would descend after a disaster. The lack of law and order was too much for some people to resist. They would take advantage, and if anyone got in their way, things could get dangerous quickly. When Ashley insisted she meet her mom somewhere, Bryce only cared that they picked a place miles from any risk of trouble.

"Okay," Ashley said, returning to them with three plastic badges on lanyards marked GUEST in big red letters. "The guard remembered me and buzzed the main office. A production assistant is coming to meet us at the gate to escort us to a place we can wait comfortably."

Bev took the fancy badge, fingering it with a look of awe on her face. "Well, look at that," she said before turning to Floyd. "We're moving up in the world." Bryce watched as Floyd responded with a yawn. The dog was calm and relaxed, exactly the way she wanted to see him.

FOR THE LAST hour as Drew drove them along clogged surface streets toward the famous Sony Pictures Studio lot, she watched Tess wringing her hands. The woman became more and more animated the closer they got. As they crossed into the Culver City area of Los Angeles, Tess was all but hopping in her seat from anticipation. With a clear lane ahead of them at last, they would be at the gate in less than five minutes. "Please let her be there," Tess said repeatedly under her breath.

"She will be," Drew assured her, willing her words to be true. "Keep thinking positive. It's gotten us this far."

Surprising Drew, Tess touched her arm, giving it a squeeze. "You've gotten us this far," she said. "And I will always be grateful."

Not expecting the praise, Drew shrugged. "Well, I'm not sure that is warranted," she said, unsure why admiration from Tess made her uncomfortable. "Most people would have done the same."

"Would they?" Tess asked, and when Drew glanced at her, the woman was studying her closely. "I am not so sure. You're more special than you realize." Drew felt herself starting to blush. Hearing words like that, especially from someone lovely like Tess Landish, wasn't something she was used to in her life. Before she could deflect the compliment, Tess kept going. "I know you're thinking of a way to change the subject, but I won't let you yet. You need to hear what I have to say."

Drew raised an eyebrow. "Hear what?" she asked, not sure she could handle more accolades.

"Hear that you're amazing," Tess said. "Not only have you helped me when you didn't have to, but for God's sake, you brought a healthy baby boy into the world today."

Not sure what to say, Drew kept her mouth shut as she made the last turn that would lead them to the main gate. She hoped with a bit of luck Tess would run out of steam and let the conversation move on. Instead, the woman leaned across the center console and kissed Drew on the cheek before whispering in her ear. "I've never met anyone like you."

Unable to help it, Drew felt her body react to the warmth of Tess's breath on her cheek. As crazy as the day had been, it didn't erase the fact she had spent the day with one of the most beautiful and charismatic women alive. The fact Tess thought she was not only amazing but also willingly told her so only made Drew more attracted to the actress. *Work will be interesting tomorrow*, she thought. *Or whenever Tess is ready to return to the set.* Even though there was a natural disaster in one part of Los Angeles, it didn't mean the world stopped in all the rest. When it came to the entertainment industry, the show must go on.

"Oh my God, I see them!" Tess suddenly yelled, making Drew jump.

"Where?" she asked, and Tess pointed. Drew saw a trio of women who could not look more different from one another. One blonde, one dark-haired, and one wearing what looked like a filthy LA Dodgers baseball hat. And a black and white dog on a leash. They looked like they were waiting for someone or something coming from the direction of the gate and paid no attention to the street. To complicate things more, they would have no way of knowing what kind of car Tess would be riding in. When Tess realized Ashley hadn't noticed them approaching, she turned to Drew.

"Honk or something," she asked. Drew complied while Tess rolled down her window and called Ashley's name.

First, a car horn honked, and out of reflex, Ashley started to look. She wanted to hear her mom's voice so badly that at first, she thought she imagined someone calling her name.

"Ashley," Bryce said, pointing down the street. "Is that your mom's car?"

Looking harder, the car was utterly unfamiliar, but the woman with the long, blonde hair leaning out the window was definitely the face she loved the most. "Mom!" Ashley yelled, running in the direction of the white Pathfinder. Before the vehicle even stopped moving, the passenger door flew open, and Tess Landish jumped out. She raced toward Ashley, and in another moment, they were hugging each other, crying and laughing. Nothing had ever felt as good as having her mom's arms around her. All the fear and worry and panic seemed to wash away as they stood there on the sidewalk holding each other. Amazingly, they were both safe and back together.

Finally, Tess pulled back and took Ashley's face in her hands. "Let me look at you," she said, her eyes roaming over Ashley. "You're sure you are okay?"

Ashley covered her mom's hands with her own. "Yes," she said, nodding. "It almost seems impossible, but yes, I'm okay." Feeling a rush of emotion in the wake of all that had happened, more tears ran down her cheeks. "But I never would have made it if not for Bryce." Looking over her shoulder, she saw the woman who was nothing short of her hero standing back to give Ashley and her mom space. A huge smile was on her face, and it warmed Ashley's heart to know Bryce was moved by their reunion. Putting an arm around her mom's shoulders, Ashley started to lead her toward Bryce. "Come meet her, Mom."

"Yes, I want to meet her," Tess said as she broke away from Ashley and marched straight up to Bryce. Without warning, Ashley watched her mom wrap the woman in a giant hug. The look of surprise on Bryce's face was priceless. The big, strong, and courageous Marine was at a loss of what to do in the grasp of her mother's love. Enjoying the sight,

Ashley basked in the feeling of relief that continued to wash over her. Things would never be the same, that she knew. There were things she saw that she would never be able to forget, but she was choosing to live in the moment.

Feeling someone come up beside her, Ashley looked to see a shorter, brown-haired woman standing with her. "Clearly, you are Ashley," the woman said, holding out her hand. "I'm Drew. And it's very good to finally meet you."

Ashley processed what the stranger said as she shook her hand. "Drew?" she asked. "As in Drew Andersen, the author of the book mom's movie is based on?"

The woman nodded. "Yes," she replied. "One and the same. I was on the set with your mom when the earthquake rattled things."

Ashley shook her head, not quite sure she understood how the famous author ended up with her mom. "Where were you guys shooting today?"

Rubbing her jaw, Drew sighed. "South Los Angeles."

Her eyes going wide, Ashley could hardly believe it. "And you drove her all the way?"

Drew shrugged. "She didn't have a car. When she couldn't reach you, I agreed to drive her to find you," she said.

Ashley was about to point out how incredibly generous it was giving her mom a ride across Los Angeles, especially in the middle of all the chaos, when Bev and Floyd came up to them.

"Does this mean we aren't going to go on the studio lot?" Bev asked, clearly disappointed.

Sorry to let her down, but no longer wanting to stay, Ashley put her hand on Bev's arm. "I'm sorry," she said. "But I want to go home."

Bev nodded, fingering the temporary guest pass around her neck. "Can I keep this as a souvenir at least? Something to remember our crazy day."

Ashley smiled and leaned closer. "Keep it. I won't tell if you don't tell," she said happy to see a twinkle come into Bev's eyes.

The woman grinned. "Good. Lost everything in the flood, you know. I need to start rebuilding my stash."

14

*W*ith Bev and Floyd on their way to find other street friends, and while Ashley with her mom continued to reassure each other they were okay, Bryce scanned her phone's mapping app. She needed to figure out how far she was from her motel. Not familiar with the Culver City sections of Los Angeles, she was a little turned around. Fatigue didn't help. With everyone safe and back together, the stress and physical exertion of the day were catching up to her. Although Bev wasn't much heavier than running with a full backpack in Marine Corps boot camp training, Bryce still burned significant energy reserves. Not to mention how thirsty she was. Getting back to her motel room, drinking a gallon of water with her head under the tap, and then crashing on the bed sounded like heaven to her. When the phone's results came back with the best land route, which was only two miles southwest, she was set. Leaving Ashley behind would be hard, but the woman didn't need her anymore with her mom there.

"What has you so engrossed in your phone?" Ashley asked, coming up beside Bryce. Almost casually, she ran a hand up her arm, and Bryce wasn't even sure Ashley realized she had done it. The gesture had a familiar, almost intimate quality to it. The craziness and shock of the day had brought them closer. Rapidly. Bryce read somewhere extreme circumstances could do that.

The sudden closeness made it harder for Bryce to leave, but she hoped she would see Ashley again soon. *Maybe even a normal date?* she thought. *One without a natural disaster.* "If you think you're okay now," she said. "I'm going to start walking to my motel."

A look of surprise, with a hint of fear, appeared on Ashley's face. "What?" she asked, starting to frown. "You can't go."

"What did I overhear?" Tess asked from where she stood near the woman who drove her across Los Angeles to get to Ashley. A quick introduction and Bryce had learned she was Drew Andersen, the famous author. Tess shook a finger at her in a way that made Bryce feel like a kid again, yet the action was obviously meant with affection. "You are not walking anywhere, Bryce, that's for sure."

Just then, a woman came out of the Sony Studio's gate. She carried a clipboard, walkie-talkie, and an air of efficiency. "Ms. Landish?" she said, approaching Tess. "I'm Rachel, the production assistant Sony has assigned to you. Would you like to come with me? There is a lounge open, and I can get you whatever you might need."

"Wait one second," Tess said before looking to Drew. Bryce saw a warmth come into Tess's eyes. "Drew, as much as I will eternally appreciate you for driving me all over Los Angeles, I'm going to ask transportation to assign me a limousine from the carpool. Everyone is ready to go home." She softened her voice. "Including you."

Bryce noticed Drew's eyebrows lifting. Clearly Tess's request for a different ride surprised her. *I suppose after being the one to help Tess all day, she didn't expect it to end so abruptly,* she thought, wondering what the relationship between the two women was precisely. On the run in the canyon earlier that day, but what felt like a lifetime ago, Ashley mentioned her mom working on a new film about a famous book. She had been worried about how it might go when the author found out Tess hadn't read the book. *Apparently, things went okay.* Still, she watched the author square her shoulders. "Well, on that note, I think I'll head home and see what kind of damage I have to deal with at my house," Drew said, and Tess covered her mouth with her hand.

"Oh, Drew, I'm so sorry. I never thought to ask you where you lived," she gasped. "Or if there was anyone you were worried about." Tess grabbed Drew's arm. "I have been so selfish. And you have been so wonderful."

Drew responded with a smile, her eyes holding Tess's. "It doesn't matter. My family is all in Texas, and my place is a new house in the hills above Malibu. I've hardly had time to move in, let alone call it home." Bryce watched as the look between the two women went on for a beat. If she didn't know better, there was a spark there too. Maybe not as strong as she felt for Ashley, but something. Finally, with a blush, Drew broke away. "Well, take care. I'll see you on the set."

BITING HER LIP, Tess wasn't sure what to do. Drew had proven to be her rock all day. Calm, resourceful, and willing to do whatever was needed to help. Tess hadn't realized it, but suddenly parting ways with her would leave a void. Having her near had helped comfort Tess. Still, she couldn't exactly keep monopolizing the woman's time and attention indefinitely. *For crying out loud, we barely know each other,* she thought. *So why do I feel so attached?* Finding herself having to fight back emotions, Tess plastered on her famous smile to hide how she felt. "Of course, you should head home," she said. "I can't imagine I'll be getting any word on call times for the morning with the phone lines down. But the state of emergency can't go on forever."

"No, certainly not. Not in Los Angeles," Drew agreed, starting to back away. If Tess wasn't mistaken, Drew appeared hesitant to leave. *Does she have new feelings to deal with too?* Tess wondered. For some reason, she really hoped so. As complicated as the reality of an attraction between them might be, Tess wasn't ready to be done with Drew Andersen. Their relationship might have started off rocky, but over the last eight hours, things had changed. *And I look forward to exploring some of these feelings. But asking her to come to stay with me now to make me feel more secure doesn't make any sense.*

For the moment, they both had other things to do. "Well. See you soon then," Tess said. "Drive safely. Please." Smiling, Drew nodded and turned to leave. Unable to let her go yet, Tess took two steps and grabbed the woman's shirt sleeve. "And maybe, you know, try to get a call through to me? To let me know you're home safe and that everything is okay for you." She shrugged, suddenly feeling a little foolish for asking Drew to check in with her. "Or at least a text." Drew might not feel anything toward her, but Tess would still worry about her. "Anyway, in case I can help with anything. I owe you."

"You don't owe me anything," Drew said, smiling but with seriousness to her tone. "I wanted to help you, and I'm glad everything worked out and your daughter is safe." Without another word, she kept walking to her Pathfinder. Tess watched her go, uneasy with her leaving, while Ashley came up beside her.

Her daughter wrapped an arm around her waist. "I'm

impressed with your friend Drew. She's special, isn't she?" Ashley asked, and Tess nodded.

"Surprisingly so," she said distractedly, waving as Drew pulled away from the curb. She watched it until the vehicle turned the corner and was out of sight. Only then did Tess refocus on the task at hand—getting the three of them to her home. She turned to the production assistant holding her walkie-talkie in her hand. "Any luck on getting us a car?"

Rachel gave a brisk nod. "It's on the way," she said. "Although the carpool operator did want to warn you traffic everywhere is a mess. The trip home could take a long time." Tess didn't bother to tell the woman she was well aware of the state of the traffic problem. Only thanks to Drew's patience, excellent driving skills, and ability to navigate in chaos was she able to be back with Ashley at all.

Tess nodded. "I understand," she said with a glance toward Bryce. "I want you to come to stay with us for a while. It's the least I can offer."

"Really, that's unnecessary," Bryce started, but Tess shook her head.

"Don't try to change my mind. My house in Beverly Hills has seven bedrooms," she said. "There's plenty of room for all of us. Frankly, I'm rattled. Having you around will help."

Ashley hugged her mom a little tighter. "Same with me," she said, looking at Bryce. "Thanks, Mom."

Pleased everyone was on board with the plan, Tess saw the black limousine come out of the gate toward them. The sight filled her with relief. Finally, they were going home.

FIFTEEN MINUTES LATER, Ashley sat in the back of the limousine with her mother waiting for Bryce to get her stuff from the low-end motel room where she had stayed the night before. "Thank you for letting us come stay with you for a while," Ashley said, making her mom smile.

"I'm not letting you more than I am insisting," Tess said. "I wouldn't be able to stand being alone and not knowing where you were." She reached out a hand, and Ashley took it. "I was terrified."

Ashley squeezed her mom's hand. "So was I, but it's okay now." *Thanks to Bryce,* she thought, looking out the window to catch sight of Bryce stepping out of the room with nothing but a large, green military duffle bag. Realizing that was all the woman had made Ashley a little sad. During their long talk on the phone the night before, Bryce revealed her father had recently passed away. The house she grew up in was sold to pay hospital bills. Even though Ashley thought she heard traces of sadness in her voice, Bryce had played off the loss, saying that it didn't matter because she was due to go back to the Marine Corps soon. Still, the one bag seemed like so little in the grander scheme of things. Not that Ashley needed material possessions, although she wanted for nothing growing up. She simply hadn't wanted much. Many children, including some of her peers, were spoiled rotten living the plush life she did, but the desire for fancy clothes or expensive cars never interested her. Probably because her mom didn't put much stock in it either. They lived a simple enough life while Ashley grew up. It was true, the house in Beverly Hills was large, with a pool and a part-time housekeeper, but it was only to keep up pretenses in a lot of ways. If she and her mom were suddenly put in the position to live with much less, Ashley knew they would persevere.

Not as well as my rough and ready girlfriend though, Ashley thought, holding Bryce's hand once she was back in the limo. She paused. *Did I just think of her as my girlfriend?* Although it seemed impossible to be so attached that quickly, Ashley did not doubt that she wanted the woman to be a big part of her life. The fact Bryce was in the military would be something to overcome, but Ashley already knew she was worth the effort. *She risked her life for me.* Ashley was convinced the act was more than out of duty to help others. The way Bryce looked at her, even before the earthquake, made her think there was more.

Plus, there was the way Bryce sat close to her and held her hand as they rode toward Beverly Hills. That heat Ashley felt from the contact was much more than friendly. There was chemistry between them. She was sure of it.

"Sorry about all the traffic, ma'am," the limo driver said, interrupting Ashley's thoughts. "But it's been a hell of a day. That little earthquake caused people to start acting stupid."

Ashley watched her mom frown. "Not sure I'd have called it a little earthquake," she said. "Not if you were in the middle of it."

"Right," the driver corrected. "Of course not. Even a four-point one shake can cause problems. Wasn't the "big one" though is what I meant."

Ashley and all Los Angeles were aware of the threat of the "big one." A cataclysmic earthquake that leveled the city. There was even an official Earthquake Preparedness month. Still, after feeling the shock of being near the epicenter of even a small quake, Ashley didn't believe the average person could fathom the experience. She hoped the scientists were wrong in their calculations that the area was due for a massive disaster.

Even though no one else in the car responded to his comments, the driver kept talking. "That wasn't the worst part today though. Did you hear?" Ashley didn't answer. She had a pretty good idea of what the man was about to say. After a beat, he tilted his head, clearly confused by his passengers' lack of curiosity.

"What was the worst part?" Ashley finally asked to get the conversation over with and move on.

The driver shook his head as if disbelieving what he was about to say was possible. "A tsunami," he answered. "Like out of a movie. Here in Los Angeles. Can you believe it?"

Ashley could see the wave crashing into the boardwalk all over again. "Yes, I can," she said, and they were silent the rest of the ride home.

15

Standing in the kitchen of her intact home opening a cold bottle of Sauvignon Blanc, Drew looked back over her crazy day. To think she was looking at dailies with the film's director and trying to decide what to do with Tess at the start of the day. It was a decision she was fretting over until the woman showed up at the door of the trailer confessing she read Drew's book. For some reason, that action had touched Drew. *Is that why I jumped at the chance to drive her to find her daughter after the earthquake?* she wondered. *Or is there more there I'm not willing to face?* She couldn't be sure. After twenty years of reacting to emergencies, she wasn't lying when she told Tess it was second nature to help. Thinking back over their conversations in the car, Tess hadn't gone along with her explanation that instinct was the only reason Drew acted as she had. Pausing, she tried to recall the woman's exact words, but in the mix of all the chaos, she couldn't come up with it. *Only that she thought I was special.* She frowned. *Could the beautiful, talented, and extremely sexy Tess Landish think that about me?* It seemed unlikely. She must have misunderstood. *And I need to make sure I don't start doing crazy things that will embarrass me later.*

After pouring a glass of white wine, she wandered into the living room that overlooked the vast expanse of the Pacific Ocean far below. When she bought the house a few months ago, her brother teased her about it. "I said to buy a house in Malibu," he said. "Not on some cliff looking down on it." Watching the white lines of waves rolling in, she was glad she didn't listen to him. Although the tsunami that hit further south hadn't touched Malibu, the thought it could have made her shiver. *What a horrible, scary thing to have happen*, she thought, taking a sip. The cool liquid tasted refreshing after a very long day. *Thank God Ashley was all right.* She paused, thinking about Tess's daughter and the woman who saved her. *Bryce. The Marine.*

The obvious connection between the two had surprised Drew. Tess made it sound like they barely knew each other, but the chemistry between them was unmistakable. Although she had long brown hair and a gentle nature about her, Bryce had some more masculine mannerisms that would have clued Drew in that she was likely a lesbian. *But I never would have guessed Ashley liked women*, she thought. Although not a fan of news from the internet, she didn't remember ever seeing headlines about Tess Landish's daughter being gay. She hadn't even seen it on a tabloid in a grocery store line. Considering how much Ashley touched Bryce, even in front of the studio's production assistant, she assumed it wasn't a secret. *Maybe it's not as big of a deal as I remember things used to be.* Growing up in a small town in Texas, being queer was a bad thing. So much so, Drew never let herself go there in her mind as a teenager. Even after she moved away, the reservations stuck with her as an adult. Standing at the window tonight though, thinking about the day and especially about Tess, made her think about the topic again.

A few times working at the hospital, Drew found another woman attractive. She always chalked the feelings up to respecting the other person's skills as a nurse or a doctor. One thing was for sure though. She never acted on any of her emotions. Even when she woke up from a dream where she was touching another woman, one that left her feeling aroused and a little confused, she refused to pursue it. Instead, she kept to herself, and never dated or let anyone get close to her. There were many lonely moments over the years, but she got through by throwing all her energy into work. *But I don't have work to distract me 24/7*, she thought. *And now there is suddenly Tess in my life to confuse me.* The lead actress in the movie meant so much to her. *I'm too old to start thinking about a relationship with anyone, especially a Hollywood megastar who happens to be a beautiful woman.* As she sipped her wine, she made a resolution—steer clear of Tess Landish.

RIDING in the limo up the long, sweeping driveway, Tess Landish's multi-million-dollar house in Beverly Hills was like nothing Bryce had ever seen except on television. Aside from being behind eight-foot walls and a black iron gate, the building was enormous. Compared to the modest two-bedroom ranch house where Bryce grew up, the place was a palace. Add in a perfectly manicured lawn with gorgeous flora everywhere she looked, and it was enough to make her feel a little out of her league. Clearly noticing Bryce's awe, Ashley leaned in close. "Sorry," she said. "It's a little over the top outside, but I promise the look is all for show. My mom's not a diva." Bryce believed Ashley's words even after only knowing Tess for a couple of hours. Considering who she was, Ashley's mom seemed genuine and well... normal.

Although as big inside as it looked outside, the house itself felt homey and modest. Tess had filled it with oversized furniture that looked comfortable and inviting. Rather than the furnishings looking like they came from a museum, Tess's choices were practical. Aside from the size, nothing about the place would make a person guess it belonged to one of the most famous actresses in the world. As they walked inside, Ashley asked Bryce if she wanted a tour, and her answer was easy. "If it starts in the kitchen, and I can have something to drink," she said. "Then yes." Both Tess and Ashley laughed.

"Since it's you Bryce, I imagine you are talking about water," Tess said. "But I want something a hell of a lot stronger." Putting her hands on her lower back, she stretched. "First though, I am going to go take a shower and see if I can relax a little. Are you two okay?"

Ashley hugged her mom. "We are okay now," she said. "I love you."

"I love you, too," Tess said, holding Ashley tightly for a moment. "I am so glad to be home and have you here with me." She waved in the direction of what Bryce hoped was the kitchen. "Help yourself to whatever you want. I'll be right back."

After Tess left them alone, Bryce followed Ashley into the huge kitchen. While she got her drink of water at last, Ashley skipped straight to the wine. As they both drank, Bryce looked around. The cabinets, backsplash, and quartz countertops were in shades of gray and white with black accents. Everything looked modern, efficient, and expensive. "Did you grow up here?" Bryce asked, and Ashley shrugged.

"Some," she answered. "From fifteen until I moved away to go to college and live on campus. Moving into someplace this fancy did take some getting used to, although ..." She smiled. "The pool is fantastic."

Bryce nodded. "From what I've seen so far, I can imagine."

Suddenly, Ashley sobered. "Although, I am not sure I

want to think about anything to do with water right now," she said, her voice shaking a little. "What happened on Venice Beach..." She let her words fade. Acting purely on instinct, Bryce set down her glass before wrapping her arms around Ashley to pull her closer.

"I know," she said, kissing her forehead. Knowing how hard it was to compartmentalize tragedy, Bryce wished Ashley had never witnessed the scene at the boardwalk. "There was nothing we could do," she whispered. "We tried, so don't blame yourself for anything."

Ashley nodded, wrapping her arms around Bryce's waist and resting her head on her shoulder. "I know," she said, but there was enough doubt in her voice to worry Bryce a little. Being a sensitive and caring woman with a huge heart, the tragedy would take a long time for Ashley to get over. If she ever could.

Lifting her head, Ashley looked into her face. "I know I've already said it but thank you for saving me. For all that you did." With their lips only inches apart, the desire to kiss her made Bryce ache. The last thing she wanted was to take advantage of the situation. Ashley was emotional. Vulnerable. So, she hesitated for a moment. Then, the reality she nearly died that day washed over her. *Died without telling this woman I am so attracted to how I feel*, she thought a moment before she leaned in and kissed her.

IN HER GIANT MASTER BATHROOM, standing under the dinner plate-sized showerhead, the hot water and steam helped Tess feel somewhat normal again. Although she didn't think she would be able to relax entirely for days, if not months after the fear she felt, the tension in her shoulders lessened under the spray. Only the draw of how good a glass of wine would taste lured her out of the shower. As she wrapped her wet hair in a thick, white towel and then slipped on her plush, navy blue, terrycloth robe, Tess hoped Ashley and Bryce would be in the kitchen. Spending more time with her daughter would go a long way toward making her feel better. Plus, she was eager to know Ashley's friend better. The attraction Ashley mentioned at dinner only the night before seemed to have become something deeper over the course of the day. Tess wasn't sure what to think about that situation. Her only concern was things were moving fast only because the two women's emotions were intensified. It seemed their life and death experience helped them bond. There was no way to know what they would be like together under normal circumstances.

But there will be time for that later, and honestly, who am I to judge these things? she thought, starting to walk through the house to the kitchen. *I've never been able to sustain a long-term relationship with anyone. Maybe an intense situation is the key.* The idea made her slow her steps. If that were true, it might explain why she couldn't seem to stop thinking about Drew. As much as she was trying to deny the feelings, Tess missed Drew. The day they spent together was crazy and scary but somehow made her feel close to the woman. She felt like they had bonded too and if she were to be honest, a deep longing inside her wished she asked the woman to come to stay with them for a night. Somehow having her resourcefulness nearby would have been a comfort. *Oh, let me be honest, I want her here for more than her resourcefulness. I miss her smile, her voice, and, frankly, how she makes me feel.*

Tess figured out over a decade ago that she preferred being around women much more than men, including romantically. Exploring her feelings had proved next to impossible if she wanted to maintain her girl-next-door, sweetheart image. Not that she found herself attracted to many women or men for that matter, but occasionally, when she met someone intelligent and talented, she would take notice. *Someone like Drew Andersen,* she thought with a sigh. Unfortunately, aside from all she did for Tess, that didn't mean the woman felt any attraction toward her. As Drew said more than once, she was wired to aid people. *She stopped in the middle of traffic and helped a stranger have her baby today, for God's sake. What more proof do I need?*

With a sigh, Tess started into the kitchen but stopped when she saw Ashley and Bryce. They were wrapped in each other's arms sharing a kiss. It was the first time she had ever seen her daughter kissing someone, and although there was heat to the embrace, there was a tenderness to it also. Enough to reassure her Bryce's attraction was sincere. She wasn't there simply to sweep Ashley off her feet but truly cared about her daughter.

Quietly, Tess backed up the way she came and walked toward the kitchen as noisily as possible the next time. "Ashley, sweetheart," she called out. "Did you leave some wine for me?"

When she entered the kitchen again, the two women had stepped apart, but the glow around them was impossible to miss. "Oh, a little," Ashley said, her voice pitched a little huskier than usual. "How was your shower?"

"Bliss," Tess said, taking the wine out of the fridge. "Although I don't know if I'll even get past how afraid I was today." Feeling a wave of gratitude, tears welled up in her eyes. "I wouldn't be able to stand it if I lost you."

Ashley came closer, wrapping her up in a hug. "You didn't lose me," she said. "And I didn't lose you. We both had heroes watching over us today." Returning the hug, Tess let her daughter's words sink in. There was a hero in her life, and suddenly she realized no matter the costs, she needed to tell Drew the truth about her feelings. That she was attracted to her and wanted to know her more. A lot more.

16

---

inally, after a long three days of waiting impatiently for the city to declare it safe to return to the area, Ashley went back into her coffee shop. Walking among what remained of the once warm and cozy space she designed herself, she heard the insurance agent scribbling notes on his clipboard. Bryce stood nearby but was sensitive enough to give her space. Ashley's emotions were as devastated as the shop. Even though the two-story building withstood the power of the wave slamming into it, all the window glass was entirely wiped away. With nothing to stop it, the wave filled the space with a mad rush of ocean water. Based on the stains clear to the ceiling, everything was under water at one point. *And totally ruined,* she thought, then reminded herself she was one of the lucky few along the boardwalk who survived that day. *All I should focus on is being thankful everyone I love is okay.*

"Well," the insurance agent said, pulling a form from his clipboard. "I'm sure you can see the situation for yourself, Ms. Landish. Your coffee shop is irreparably damaged." As Ashley took the paper he held out for her, words could not express how she felt. Like he said, she could see for herself, and it broke her heart. "Luckily, your business insurance coverage is top tier. You will be reimbursed for everything." He gave her a gentle smile, suddenly appearing more sympathetic than he had throughout the process. "Think positive, Ms. Landish. This doesn't have to be the end of your business venture."

"Thank you" was all Ashley could think to say as Bryce approached, slipping an arm around her shoulders. The show of support felt good, and she looked forward to when they could be alone. Proving to always be steadfast, Bryce's strong shoulders would be a perfect place to cry.

The agent started toward the door, stepping gingerly over the glass and other debris. "Reach out to us when you find your new location," he said. "And I'll come to appraise everything for coverage again."

Ashley blinked, not understanding. "New location?" she asked. She had every intention to keep Landish Coffee on the Venice Beach boardwalk. The perfect location was one of the things she attributed to her success. Gutting and remodeling the coffee shop would take time, but she hoped she could upgrade some things with the extra insurance money.

Pausing, the agent shook his head. "I thought you knew," he said. "The building, as well as ninety percent of the others along the block, have been determined unsafe for occupancy. Eventually, everything will be torn down and replaced, but that will take months at best. Maybe a year."

"A year?" Ashley repeated, a sinking feeling in her stomach. The news kept getting worse by the minute.

The agent sighed. "Yes, unfortunately," he said. "Marina Del Rey and the other neighborhoods along the coastline affected sustained millions of dollars of damage. Recovery will take time and money."

As the words sunk in, Ashley felt tears welling up in her

eyes, but she fought to hold them back until the man was gone. She was more discouraged than ever, but it wasn't the agent's fault. "Thank you for coming out so quickly."

"Of course," the agent said as he departed.

Once he was gone, Ashley fell against Bryce, letting the woman wrap her arms around her. "What am I going to do?" she sobbed into Bryce's shoulder. "My coffee shop was my second home."

Bryce ran a hand over Ashley's long hair. "I could see that," she said. "We will figure out something."

Suddenly, Ashley heard a long, low whistle. "Woo hoo," a woman said from where the front door used to be. "I can't believe how bad everything looks." Lifting her head, Ashley was surprised but very happy to see the gap-toothed smile of her friend Bev. "Yeah, I came back. I was wondering if any of my stuff might be lying around. You never know what might turn up."

"It's wonderful to see you," Ashley said. Floyd appeared at Bev's side before Ashley could ask about him. His tail wagged, making him look happy to see Ashley and Bryce. "And you too, Floyd." Realizing the woman and her loyal companion were happy and healthy despite all that had happened helped Ashley. *Things will improve*, she thought. *Just like Bev, I need to keep a positive attitude.* And as the woman said, a person never knew what might turn up.

FINDING a chance to talk to Drew proved to be a challenge. At first, Tess chalked up the disconnects to the rush of everyone getting back into shooting after losing time. Drew was busy, and Tess, still playing catchup herself from joining the project at the last minute, worked hard around the clock. After a couple of days though, Tess started to get a sense

Drew intentionally avoided her whenever they might end up alone together. The complete one-eighty made no sense. After their traumatic day together driving across Los Angeles to get to Ashley, she felt they had bonded. Tess began to realize Drew had not.

Testing her theory, Tess intentionally waited to go to the craft service table for a bottle of water until she saw Drew approaching to get her usual ten o'clock coffee and donut. With her back turned, the writer didn't see Tess coming. "Hi," she said, stopping beside Drew. "Seems I haven't had a chance to talk to you much the last few days." She purposefully made eye contact. "How are you?" Tess wasn't sure what she expected, but her worst fear was confirmed when Drew blushed and started to back away. Somehow over the last few days, she had done something to put the woman off, and Tess had no idea what. Confused, her first instinct was to give some blanket apology and drop it, but she caught herself. Drew was important to her, made her feel emotions too significant to ignore, and she wouldn't let their friendship be swept under the rug. "Can we go somewhere and talk for a minute?"

"Uh," Drew said, glancing around as if trying to find an excuse to escape. Not finding anything, she frowned. "Sure."

Working hard not to be discouraged by Drew's unhappy expression, Tess pointed in the direction of her trailer. The crew was in the middle of setting up the next scene, leaving a little time for the actors to relax. "Maybe take a minute in my trailer?" If Drew looked uncomfortable before, the suggestion made her more so. Any second, Tess thought, the woman would turn and make a run for it. *What in the world happened to us?* she thought, knowing she had to get to the bottom of whatever was wrong, or the uncertainty would drive her crazy.

After another beat of hesitation, Drew's shoulders slumped, and she nodded. "Okay," she said. "But I only have a couple of minutes."

"Then I'll be quick," Tess replied, leading the way across the parking lot to the trailers. Once they were inside hers with the door closed, Tess felt confident they would not be overheard. She needed to be direct and not have to watch what she said. If Tess only had a couple of minutes, there was no time to work up to what she wanted to say. Even if her confession backfired, at least Tess would have expressed what had kept her awake the last three nights. Taking a deep breath, she dove in. "Thank you for giving me a minute. I know you're very busy. But there is something important I need to tell you."

Crossing her arms, Drew could not look less receptive. "If it is about you not having the role as the nurse, I think that's settled," she said. "You have the job whether I want you to or not."

Working hard to keep her resolve in the face of Drew's negativity, Tess shook her head. "No, not about the role," she said. "Nothing about your book or the movie even." She looked into Drew's eyes. "But about us."

Drew's eyebrows went up. "Us?" she asked. "Since when is there an us?"

Biting her lip to take a moment and make entirely sure she wanted to say the next sentence, Tess held her gaze. "Yes, there is an us," she said. "At least I think so." She shook her head, almost not believing she was about to confess how she felt. "Drew, I don't know how else to say this, so here it is—"

"Tess, wait," Drew interrupted. "You don't need to tell me anything."

"But actually, I do," Tess said. "Because after everything that happened, I realize I'm extremely attracted to you." She gave a little self-conscious laugh. "I can't stop thinking about you. And it might be making me a little crazy."

WHILE TESS STOOD before her baring her soul, Drew froze while her brain processed the information. What she thought she heard made no logical sense. *Tess Landish is attracted to me?* she thought, certain she misunderstood. *If there is an attraction between us, it comes from me.* Every time she looked at the actress on set, something stirred inside her. Something that scared the hell out of her. Like Tess confessed, Drew could not stop thinking about her either. Sleep proved to be nearly impossible, because she saw Tess's beautiful face whenever she closed her eyes. *But even if Tess's feelings are real and not some side effect of the situation we went through together, what can I do? Date a woman? And not just any woman, but a Hollywood superstar?* She met Tess's eyes, seeing them filled with a mix of emotion and waiting for her response.

"Please say something," Tess whispered, and Drew swallowed hard. The walls of the trailer seemed to be pressing in on her, making it hard to breathe, and suddenly all she wanted to do was run.

With a shake of her head, she brushed past Tess and went for the door. "I'm sorry," she said. "But I can't." Then, she was outside, sucking in air as she strode away without a look back. She didn't dare check if Tess was following her. The last thing she wanted was to see the hurt on Tess's face. Drew couldn't handle it. None of it. *At least not right now*, she thought. *And after I barged out of there, there won't be a second time anyway.* A strange feeling of sadness suddenly washed over her, and her steps slowed. *Maybe I should go back. Try to explain why I'm reacting this way somehow, assuming I know myself.*

A production assistant came running toward her from

the other direction. "Ms. Andersen," he said. "Here are the pages to tomorrow's shooting schedule that you asked for."

Welcoming the distraction, Drew took them from the young man's hand. "Thank you."

"Oh," the assistant went on. "One more thing. That research you wanted. Here's the phone number of the hospital nearest to the address you gave me."

Drew accepted the slip of paper from him. "Perfect," she said, glancing at the number. "Thank you."

"You're welcome," the production assistant said as he hustled away to his next task. *Making a call is exactly the distraction I need right now,* she thought, forcing Tess out of her mind and calling the hospital. After navigating a complicated phone tree and being transferred twice, she reached the maternity ward. Drew identified herself as an ex-emergency department nurse once the woman in charge of the floor came on the phone. "I know you can't tell me details," she said, crossing her fingers that she found someone flexible. "But I helped deliver a baby in the middle of traffic Tuesday morning. It was in the chaos after the earthquake."

"I see," the charge nurse replied. "And you think they may have ended up here?"

"Yes. Yours is the closest hospital. I'm assuming the parents drove straight to you since we couldn't get through to 9-1-1." When the woman didn't immediately tell her she couldn't help, Drew gave all the information she knew about the baby and mother and held her breath. Regulations were strict about divulging any medical information, but she wanted to know if everything turned out okay. Finally, the charge nurse told her to hold.

A few minutes later, she came back on the line. "Nurse Andersen, as much as I would like to help you, my hands are tied."

Drew sighed, expecting no less but had hoped for information. "Thank you," she said, ready to hang up.

"But..." the charge nurse continued without prompting. "There is a rumor going around that a Good Samaritan did deliver a baby in the back of a car near here. And if the rumor is true, we are all very grateful. Especially the parents whose baby is doing fine."

17

The phone call came. Bryce expected it sooner actually, but she had tried to ignore her quickly approaching decision. Making up her mind would not be easy. Other than Ashley's coffee shop being in shambles, the rest of the three days after the disaster were nothing but perfect. Anything Bryce might have imagined happening between her and Ashley was slowly unfolding. Her attraction to the woman grew stronger every minute they were together, which was nonstop. If she read the signals coming from Ashley correctly, the feelings were very mutual.

After the earthquake, Tess had insisted they stay with her a few nights while her nerves settled down and, even though Bryce and Ashley slept in separate bedrooms, there were plenty of steamy moments between them. Not that Bryce only wanted Ashley in her life because of physical attraction. Quite the opposite. The woman amazed her. All the qualities she found herself drawn to in college were still there, but she learned new things about Ashley too. Little details like her favorite ice cream flavor, her favorite music, and how competitive she was at everything. Plus, not only was she wicked smart, especially in terms of business, but Bryce confirmed her guess that Ashley was sensitive and kind. She cared deeply about people, wearing her heart on her sleeve. Although they hadn't talked about what Ashley witnessed at the boardwalk when the wave hit, Bryce could tell at times the memory bothered her and at some level probably always would.

On loungers by Tess's sparkling blue pool, Bryce stared at her buzzing phone, trying to decide what to do with the call. After a moment, Ashley raised her sunglasses and looked at her. "You don't look happy," she said. "Who is it?"

Unable to hide the truth, Bryce sighed. "My company commander," she answered. "I haven't checked in for a few days, so it's my fault."

"Checked in?" Ashley asked, a hint of uncertainty in her voice. Bryce mentally kicked herself for not addressing specific facts with Ashley earlier. Bryce was very tied to the military, even if she was on indefinite leave. As a highly-trained Marine, they wanted her to reenlist immediately, but Bryce stalled while she got to know Ashley better. Still, she couldn't delay things with the Marine Corps forever.

Standing, Bryce had to accept the phone call at least. "I'll be right back, and then I will explain everything," she said to Ashley before stepping through the open sliding doors into the house's great room. "Hello."

"Corporal Cooper. It's good to hear your voice," said a man Bryce knew and respected. Marine Captain Wilson Roberts was a good leader. Firm, with strict standards, but there was a compassionate component to him. If Captain Roberts didn't have empathy in his personality, Bryce would never have been able to take care of her father in his last days. For that, she would be forever grateful, which was why ducking his calls would be dishonorable. She needed to face up to her responsibilities.

"Thank you, sir," she said. "I apologize for not calling in. Things here were a little bit... unusual." The last thing Bryce wanted was to start making excuses, even if they were warranted. After all, there had been an earthquake and a tsunami.

"Are you in Los Angeles?" Captain Roberts asked. "Because I have heard reports things were more than only unusual. Were you nearby the natural disasters?"

Bryce paused, not sure how much to reveal. If she described her role in things, the fact she saved the lives of four civilians, the Marine Corps would no doubt want a written report of her involvement. Immediately.

She cleared her throat. "Yes, sir," she said. "I was in the coastal area of both the earthquake and the resulting tsunami."

When Bryce didn't elaborate, there was a beat of silence. "I see," the captain said. "Well, I'll expect a debrief upon your return. What is your ETA?"

That was the question Bryce didn't want to answer. She did not have an estimated time of arrival in mind yet. "I'm not sure, sir," she admitted. "I am working through some personal matters here." She hesitated before asking yet another favor when the Marines had already been so generous. "I'd like another week."

ASHLEY WASN'T sure what to think. From what she saw, although the phone call didn't precisely upset Bryce, it brought on a seriousness she had not witnessed before. Although Ashley was aware from their experiences three days ago that the woman was a Marine, the reality of what that meant overall hadn't really crossed her mind. As in, there wasn't any connecting the dots that Bryce could still be active in the military. *If that is the case, how can she be running around Los Angeles with me?* she wondered with a frown. *It must have something to do with her taking care of her dad before he died. But does that mean she has to go back?*

Regardless of the reason, it was clear they needed to talk about the situation. The question was when. If Bryce wasn't ready, she wouldn't push her. When the woman was willing, they would work through whatever was going on. Turning her head, Ashley saw through the patio doors and watched Bryce lower the phone from her ear, staring at it as if not sure what to do next. Ashley decided maybe it was time she refilled her glass of iced tea. *And see if Bryce wants to talk about anything.*

As she approached the doors, Bryce hadn't seen her yet, and Ashley could observe her. There were so many things she liked about the woman. Until that moment though, Ashley hadn't considered her military bearing being a big part of the attraction. Levelheaded. Confident. Strong. *But let's not forget sexy*, she thought. There was a tenderness to Bryce whenever they kissed, but a definite hunger too. *So much heat.* She wondered how long they would stay with Tess and have separate bedrooms. Every night, after making out on the couch for hours, they separated, leaving Ashley with an ache inside her. If things kept going like they were, something would have to give soon.

Not that Ashley was quick to jump into bed with someone, but the chemistry between the two of them was hard to deny. Even after only a few days, she connected to Bryce in a way she never had with anyone else. They got each other's jokes and seemed to like so many of the same things. Still, that didn't necessarily mean they needed to sleep together, and as Ashley walked toward the house, she resolved to keep working on getting to know Bryce before taking all her clothes off.

Finally noticing Ashley as she neared the door, Bryce smiled. "Hey," she said. "Had enough sun?"

Deciding she wasn't quite ready to talk about anything serious yet, Ashley closed the distance between them and wrapped her arms around Bryce's shoulders. "I came in for more tea," she said. "But if you're done at the pool for the day, I'm okay with that too."

Bryce put her hands on Ashley's hips and pulled her closer. "Whatever you want," she said, leaning in to kiss her. The caress was a gentle brush across her lips but with a promise of more behind the touch.

A tingle ran through Ashley, and she felt her resolve slipping already. "Whatever I want?" she murmured against Bryce's lips. "That's wide open." Chuckling softly, Bryce nuzzled her neck, leaving a trail of hot kisses. Ashley felt more than a tingle and gasped when Bryce nipped at her hot skin.

Bryce kissed her way up to Ashley's ear. "What do you want, Ashley?" she whispered, and Ashley felt her resolve melt a little more. Her mom was on the movie set for another couple of hours at least and would text when headed home. Plus, they were grown adults, and even though she always felt like a kid again around her mom, they most definitely were not. As Bryce's hand roamed up her back, stroking the bare skin barely covered by her bikini top, Ashley had to work to suppress a moan. It would be so easy for the woman to untie the string, leaving Ashley's breasts bare and ready to be touched. She could feel her nipples tighten at the image of Bryce's mouth on them.

When the familiar ache started low on her body, Ashley knew what she wanted. "I want you, Bryce," she whispered. "I want you."

. . .

NOT HESITATING, Bryce lifted Ashley in her arms to carry her down the long hallway to the bedroom. Every fantasy she ever had while staring at the ceiling in the military barracks night after night came rushing into her mind. There were so many ways she wanted to touch Ashley, arouse her, and ultimately take her until she came.

Ashley wrapped her arms around Bryce's neck, letting out a little cry of surprise and excitement. "I love how strong you are," she said, her voice low and thick with anticipation. "There are so many things that make me crazy about you."

Smiling, Bryce liked the sound of that. "Really," she said. "Well, you make me crazy too. You're so damn hot in that bikini, for starters." Coming to the bedroom she had been sleeping alone in since they arrived at Tess's house, Bryce gently kicked the door open. In three steps, she set Ashley on the giant king-sized bed, appreciating how incredibly sexy the woman was while grabbing the hem of her tank top.

With a sultry smile, Ashley reached behind her back. "This bikini?" she asked, making Bryce pause. "Wouldn't you rather it be on the floor instead?"

Licking her lips, Bryce nodded. "Yes, I would." In one deft move, the bikini top was off, and Ashley laid back in all her magnificent glory. She wore nothing but a small pair of bottoms, and at that point they were more of a tease than for modesty. "You are so incredible."

Ashley arched her back, lifting her full breasts and tight nipples. "Well, don't make me wait," she said. "Take off your shirt." Happy to oblige, Bryce finished pulling the fabric over her head, leaving her chest bare. She heard Ashley gasp. "My God, Bryce. You're perfect."

Without comment, Bryce climbed onto the bed and covered Ashley's body with her own, reveling in the sensation of burning skin on skin. Nothing she could have imagined compared to the feeling of finally having Ashley under her. As her thigh parted Ashley's legs, she felt the woman tremble. The wetness between her legs soaked through the fabric of her bikini bottoms and felt hot on Bryce's skin. It was her turn to gasp. Never would she have thought she could turn Ashley on so much. All she wanted at that moment was to bring the woman as much pleasure as she could and lowered her lips to kiss her again.

Their mouths melded together, desire building between them as their tongues teased each other. Bryce could not get enough of her, taking the burning kiss deeper with an intensity that made Ashley moan as she bucked her hips against Bryce's thigh. In answer, Bryce started to rock her body, pressing against Ashley's center with each movement. Even through the bikini, Bryce felt how swollen and ready the woman was. "I want to know how wet you are," Bryce breathed against Ashley's neck. "I want to feel you."

"Oh yes," was Ashley's only response. Forcing herself to relish every moment, Bryce slowly moved her hand down Ashley's body, trailing her fingertips over the woman's hard nipples. Taking her time, she teased them until Ashley arched higher to press against her hand.

"Do you like that?" Bryce asked, and Ashley moaned.

"You're driving me wild," she said, her voice thick with need, and encouraged, Bryce kept going until she felt the small patch of neat hair between her legs. Brushing her fingers over the curls, she made herself go slow, to take in every part of the pleasure she wanted for so long. Ashley whimpered. "You're teasing me." The sound of her voice pushed through any of Bryce's restraints. Sliding lower, she slipped two fingers through the wetness of Ashley's lips to find her throbbing clit. The slightest touch and Ashley's body started to tremble.

Slowly, Bryce started to circle with her fingers. "Right

here?" she asked, knowing the answer but wanting to hear the words.

"Yes," Ashley said. "Right there. Don't stop."

Moving her hand faster, Bryce waited until Ashley's breathing grew ragged before letting her thumb graze the tip of Ashley's clit while she moved lower. Her fingers found Ashley ready, and as she slid two deep inside her, she cupped Ashley with her palm. Pressing harder, while she moved in and out of Ashley, the rest of her hand provided enough friction against her center to make the woman start to shake. She lifted her hips in rhythm with Bryce's movements. "Are you going to come, Ashley?" Bryce asked, moving faster and faster, pressing deeper and deeper. "I want that. You have no idea how much I want that."

In response, Ashley raised her hips to press Bryce harder against her while she grabbed a handful of Bryce's long thick hair. "I'm so close, Bryce," she said, her voice shaking. "Oh God. It's happening. Yes." Stopping mid-thrust, Ashley let out a scream of pleasure while Bryce felt her body grip her fingers a moment before starting to throb around them. Knowing she had made the sexy, beautiful, and wonderful woman come hard, Bryce could not have felt more fulfilled. It was everything she wanted.

18

*C*omposing herself after Drew's frantic exit from her trailer, Tess threw herself into the final scene of the day. With minimal blocking required, there wasn't much to the acting in terms of action, but her heartfelt dialogue needed all her emotional range. She would have to make herself entirely vulnerable for it to work. The audience had to feel what the character experienced in the dramatic moment—angst, desire, and above all, disappointment. As luck would have it, Tess didn't have to dig very deep to find those emotions. She suddenly found herself experiencing them in her own life. Confessing to Drew proved an utter failure, and although Tess hoped to somehow apologize before the scene for her emotional ambush, the woman was nowhere around. *Maybe just as well*, she thought before focusing on the director's explanation of what he wanted. *The last thing I need to do is embarrass myself and make her run away again.*

When the final 'cut' for the day was called, Tess closed her eyes to gather herself. Laying out all her feelings for the world to see, even in make-believe, exhausted her.

"Amazing work," she heard the director say as he approached. "As always, of course."

Opening her eyes, Tess smiled at him. "Thank you. But it's easy when I have such a rich character to play and a wonderful script to draw from," she said, meaning every word. The movie was proving to be the best she ever worked on.

"Well, you're certainly making it look that way," he said, holding out some colored sheets of paper. "A slight change to the schedule, by the way. The weatherman is predicting thunderstorms tomorrow, so we are moving to another indoor scene." Tess took the pages, giving them a quick glance. She immediately recalled the action and felt her stomach tighten. It was the first of many emergency room scenes where she would be required to act like she knew how to be an experienced ER nurse. Since the last time she was even in a hospital was twenty-eight years ago, when Ashley was born, she was nervous about everything looking realistic. Noticing her reaction, the director put a hand on her shoulder. "Relax, Tess. We will spend the first part of the morning walking through everything until you're comfortable."

Tess nodded. "I appreciate that," she said, but the short rehearsal on set was not the only thing she needed. *I need to talk to Drew*, she thought. *To have her coach me. Going through the motions won't be enough to come across as authentic.* "Have you seen Drew? I noticed she didn't sit in on the last scene."

Glancing around, the director frowned. "You know, you're right. She wasn't at the camera viewer with me," he said. "That's odd. I wonder what's up."

Tess had a pretty good guess. *She doesn't want to be anywhere near me right now*, she thought, feeling more disappointed than ever. *I really scared her off.* "Well, maybe I'll check with the second AD and see if she knows where Drew is hiding. I really would like some of her input."

"I'm assuming you're talking about tomorrow's scene," Drew said from somewhere behind Tess. "And I agree. You can't do it without some detailed explanations behind why you are doing each action."

Turning, Tess saw the woman standing at the edge of the set. Her arms folded with no hint of friendliness in her eyes. Whatever bond they developed while racing across Los Angeles appeared completely erased. Tess had only herself to blame. By cornering Drew and putting her on the spot, she forced the writer to put up even more walls.

After a beat, Tess resolved to start working on pulling them back down enough they could at least be friends again. "Are you offering to help me learn the part?" Tess asked, holding her breath, waiting to hear if Drew would at least do that. Her coaching would be for the betterment of the entire film.

Before Drew answered, the director clapped his hands, rubbing them together. "I'll tell you what," he said. "How about you talk it out over a nice dinner? Name the place. Italian? Mexican? Thai? Whatever you want, and I'll get a PA to set up a reservation, compliments of the studio, of course."

NOT QUITE SURE how the circumstances came about, Drew found herself behind the wheel of her Pathfinder driving Tess Landish somewhere once again. *And it feels totally normal. Like we do it all the time,* she thought, pulling away from the parking lot of the rundown apartment building where they filmed all day. *Although I don't know what I was expecting. It's not like she would attack me out of sheer lust.* The thought almost made her laugh it was so ludicrous. If anything, Tess's posture made Drew think the woman was uncomfortable with the situation. She was about as far against the passenger door as possible without making it look too weird. *Because she doesn't want to freak me out again and is giving me all the space she can.*

Back on the set, when the movie director insisted they discuss the next day's complex scenes over dinner, Drew met Tess's eyes. All the awkward surprise she felt at the sudden turn of events was on Tess's face too. *But there was more*, she remembered. Tess's look had a pleading quality to it as if begging Drew not to say no. With her mouth suddenly dry, Drew didn't speak for a moment, leaving Tess to drop her eyes and blush at the idea she was about to be rejected. "Maybe that's not such a great idea—" Tess started saying after a beat, but Drew took a step forward before the actress could finish her sentence.

"I think dinner is a good idea," she blurted, louder than she intended, startling herself. Tess and the director both looked at her with surprise at her outburst. "I mean, it's only that I'm starving. And would rather not have my dinner be an overripe banana with a Coke Zero from the craft service table." When a smile of relief crossed Tess's face, Drew found herself smiling too. There was no reason they couldn't find a way to work together as friends. *We will put Tess's crazy confession behind us like it never happened*, she thought. *I'm sure she regrets saying it anyway and has come to her senses.* A pang of disappointment at the idea Tess would have changed her mind about what she said earlier gave Drew pause. For some reason, she suddenly wasn't sure that was what she wanted. *Too late now. I ran away.*

"Let me grab my purse, and we can go," Tess said, moving in the direction of the apartment's door before she pulled up short. "I'm sorry, that was incredibly rude of me assuming you would drive. Let's decide where we can meet, and I'll—"

Shaking her head, Drew interrupted again. "No," she said.

"That makes no sense. Of course, I'll drive you. But that means you pick the place." Tess smiled, her eyes twinkling, and her beauty radiated like a wave over Drew. What she said clearly made Tess happy. A desire to find ways to see that look over and over again caught Drew by surprise. So much so, she puzzled over it as she drove them through West Hollywood. *If I do like Tess as something more than a friend, why did I run away?* she wondered, stealing a glance at Tess. *And where do I go from here?*

"I hope you like sushi," Tess said, bringing Drew back to the moment. "Because I picked a perfect little place not far from here, and I promise the food is delicious."

Drew bobbed her head. "I like sushi a lot."

Visibly relaxing, Tess pointed at the next cross street. "Good," she said. "They know me and are discreet."

"Of course," Drew said, not realizing until that moment how hard it might be for Tess to go out for dinner. Once recognized, Tess drew attention. She remembered the crowd forming on the street around Tess after the baby was delivered. The pair literally had to flee to avoid a scene. *What an interesting life*, she thought, glad that as an author she could be moderately famous, but no one would ever know that was the case by looking at her. Then, a new thought occurred to her. If Tess lived a life where everyone watched her every move, her confession in the trailer was an even bigger deal. *She risked a lot telling me how she felt.* As they made their way to the restaurant, the realization only confused Drew more.

WITH A BIT OF LUCK, they were able to park nearby and slip in through the restaurant's backdoor without a scene. "Irasshaimase," the owner said as he ushered them to a special secluded space where gold silk curtains hid the entry. A discreet entry was an arrangement set up years ago with the restaurant and used by several celebrities. She was glad the space was available on such short notice.

Once they sat on the plush, red cushions around a short black table, with sake poured and their order given, Tess prepared herself. Addressing the elephant in the room sooner rather than later would hopefully allow them to enjoy the meal together. Taking a deep breath, she got straight to the point. "Drew, I want to apologize for earlier in my trailer," she said, trying to catch her eye. "I never intended to make you uncomfortable. I am sorry." For a moment, Drew didn't react other than to study Tess's face while her eyes gave nothing away. "Can we put it behind us?"

Slowly, Drew shook her head. "Please don't apologize," she finally replied. "I was rude to leave like I did while you were only being honest." Tess watched her swallow hard. "You were being honest, right?"

Unable to help herself, Tess reached across the table to take Drew's hand. "Yes," she said in a rush, relishing the feel of Drew's warm skin. "Every single word." Drew continued to shake her head but didn't pull back her hand.

After a second, she gently returned the caress, rubbing her thumb over the back of Tess's hand. "It just I... I can't do this..." she managed to say, pausing for a second while she looked at their clasped hands.

Tess guessed a million thoughts were running through Drew's head, because the same was happening to her. The words 'I can't' hung in the air while Drew exhaled a long breath. She was clearly trying to gather herself to say something more. Tess forced herself to be patient but struggled because Drew's answer mattered so much. No matter what it was. Finally, Drew looked ready to speak again.

"No, that's not what I want to say. It's not that I can't. It's that I don't know how to do what you're wanting."

To be sure she understood, Tess leaned closer. "What do you mean?"

Drew held Tess's hand tighter. "I mean, I'm incredibly attracted to you too," she said. "But I don't know what to do about it. I've never... I mean..." She sighed. "Why is it so hard to explain? I'm a writer for crying out loud. I'm trying to say, I've never had a relationship with a woman, or really with anybody."

Her heart pounding, Tess had so many things she wanted to say, she didn't know where to start. The moment she began to tell Drew they could work it out, the restaurant owner whisked in between the curtains. He carried two white ceramic plates of sushi. Drew jerked her hand back as if she had been burned while Tess politely smiled at the man's entrance.

Out of the corner of her eye, Tess saw Drew blushing. "Here you are," the owner said, setting multiple dishes on the table. A variety of delicacies filled them. "Will there be anything else at the moment?"

Keeping her frustration in check at the unlucky timing, Tess shook her head. "Thank you," she said. "We're fine for now."

"More sake?" the owner asked, pushing the edge of Tess's patience. She could almost feel Drew withdrawing into her shell.

"No, thank you."

The owner nodded, backing through the curtains. "Enjoy your dinner." As soon as he disappeared, Tess looked at Drew, seeing what she was afraid she would. The woman had dropped her eyes to study the food, neither hand on the table. Everything about her posture let Tess know the previous conversation was over.

Watching Drew pick up a bite of sushi with her chopsticks, Tess let out a sigh. "Are we ignoring what we were saying?" she asked. "Because I don't want that."

Lifting her napkin to cover her mouth while she chewed, Drew wouldn't meet Tess's eye. "I think we should focus on why we came here and get busy with the script," she said. "Okay?"

Remembering how Drew fled her trailer earlier, Tess didn't want to press, so all she could do was nod and start on her dinner.

19

*G*rabbing her phone from the nightstand to check the time, Ashley sighed with disappointment when the thing read seven a.m. She was hoping the time was earlier, and the fact the sky was dark outside wasn't because of the weather. Pausing to listen, she heard the patter of rain hitting her bedroom windows. Groaning, Ashley turned to face Bryce as the woman stirred beside her. "What's wrong, babe?" she asked, rubbing her eyes with her fists in a way that Ashley found adorable. Her badass Marine was trying to wake up with a serious case of bedhead.

"It's still raining like crazy," Ashley answered. "Honestly, I think the whole city is going to wash away if the weather doesn't let up." Three days of rain in March wasn't necessarily unexpected in Los Angeles, but thunderstorms with torrential rain were unusual. Especially since anything other than blue skies and sunshine made people act silly. No one was quite sure how to handle it and the news was having a field day. Accounts of swamped cars blocking streets, and even some freeway exchanges, had sent driver's tempers escalating out of control. The chaos turned into epic traffic jams. Not that Ashley intended to drive anywhere, but she itched to go for a run. The weather made that unappetizing. Plodding along in wet running shoes was incredibly unpleasant. Not that she minded being cooped up with Bryce in her mom's giant house. They binge-watched seasons of detective stories, ate whatever was near enough that they were willing to go out and get, and had a lot of sex.

"I'll go make coffee," Bryce said with a yawn, but Ashley pushed her back onto the bed. Seeing the woman lying there wrapped in the silk sheet, Ashley was tempted to slide under the covers and give Bryce a proper wakeup. The sexy woman, even looking sleepy, turned on Ashley pretty much all the time. That morning was no different. Only the hope she would catch her mom before she left for the studio kept their pajamas on for the moment.

Giving Bryce a peck on the lips, she sprang out of bed. "I'll go grab us coffee," she said. "I want to see if Mom's still here."

Bryce nodded. "I'll check the weather forecast," she said. "Maybe we can catch a break."

"Thank you," Ashley said over her shoulder before wandering down the hall to the kitchen. Stepping inside, she saw her mom rinsing a cup. "Good morning."

"Well, good morning," Tess said as Ashley walked over to hug her. "If I had known you were up, I'd have waited to see if I could talk you into making me a latte."

Ashley smiled as she let go. "Are you in a rush?" she asked, turning to the expresso machine. "It will only take a second, and you can always take it to go."

Clearly not needing to be talked into saying yes, Tess sank into one of the chairs at the kitchen table. "If you insist," she said with a laugh. "So, how are you? We haven't had time to talk the last few days, and I miss you."

"I miss you too," Ashley said. "We talked more when I

wasn't living here." She worked the levers to build up steam for the milk. "But honestly, I'm excellent. Bryce is wonderful." She added the espresso. "Although the rain is making us both nuts. We want to go for a run or something. Anything to get out of here for at least a few hours." Ashley finished the latte, added a fun bit of artwork to the foam, and set it in front of her mother. "Ta-dah."

Tess picked up the drink. "You and Bryce could always come to the studio lot this afternoon," she said. "Although you will want umbrellas. The director is exercising his artistic license as leverage to make a change to a scene. Outside in the rain."

Ashley lifted her eyebrows. "What's that all about?"

"The reunion of the two main characters scene was moved up," Tess explained. "It was going to be shot later, but with the rain, he wants to make it more dramatic." She shook her head. "I'm not sure how romantic it is to passionately kiss in the middle of the street during a thunderstorm, but he's the boss."

"Interesting," Ashley said, liking the sound of seeing her mom work. "We'll come by."

WATCHING the wipers race back and forth on the windshield of her Pathfinder, Drew sighed. Like everyone else, she was sick of the pounding rain. Three days of steady downpour and gray skies not only did havoc on the city but made driving dangerous—from the weather as much as from road rage. Drivers were frustrated, including her. It amazed Drew how easily a person got accustomed to bright and sunny seventy-five-degree weather every day. *Especially in March*, she thought, growling as she noticed bright-red taillights turning on along Highway 1 ahead of her. *We should all be thinking about spring flowers, not a monsoon—damn global warming.*

Slowing considerably with the traffic, Drew tried to be patient, but doing so wasn't easy. Today she particularly wanted to get to the set early to talk to the director about his plan for the day. They needed to speak before wasting time setting up shots they might not use if she got her way. He wouldn't like her butting in on his creativity, but she wasn't on board with his suggested changes to her script. What he proposed deviated from the novel too much. It was as simple as that. The characters, as she wrote them, would never run through the rain to share a passionate kiss. The nurse was especially reserved. *This isn't some Nicolas Sparks novel,* she thought, blowing out a frustrated breath. Although she wrote a love story that drove parts of the plot, at no point would they act so spontaneously. *Or so romantically.* She sighed. *Because let's face it, I'm lousy in that department. I sure proved that point.*

Ever since the sushi dinner with Tess, Drew replayed the entire evening repeatedly in her mind. In the middle of the night, when she stared at the ceiling unable to sleep, she couldn't help but wonder where things would have gone if the restaurant's owner hadn't come in right when he did. The instant before the interruption, she and Tess held hands and confessed their attraction to each other. *And then, as soon as someone could see us, I panicked,* she thought. *And I had no reason to.* Even though Los Angeles, especially West Hollywood, where they were, was very open to women loving each other, Drew still felt embarrassed to be caught. So much so she refused to return to the topic again that night and for the next three days. Although she hated to admit it, she avoided Tess as much as possible. Occasionally, their eyes would meet across a set before filming started. The actress's look would be questioning and then hurt when Drew didn't do anything but turn away. *Like a coward.*

Crawling along on the highway, Drew realized she would be too late getting to the set to stop the director. At the rate the cars were moving, and with no idea what was wrong, the drive could take her anywhere from minutes to hours to arrive. With no other options, she would have to get the director on the phone and plead her case while she sat there waiting for things to move. Asking her vehicle's nav system to dial his number, she listened to the ringing. *He can see it's me and doesn't want to debate the change again,* she thought as the call rolled over to voicemail. After leaving a short, and very terse message for him, Drew tried to figure out what to do next. Traffic wasn't cooperating, and if things didn't change soon, the scene could well be shot by the time she made it to the lot.

I need someone to advocate on my behalf, she thought biting her lip, because there was only one person who could help her. Tess. Her heart rate doubled at the idea of talking to her. *But what else can I do?* Having the nav system call Tess, Drew held her breath. There was always the chance the actress would ignore the call too. *I haven't been treating her very nice so why should she help me?*

"Drew?" Tess asked as soon as the call connected. "What's wrong? Are you okay?"

Swallowing hard, Drew had to force her voice to stay casual. Hearing Tess over her car's speaker made her stomach tighten with anxiety but also excitement. "I'm stuck in traffic," Drew answered. "So, I need a favor. I know you don't have any reason to—"

"Anything," Tess interrupted. "For you."

. . .

As the town car pulled up, Tess jumped out of the backseat, ignored the pouring rain and made a beeline for the movie director who was walking with the lead cameraman. Holding umbrellas, they were pacing the blocked off street, undoubtedly working through the details of the dramatic scene planned for the morning. *The scene that Drew hates,* she thought. *And asked me to at least delay until she arrived or maybe quash altogether.* Not that Tess had any honest opinion about the part either way. She could see both sides of the argument. Drew was right that the scene wasn't in the novel and might be a bit over the top for the character Tess played, but that was the movie business. If the director wanted her to run down the street in the rain to kiss her costar, then that's what Tess would typically do. *But not this time. Not if it matters so much to her.*

"Well, hey there, Tess," the movie director said as she approached. "Are you crazy? Why don't you have an umbrella? You're getting soaked."

He moved to hand her his, but Tess waved him off. "Thank you, but I'm fine," she said. "Hair and makeup will dry me off in a minute. I need to talk to you about the morning's scene." She squared her shoulder because contradicting the director wasn't commonly done, but she was about to try it. "I'm not sure how I feel about it and suggest we don't do it."

The director rolled his eyes. "Don't you start in on me about it too," he said. "I see Drew's been calling my cell all morning, and I don't need to listen to her voicemails to know what they say." He shook his head. "But I'm not cutting the scene. Tess, you shouldn't want me to."

Grinning, the cameraman nodded. "He's right," he said, obviously excited about the shot. "When I'm done capturing the moment, the action will be the most powerful scene in the movie."

Frowning, Tess crossed her arms. Having worked with the cameraman before, Tess knew he was magical with using the light and shot great angles. For the most part she considered him a friend. Still, in her opinion, his boast went a bit far. "More powerful than when my character saves the ten-year-old boy who comes into the ER dying after a car crash?" When the cameraman didn't answer, she smiled to lighten her statement. "Okay, to be fair, for some test audiences, the romantic scenes will be the highlights." She returned her look to the director. "But the kiss isn't even in the book."

"Well, it should have been," the director growled. "The book might have a love story, but it's not exactly filled with a fiery passion." Tess wasn't sure what to say. What he said was true. Drew's novel was tender and straightforward in how the two characters fell in love but felt perhaps too timid at times. A thought occurred to her. *Kind of like Drew herself,* Tess reasoned. *Shy. But does that mean there isn't a fiery passion inside her too?*

Regardless, she couldn't let the scene happen without talking to Drew. "I'm sorry, but I think we need to stay true to the book."

The director shook his head but didn't answer while they stared at each other. After a beat, the cameraman shifted his feet, clearly uncomfortable at the standoff. "So, what's the plan?" he mumbled. "Is the scene in or is it out?"

"Start blocking the scene," the director said, looking at Tess. "But keep the cameras inside until I talk to Drew." He narrowed his eyes. "Unless you're willing to? Maybe convince her the scene really will bring tears to the audience's eyes. It could win you an Oscar."

20

With a drive that should have taken thirty minutes but ended up being sixty, Drew felt filled with anxiety when she finally arrived. Having to park further away than she wanted because they had blocked the street for the shot, she could not get out of the Pathfinder fast enough. No word from Tess had her worried the worst had happened already, and the scene was in the can. Still, as she popped up her umbrella and went around the corner to see where the craziness was supposed to happen, no one was there. Not as if everyone left because cables were running to a generator, and the ever-resilient craft service table crew were set up under a popup canopy. Marks on the asphalt let her know they had done some prep, but there was no one getting ready to shoot a scene. *Has Tess been that convincing after all?* she wondered, hoping it was true and the whole ridiculous thing was canceled.

"Drew," she suddenly heard behind her and, turning to look, saw Tess coming toward her. Although she held a blue and white umbrella over her head, her hair was wet.

So are her clothes, Drew thought with a frown as she

walked to meet Tess. "What happened? You look like you were standing in the rain."

Tess laughed. "That's because I was," she said. "While I pled your case." She sobered. "Which is what I want to talk to you about."

Drew raised her eyebrows. "Really?" she asked. "Why? It looks like it was called off."

"Not exactly," Tess said. "Come with me to my trailer?" When Drew hesitated, unsure what to think about the woman's words or her invite, Tess shook her head. "We will only talk about the film."

Feeling her shoulders relax, Drew nodded. "Okay," she said. "But you're making me curious. Why am I talking to you about the situation? And not the director?"

Tess nodded toward her trailer and led the way. "Let's go inside," she answered. Not sure what was going on, all Drew could do was follow. By the time she had shaken the water off the umbrellas and stepped under cover, her impatience got the best of her. She wanted to know the bottom line.

"Explanation? Please?"

Sitting on the couch, putting a towel around her shoulders, Tess sighed. "Drew," she said. "The new scene needs to stay."

"What?" Drew started to shake her head. "No way. We went over that." It felt like a double-cross. "The scene isn't even in the book."

Tess's face stayed calm. "I know you don't like the idea of the passionate scene," she said. "But it will make the movie better, I promise." That was the last thing Drew wanted to hear coming from Tess. She had thought the woman was on her side, but apparently not. Without bothering even to say goodbye, she headed for the door. "Stop." Tess moved quickly from the sofa to take her arm. "Please. Hear me out."

Something in the tone of Tess's voice made Drew pause.

"All right," she said, turning around. "But I'm not going to be convinced." With her hand on Drew's arm, Tess didn't move back to the couch. Unable to help from reacting to the touch and their closeness, Drew sucked in a breath, willing herself not to get distracted.

Tess's face was earnest. "I'm going to be very blunt," she said. "And I apologize if what I'm going to say hurts your feelings."

Staying by the door, Drew was curious where the conversation would go. "Blunt?" she asked, and Tess nodded.

"Yes, blunt," she said. "Drew, you're a special woman. You already know how I feel about you, but I promised to keep that out of it. However..." Drew waited with no idea what Tess would say next. The woman took a deep breath. "My character's thoughts in your book carry the smoldering desires on the written page, but that won't work here. The movie audience needs to see the passion. To feel it for themselves."

Drew furrowed her brow. "But you are pulling off the looks of desire well enough," she argued. "I don't see why a single kiss will make the difference."

"Then let me show you," Tess said, moving even closer before Drew could react. Suddenly, the woman's lips were on hers, and a jolt of something she had never felt before ran through her. Heat like white lightning that made her stomach flutter. Desire in waves she never knew possible. A part of her wanted to pull away, but another part, a stronger part of her, wanted to lean in. Kissing Tess back, wrapping her arms around her waist, Drew fell into the embrace completely. And finally knew why the scene needed to stay.

NEVER HAVING BEEN to an actual working movie set before, Bryce was curious. Watching Ashley's mom work would be

147

interesting, and frankly, kind of cool. After all, she was Tess Landish. Hollywood megastar. Luckily, the Uber ride to the location was less frustrating than she feared, and they arrived early. From the look of things, no acting had started. Before they had walked a dozen steps, a production assistant, armed with a giant golf umbrella for them to use, was there. "Ms. Landish asked me to keep an eye out for you," the PA said, handing them two guest passes on lanyards.

"We are early. Can I check in with my mom at her trailer?" Ashley asked while she and Bryce put on their passes. "Or is she in hair and makeup already?"

"She's in her trailer," the assistant said. "I believe she is talking to Ms. Andersen about the next scene. Although no one has said to me directly, I hear there's some question about the necessity of shooting it."

"Interesting. She mentioned something about the debate this morning," Ashley said. "Well, I don't think she will mind if I pop in and say hello. It will be nice to see Drew again too."

The production assistant nodded. "I'm sure that's fine," she said. "Trailer number four. You can't miss it. One of the two biggest units." *Well, that makes sense*, Bryce thought. *Since she is one of the stars.* She followed along with Ashley as she led the way.

When they reached trailer four, Ashley gave a perfunctory knock before turning the doorknob. "Mom?" she said, sticking her head inside. "We came by early—" Bryce watched Ashley freeze in the doorway. Not sure what happened, but sensing something was a little off, she stepped closer, only to be almost bowled over by Ashley in retreat. "I'm so sorry. I shouldn't have barged in."

Then, Tess was in the doorway with her face flushed, eyes wide. "Ashley, wait," she said. "Don't be upset."

Ashley stopped, and Bryce saw the widest smile ever on

the woman's face. "Upset? Mom, I'm so not upset," she said. "I'm super excited for you. Maybe a little surprised, but happy too."

Tess's shoulders relaxed. "Thank God," she said. "At first, I thought the worst." She stepped back and waved them forward. "Come in, please. I don't want to talk about everything out in the open."

"Of course," Ashley said, and still not sure what happened, Bryce collapsed the umbrella and followed her into the trailer. Drew sat on the couch looking very uncomfortable. Her face was beet red, and she wouldn't make eye contact.

Tess hurried to the woman's side, taking her hand. "Drew," she said. "It's only Ashley and Bryce, and there's nothing to worry about."

In response, Drew started to stand. "I'm sorry," she said, looking ready to flee. In response, Ashley slipped her arm through Bryce's.

"Don't go," Ashley said. "We will take off so you two can be alone. Please don't leave on our account." Before Drew or Tess could respond either way, Ashley hustled Bryce back the way they came. "Bye, Mom. Bye, Drew." She closed the door and rushed them both down the steps.

Once away from the trailer, Bryce's curiosity got the best of her, and she pulled Ashley to a stop. "Okay, will you explain to me what's going on?" she asked. "Why did Drew look so..." Suddenly, the word came to her, and everything fell into place. "Guilty." She grinned. "Just what exactly were they doing when you opened the door?"

Ashley playfully pushed her shoulder. "Not that," she said with a laugh. "Thank God. I mean, I'm happy to see Mom involved with someone." She shook her head. "But there are limits."

· · ·

GENUINELY THRILLED to see her mom passionately kissing someone, even another woman, Ashley wondered when their relationship started. *Maybe on the day of the earthquake?* she thought, walking under the umbrella with Bryce. Talking to her mom about what happened during the eight hours she was trying to get to Ashley, Drew was her mom's hero that day. *Like Bryce was mine.* She certainly made an intense connection with her, so there was no reason her mom couldn't have done the same. From what Ashley knew about Drew, which wasn't much other than she was a fantastic writer and super helpful to her mom, she seemed nice. *I'll have to get to know her better. Maybe the four of us can go to dinner after filming today.*

Crossing the lot, she decided they would hang out at the craft service table while waiting for the filming to begin. While they stayed undercover to avoid the rain, enjoying a fresh cup of coffee and a pastry, Ashley noticed the movie's famous director talking to someone. They stood in the rolled-up doorway of one of the warehouses edging the set. Not wanting to act like a total fan, although she was, Ashley nonchalantly nodded her head in the man's direction. "Don't be super obvious, but there's the movie's director. You might have heard of him," she said, and when Bryce slowly turned to look, she saw the woman's eyes widen.

"Wow. No kidding," she said. "I really like his dramatic action stuff." As if feeling their eyes on him, the man looked over. A smile lit up his face when he recognized Ashley. Although they only met a couple of times over the years, he remembered her.

Strolling over, he shook his head. "Ashley," he said. "Wow, you have certainly grown up. And are as beautiful as your mother."

"Thank you. I didn't know if you'd remember me."

The director laughed. "Hardly a problem when you look

so like her," he said. "Are you sure you don't want to be in a movie? I have one coming up I think you'd be perfect for."

Ashley smiled. "Sorry, no, not really," she said. "Movies are Mom's business, and I never felt like it was something I wanted to do."

"Fair enough," the director said, looking at Bryce.

Ashley put her hand on Bryce's arm. "This is my girlfriend, Bryce Cooper."

Bryce held out her hand, and the director shook it. "You make excellent movies, sir," she said. "I especially liked *Modern Patriots*. A solid portrayal of what the military is like these days."

The director lifted an eyebrow. "I take it you're military then?" he asked. "What branch?"

Ashley watched as Bryce lifted her chin, a proud look coming over her face. "United States Marine Corps, sir," she said. "1st Reconnaissance Battalion."

It was the director's turn to look impressed. "Remarkable," the director said, shaking Bryce's hand with even more vigor. "It's an honor to meet you."

"Thank you, sir," Bryce said, taking her hand back. "The honor is mine."

The director nodded. "Listen, I have to get the day started. We're behind, but maybe we can talk later?" he said. "I'd be very interested in your perspective on some military questions I have." He smiled. "Assuming you're allowed to answer them."

Bryce smiled too. "I'll do my best, sir," she said. "Although some things are classified, of course."

"Right, of course," the director said, turning to go. He paused. "And thank you for your service."

"You're welcome," Bryce said. The minute the director was out of earshot, Ashley met Bryce's eyes. They had yet to talk about the military in detail, and she had questions she needed answered.

"Bryce," she said. "I think it's incredible that you're in the Marine Corps. But I feel like there are things you're not telling me."

With a sigh, Bryce nodded. "I'm sorry. I have been evasive," she said. "It's simple. You know I'm in the Marine Corps." She paused, a tenderness coming into her face. "And I'm on leave until the end of the week."

Ashley wasn't sure she liked what that might mean. "And then what happens?" she asked, a nervous tightening in her stomach.

Bryce sighed. "And then I have a really big decision to make."

21

*A*s the rain continued to pour, Tess stood under a broad umbrella held by a production assistant. There really wasn't any point in trying to protect her from the rain, in her opinion, considering she ran down the block three times already and was soaked through. Still, she let the PA do his job while she did her best to mentally prepare for another take of the much-debated romance scene. The task wasn't easy. Drew kept invading her thoughts and in the very best possible ways. After the nearly catastrophic interruption by her daughter and Bryce, Tess sat beside Drew on the couch again and worked to calm her down. "Can we talk about what is upsetting you?" she asked. "I know they are waiting on us, but I don't want to leave things like this. What are you thinking?"

Drew shook her head. "I know it doesn't make sense considering I wrote over a hundred thousand words in my novel," she said while they sat there together. "But I can't find the words to what I'm feeling. Everything is all jumbled into such a mixture of crazy emotions."

Gently taking Drew's hand, loving the warmth of her skin, Tess waited for her reaction. When she didn't pull away, she kept the conversation going. "Crazy how?" Tess asked, very much wanting to understand. Anything to keep the woman from running away again. "I'm listening."

Drew gave her a shy smile. "I know you are," she said. "And being incredibly patient. I'm sure you're frustrated with me."

Tess squeezed her hand, and looking into the woman's face, she wondered what she could do to get through to her. How to let her know she wasn't in a hurry. "I'm not frustrated," Tess said. "Please don't think that. I only want to spend time with you." She moved a little closer. "And see where our feelings can go. But I need you to want that too."

Squeezing Tess's hand in return, Drew gave her a tentative nod. "I think I want that too," she said before shyly locking eyes with Tess. "But I have a confession."

"A confession?" Tess raised an eyebrow. "Okay, now I'm curious. What is it?"

Color rose to Drew's cheeks, and Tess watched her swallow hard before daring to say what she wanted. "I want to kiss you again," she said in a whisper. "Like we were before Ashley surprised us."

Never wanting anything more, Tess took Drew's face in her hands. "Then, kiss me," she said, and Drew did with the passion Tess craved. As the kiss grew hotter and Drew less tentative, Tess slowly slid her leg over until she straddled Drew.

With a gasp, Drew broke the kiss. "Oh God," she said, rubbing her hands against the fabric of the couch as if not sure where to put them. "I'm not sure I'm ready for this."

"Do you want me to stop?" Tess asked, her voice breathless as desire rippled through her body. Being so close to Drew, to feel her body, could quickly drive Tess crazy, and she prayed the woman wouldn't push her away. "It's up to you." Licking her lips, Drew raised her hands to tentatively trace the edges of Tess's breasts through the fabric. Tess trembled with pleasure. "That feels so good."

Clearly encouraged, Drew pressed harder. "Is this too much?" she asked, and Tess shook her head.

"No," she answered. "Definitely not. Do you want me to unbutton my blouse?"

Drew's hand froze. "No," she squeaked. "I mean, yes. God, I don't know." She blushed. "I'm not sure I'm ready when anyone can knock at any time."

Sensing the woman was overwhelmed and not wanting to ruin things, Tess covered her hands with her own. "Then we will wait," she said, and after a few more incredible kisses, Tess slid off Drew. "I probably should check in and let them know you're okay with shooting the scene anyway."

As soon as she said the words, there was a knock at the trailer door. "Ms. Landish," came the familiar voice of her personal production assistant. "Do you have a minute? The crew is waiting to hear the plan for the morning."

Pecking Drew on the lips one last time, Tess stood. "I'll be right out," she answered. "But you can tell them the scene is a go."

STANDING with Bryce and Drew a distance from the action to ensure they weren't in a panning camera shot, Ashley watched her mother run down the wet street. The costar, a Hollywood A-lister in his own right, stood at his car. The door was open, and he moved as if he was about to leave. "Wait," Tess called out to him. "Please." The costar turned at the sound of her voice, surprise followed by happiness on his face. Looking uncertain, he stepped in Tess's direction, and the two collided into a passionate kiss. Water poured down from the sky, drenching them both. The rainstorm had luckily not abated, although the forecast of a break coming later in the day had people worried. Everything went perfectly, and even though it was all make-believe, Ashley felt the emotion behind the scene. *The director was right. The audiences will love the passion coming off the two characters*, she thought. *I'm glad they talked Drew into letting them shoot it.*

She glanced over and noticed Drew staring at the action, clearly as enthralled as she was. Unable to keep from smiling at the memory of seeing her mom and Drew on the couch making out, she smiled. The sight of them with arms wrapped around each other in a passionate kiss had caught her entirely off guard. After hearing Ashley come in, she couldn't think of a time when her mom had looked so surprised. *Of course, I did barge through the door*, she thought. *And it could have been worse. At least they had clothes on.* She made a mental note to be a little more careful around them in the future. As attractive as her mom was, Ashley wasn't keen on catching her naked with someone.

"Cut," the director yelled, and as Tess and her costar stepped apart, everyone waited, holding their breath to hear the man's verdict. Even though they wore raingear, and the cameras were wrapped in plastic to protect them from the rain, everyone looked a little miserable. The outcome from the last scene hung in the balance. Finally, the director smiled. "Brilliant. Exactly what I wanted." He clapped his hands together. "Now, let's break everything down, and all go get dry."

As people followed his directions, Tess joined Ashley and the others. Her production assistant rushed over to wrap the actress in a large towel, and Drew stepped closer to share the umbrella she carried. "That was great, Mom. Really captured the emotion," Ashley said while Tess squeezed water out of her long blonde hair.

"Do you think so?" she asked. "That last take felt right. Thank God. If I had to run down the street and kiss him again, I was bringing him a breath mint."

The group laughed. "I imagine that can be an occupational hazard at times," Bryce said with a grin, and Tess nodded.

"Among other things. The stories I could tell you."

"I bet there are some I haven't even heard," Ashley chimed in. "Why don't we all go to lunch and share? Or are you shooting more today?"

"Nothing else today," Tess said, glancing at Drew. "Are you interested in lunch?" she asked. Drew smiled, meeting Tess's eye. The moment between them held for a second before Drew answered.

"I think that would be perfect," she said, and Ashley watched her mom smile.

"Then let me go back to my trailer so I can get dried out," she suggested, starting to walk in their direction. "And go somewhere fun. Anybody interested in heading downtown?"

"Perfect," Ashley said as they walked, snuggling closer to Bryce to stay under their umbrella and enjoy the woman's touch. Ashley loved seeing Drew and Tess ahead of her doing much the same. Not nearly so obviously, but after seeing the kissing earlier, Ashley knew what to look for, and she could see the tenderness there. The chemistry between them. *This will be something interesting to watch*, she thought, excited for her mom. *She deserves to find someone wonderful.* Thinking of wonderful people, she leaned in to kiss Bryce on the cheek.

Bryce grinned. "What was that for? she asked. "Not that I'm complaining."

"For being wonderful," Ashley said. "Is that reason enough?"

Wrapping her arm tighter around Ashley, Bryce nodded. "It is for me," she said. "You can kiss me anytime you want."

. . .

AFTER A SHORT RIDE downtown in Drew's Pathfinder, Bryce followed the others into the Ritz-Carlton Hotel. "That was cool, watching how a movie is made," Bryce said after Tess gave her name, and they were shown to a table near the back. The actress had decided to take them downtown to Savoca, a restaurant popular with local celebrities. Bryce worked hard to keep from looking in every direction as they got settled. Still, she was pretty sure she spotted the actress in her favorite sitcom only one table over. Refocusing on the group, Bryce picked up where she left off. "I didn't know how scenes were shot. There's a lot more to it than they depict on television. But you made it look easy."

Tess nodded. "Thank you. And yes, it's not as simple as it looks. I'm lucky. Our experienced team is truly making it all go smoothly," she said, pointing to a thick leatherbound menu. "Can you please hand over the wine list? We need something extraordinary to celebrate a very special day."

Ashley, sitting beside her mother, bumped her shoulder. "Oh, really," she said with a smile. "A very special day?" She winked at Bryce. "Other than shooting a great scene that audiences will love, you mean?"

Bryce watched as Tess didn't even look up from the wine list. "Behave yourself, daughter of mine," she said. "I need to teach you to knock."

"Yes, mother dear," Ashley said. "But I did knock." She laughed. "Briefly."

Peeking over the top of the list, Tess was smiling too. "I'll just learn to lock the door next time." Enjoying the exchange, Bryce glanced at Drew. The woman was bright red but thankfully smiling.

With a shaking hand, Drew reached for her glass of water. "If you're going to keep talking about it, I'm going to need that wine to get here soon," she said before taking a long swallow. "I'm not used to it."

Laying down the menu, Tess touched the back of Drew's hand. "If it bothers you, I promise we will stop joking about it," she said. "And as for wine, I will get us two bottles. Even if it means we have to take a taxi back and get your car tomorrow."

True to her word, as the multi-course lunch went by, Tess ordered two bottles of champagne, which tasted better to Bryce than she remembered. *Of course, it might have something to do with the quality of the bottle too*, she thought, trying to think of the last time she had bubbly. At best, whatever she had was probably from a convenience store. *This is stronger stuff than I remember too.* Even after a plate of melt-in-your-mouth pan-seared sea bass, she could feel the effects of the champagne. *So much I swear the room is moving.*

Looking at her water glass, the liquid was subtly but undoubtedly shaking. There was a slight rumbling sound, and as it increased, the silverware on the table jumped. Suddenly, Ashley grabbed her hand. "Oh God," she said, her voice tight with fear. "It's another earthquake." Before Bryce could answer her, the rumbling stopped. They all sat in silence for a minute. Then, everyone in the restaurant started talking, asking each other, "Was that an earthquake?" and "Do you think we should leave?"

Bryce laced her fingers through Ashley's to hold her hand tight. "It's over," she said. "We're okay." She looked at the other two women at the table. Tess was white as a sheet, but Drew appeared to have taken the event in stride. "Tess, are you okay?"

Slowly, Tess nodded. "I think so," she said. "But I want to go home. Just in case."

"Do you think it will happen again so soon?" Ashley asked, her hand gripping Bryce's even tighter. She knew the woman understood there was no way to predict if another earthquake was coming. *She's reacting because of what happened before*, she thought, hoping the slight tremor was the last of earthquakes for a long time. Still, a part of her wondered if Mother Nature was done, and she wished they had Floyd the dog with them.

22

*A*fter Tess left a few hundred dollar bills on the table, Drew kept a guiding hand on the woman's back as they followed Bryce and Ashley toward the restaurant's main doors. Seeing people starting to bunch in the hotel lobby, Drew was glad they didn't hesitate to go. If another tremor or worse hit and people panicked, leaving would prove to be a serious challenge. "Hey, watch where you're going," a man said when Drew bumped his shoulder.

"I'm sorry," she said, accidentally stepping on another man's toes as they weaved their way forward. "Only trying to stay up with my friend."

Bryce wasted no time getting them outside the building and onto the front steps. Once they were clear of the mass of people, she saw valets racing to fetch cars, and she groaned. Her Pathfinder was parked in some location offsite with no easy way to get to it.

Seeing the apparent problem, Tess groaned too. "Damn it," she said. "I didn't even think of this complication. What are we going to do?"

For a second, Drew wondered if Tess's fame could get

them to the front of the line but knew the actress would never use her stature to cut in on other people. They would have to wait like everyone else. Suddenly, she heard a low rumble a second before the ground shook a little under her. The sensation was so minor, if there hadn't been earthquakes already, she might not have noticed it. There was a ripple of voices from the crowd around her as people asked if others felt the movement. Not everyone appeared to have, but a few looked particularly anxious.

Coming out the front doors and pushing his way forward, one man reached the valet station ahead of the others. "I want my car," Drew heard him insist. "My wife and I need to get home to our children."

"I'm sorry, sir," one of the valets said. "You have to wait in line. We're moving as quickly as we can." As he said the words, the rumbling started again, followed by another tremor. Again, it came and went in seconds, but a few women let out tiny screams.

Tess grabbed Drew's hand. "I'm so scared," she murmured as Ashley moved closer, putting her arm around her mom.

Her face was pale, eyes wide. "Me too," Ashley said. "I only want to get out of here." With no idea what to do, Drew scanned the crowd. Fear radiated off the group of people, and as a mass, they pressed forward on the valet station.

"Give me my keys then," the same man as before growled, but Drew didn't hear the valet's response over the chorus of voices echoing his request. Drew clenched her jaw. *There is no way we can get my car,* she thought. *And things are about to get out of hand.* Walking, at least far enough to catch an Uber or taxi to take them home, looked to be their only option. She could come back and get the car later.

About to suggest that, Bryce was suddenly beside her, holding out her hand. "Let me have your valet ticket," she said. "I have an idea."

Not hesitating, Drew pulled the slip of paper from her pocket. "What are you going to do?"

"Going to get our keys," Bryce said, already moving. "Is there anything unique on your keychain?"

She nodded. "I have a small, silver hummingbird on it."

"Perfect," Bryce said before disappearing into the crowd without explaining anything else. Looking at the mass of angry people at the valet station, her claim sounded impossible. *Except it is Bryce*, she thought. *The Marine.* Once she considered everything else the woman had done in the last few days, she felt they might have a chance. If anyone could fight a mob to get what she needed, it would be Bryce.

Drew squeezed Tess's hand, putting her fear of being seen aside. It seemed silly to worry about it with everyone else focused on the earthquakes. Considering the circumstances, she didn't believe anyone would notice or care what she and Tess were doing. "We're going to be okay," she said, Tess and Ashley both nodding. "But let's move closer to the street and away from this group." As voices escalated, she knew from her emergency department experience punches would be coming soon. When that started, she didn't want them anywhere nearby.

THANKFUL the torrential rain had finally started to let up, Bryce slipped wide around the edge of the crowd until she was behind the valet station. Acting as if she belonged there, she walked into the space and considered the board of keys hanging on hooks. Overwhelmed, the valets were trying to keep the crowd under control while still fetching cars. Everyone in the group had focused on the poor guy in charge, not even noticing her taking a moment to find what she needed. Overhearing his pleas for calm, Bryce could tell the young man would cave to the demands for keys any moment. True chaos would break out as people rushed to get their vehicles when that happened. *Even more reason to act now and get out of here*, she thought, scanning the board for a silver hummingbird keychain. It stood out easily.

After she grabbed it and double-checked the ticket number to be sure, she waited until the next valet arrived with a car. A soon as he handed it over, he took off running to get another. Falling in quickly behind him she kept up with his pace even though he was in a full sprint. Bryce shook her head when she saw the multistory parking garage they headed toward. When the wave of upset drivers descended on the location, the traffic getting out of the many levels would be a nightmare. Not knowing how much lead time she had, she didn't waste a second looking for the vehicle. Pressing the panic button on the key fob, she homed in on the shrieking car alarm in seconds.

A moment later, she was driving out, the tires squealing on the concrete. Once she hit the street, Bryce saw a steady stream of men and women headed her way down the middle of the road. *Apparently, the valet gave in*, she thought creeping along to avoid the people running without much regard for traffic. *People lose all common sense when they start to panic. And it might not even be warranted.* Two small tremors did not mean another earthquake would come any time soon. Still, considering the tragedy along the coast, people were wired tight. Even she had a funny feeling about the situation. Growing up in Bakersfield, a city close enough to the famous San Andreas Fault to live with the fear of the "big one," she knew the possibility of a catastrophic event existed. There was something unusual about the repeated small tremors that seemed off to her. *Like maybe it is some warning from Mother Nature.* That premonition was even more reason to get to Ashley and the others.

Speeding up, after only a few blocks, she saw a man

waving his arms over his head to get her attention. Slowing but not completely stopping, Bryce rolled down her window. Although the man wore a business suit, she wasn't ready to trust any strangers. "What's wrong?" she called to him, and he came toward the window. "That's close enough."

He panted, clearly not used to running anywhere. "Which way to the valet lot?" he asked between deep breaths. "I need to get my car. I'm not going to be downtown when it gets worse."

Not appreciating his line of thinking but understanding why he was worried considering tall, concrete buildings surrounded them, Bryce pointed back the way she came. "About three blocks straight ahead. Parkade on the right," she said. "Good luck." Without waiting for a response, Bryce kept moving and was thankful to see Ashley with her mom and Drew standing at the corner.

Pulling over, she hopped out only to find Ashley in her arms for a tight hug. "You're always amazing," she said, a sob in her voice. Bryce hugged her back, holding out the keys toward Drew.

"We're okay, Ashley. Try to stay relaxed," she said before looking at Drew. "I don't know the city streets at all. You should drive."

Nodding, Drew reached to take the keys when a rumble started, seeming to roll over the ground lasting barely a few seconds. "Not again," Ashley said, hugging Bryce tighter. "Why do these little ones keep happening?"

Bryce didn't know, but they worried her. A lot.

BITING her lip while they waited on the corner, Tess had watched the street for the familiar white Pathfinder. For her, Bryce could not get back fast enough. Not only because she wanted to get everyone home in case there were more

165

shakes, but the crowd behind them was coming unglued. Just when she thought something might have gone wrong with Bryce's attempt to get the car, the Pathfinder turned the corner a second before pulling up to the curb beside them. The minute Bryce stepped out of the driver's seat, Ashley was in her arms. Even wanting to hurry, it made her happy to see her daughter with someone as incredible as Bryce Cooper.

Then, the earth shook again. Not much, but enough to send her heart racing. Three small quakes in a row somehow seemed a warning that worse was yet to come. "Please, let's get in the car and go," she said, working to keep her voice even. She sensed Ashley was genuinely struggling, undoubtedly brought on by her earlier experience at the Venice Beach boardwalk, and she wanted to appear as calm as possible.

Thankfully, Drew acted with the same relaxed demeanor while quickly taking the driver's seat. "Your house?" she asked when Tess settled in on the front passenger side. "And put on your seatbelt."

Tess obeyed as she nodded. "Yes, I think that's best," she said, looking into the back. Ashley was buckled in the middle seat to sit closer to Bryce. Seeing her daughter so shaken, Tess reached to touch her knee. "We're going to be okay, Ashley." She looked at Bryce. "Do you agree going to Beverly Hills is the right thing to do?"

Bryce nodded. "Honestly, anywhere but here is a win," she said. "Downtown LA is not an optimal place to be right now."

Tess had to agree. Skyrises as high as seventy-three stories surrounded them. *If anything significant starts to happen, no matter how earthquake-proof people say they are, stuff will start falling,* she thought. *Likely big, heavy stuff.* Visions of the Pathfinder peppered with massive concrete chunks threatened to put her in a panic, but she fought the fears off. There was no sense in imagining the worst case scenarios.

As if sensing her internal battle, Drew grabbed Tess's hand to give it a gentle squeeze. "Nothing but positive thoughts, remember?" she said, and Tess did her best to give the wonderful, confident, levelheaded woman a reassuring smile.

"You're right," she said, refocusing on the present moment and the situation they were in. "I'm sorry. I'm overreacting." Looking out the windshield, she saw nothing but brake lights. Cars, trucks, and busses surrounded them moving in fits and starts. Everyone had the same idea they did—get out of downtown. Much of the workforce in the heart of downtown LA lived elsewhere. Even though it was early afternoon, the series of shakes was enough to send people scattering for home. Tess shook her head in frustration. "Traffic is crazy. We could sit here for hours."

Drew nodded. "Unfortunately, you're right," she said. "Everyone wants to get on the Harbor Freeway because it's the fastest way out of downtown."

Tess pursed her lips, trying to decide what to do. *But is that the way we want to go?* she wondered when Bryce spoke up.

"Don't take the freeway," she said in a tone harsher than Tess had heard before. The woman paused, clearly recognizing how she sounded. "I'm sorry. I mean it's likely to be backed up as bad. And, well…"

Tess glanced back at the hesitation and saw Ashley resting her head on Bryce's shoulder. Her eyes were closed. "What are you thinking?" Tess asked softly but had already guessed what the Marine would say. She didn't need the military to see the risk once she thought things over. Still, she waited for Bryce to answer.

"Because if there's another earthquake, we don't want to be trapped on there."

With her eyes closed, leaning her head on Bryce's firm shoulder in the backseat of the Pathfinder, Ashley loved how solid the woman felt. *That and how she smells,* Ashley thought. Not like any perfume or something store-bought necessarily but simply her unique scent. Over the last few days, cuddling on the couch and in bed, she didn't realize how used to Bryce she had become. *Right now, she comforts the hell out of me. I swear I will stay like this until we are back at Mom's house.*

Lost in her thoughts, Ashley wasn't paying much attention to what the other three were saying until Bryce suggested walking somewhere. Ashley reluctantly lifted her head. "Wait. What? We're walking clear to Beverly Hills?" she asked, hoping she misunderstood. The distance had to be at least a dozen miles. "You can't be serious."

"I know it sounds a little much," Bryce said, taking her hand. "But not necessarily that far. We are considering all our options." Being in good shape from running, Ashley could walk for twelve miles, and Bryce certainly could, but she wasn't too sure about her mom and Drew. At the least, it would take them hours. Plus, it would be dark soon, not to mention it would be in the rain which had started up again. "We are only thinking we would walk far enough away from the traffic jam that we can find a taxi or an Uber or something."

Although that explanation sounded more practical to Ashley, leaving the car's safety and walking in the rain didn't feel right. "Why can't we wait here?" she asked, glancing around. Not a single car moved as she watched. The traffic jam had the makings of becoming something epic, even by LA standards. "I know we aren't moving, but we are safe and dry."

Apparently not the only person frustrated about the situation, Ashley heard a car horn in the distance. The sound wasn't only a honk from time to time but a long, persistent, almost angry noise. And it was quickly getting closer. "What the hell?" Bryce said, looking over her shoulder in the direction of the noise. Ashley followed her gaze and saw a black truck, taller than the other vehicles around it, coming through traffic. Raised on large tires, the truck was big and pushing through the two lanes of cars, forcing people to pull out of the way. She heard Bryce growl with frustration. "Drew, you need to pull over as far to the right as you can. The jerk isn't stopping."

"I see him. There's not much I can do," Drew said, pressing the Pathfinder up against the parked cars along the street. Ashley expected to feel the touch of another car at any second the woman was so close. Instead, all she heard was honking coming from behind as the truck closed in. The driver was relentless, pushing smaller sedans and SUVs aside with the rhino guard rack on the front. For a fleeting moment, Ashley wondered why anyone would have that sort of setup in downtown Los Angeles, and then the truck was only a few cars behind them. When a smaller pickup truck didn't yield, the driver of the bigger vehicle laid on the horn. Hating the obnoxious sound, Ashley covered her ears while watching in shock as the truck slammed into the other one. There was a crunch of metal and glass. Rather than give up, the driver of the smaller truck swerved further into the path, hitting his own horn.

Bryce shook her head. "That's not helping the situation," she muttered, and as if to prove her right, the big truck revved its engine a second before plowing forward. Unable to withstand the powerful surge of the stronger vehicle, the small truck started to slip to the side, giving its opponent enough space to swerve around him. As the drivers shouted obscenities at each other out their windows, Ashley saw what was going to happen a moment before it did. Not paying attention to the road in front of him, the driver drifted on a beeline for Drew's vehicle.

DREW HEARD BRYCE SAY, "Everybody hold on," one second before the giant truck slammed into her vehicle. Even with her foot on the brake, the impact forced her into the car in front of them and only the locking seatbelt saved her from banging her head into the windshield.

"Son of a bitch," she said as the strap dug into her shoulder. In the ER, she saw car crash victims come in with bruises across their bodies from where the seatbelt held them in place. Considering the alternative, it was a good injury to have, but at the moment, it hurt like hell. As if she did something to cause the crash, the driver of the big truck laid on his horn while flipping her off as he roared past.

Seeing enough of the stupidity, she focused on Tess. "Are you okay?" she asked, and the woman nodded although there was blood on her lip.

"I bit my lip when he hit us," she said, dabbing at her face with her fingertips while turning to look in the backseat. "Are you two all right?"

Drew glanced in the rearview mirror and saw Ashley nodding. "Just pissed," she said, with more spirit in her voice than she had since they got in the Pathfinder. "What an asshole."

Aside from being in total agreement, Drew was glad to see Tess's daughter perking up a little bit. She could tell the tremors had been affecting her more than the rest of them. For Drew they were scary and concerning, but Ashley acted terrified. Until the truck hit them anyway. That appeared to make her angry enough she stopped thinking about earthquakes.

"He sure was," she heard Bryce say although she couldn't see her in the mirror at the angle they were sitting. "Some people feel entitled and think they can do whatever they want. No matter what the consequences."

Drew was about to agree when someone tapped on her window. Startled, she looked into the face of an angry woman standing in the rain. She pointed at the small red Honda Civic in front of Drew's vehicle with a shaking finger. Even though she couldn't see all the damage, the back of the little car looked smashed like an accordion. "You hit my car," the stranger yelled through the glass. "I hope you have insurance."

"Seriously?" was all Drew could think to say through the rolled-up window. There they all were, trapped together out of fear of an earthquake, and people were starting to act like nuts.

Her face red and eyes snapping, the woman put her hands on her hips. "Yes, seriously," she said. "I finally got her paid off, and now this happens?"

Drew shook her head. "But it wasn't my fault," she said.

"The guy in the black truck didn't watch where he was going and pushed me into you."

Throwing up her hands, the woman looked to the heavens. "Why does stuff always happen to me?"

Drew could hardly believe what she heard her say. Her car was ruined too from the looks of the bent hood. The damage would be expensive to fix, and although money would never be an issue, it pissed her off the woman claimed things always happened to her. From Drew's perspective, bad things were currently in the process of happening to everybody.

Obviously overhearing the entire exchange, Tess leaned over Drew's lap to look out the driver's side window. "Listen," she said, with a little more grit than Drew was used to hearing. "We are all victims here, so cut us some slack."

The woman's mouth fell open as she stepped closer to the car window. "My God, are you Tess Landish?" she asked a moment before grabbing at her lower back. "Oh, my poor back. I felt something pop when you hit me."

That was the last straw. "You have got to be kidding me," Drew said, unfastening her seatbelt.

Tess grabbed her arm. "What are you doing?" she asked, and Drew nodded at the crazy woman on the other side of the door.

"Did you hear what she said? I'm getting out so I can talk some sense into her," she said. "It's all getting ridiculous."

"DREW, DON'T," Tess said, not letting go of Drew's arm. "I can promise you, engaging will only make it worse. Ask for her name and number. I can have one of my assistants look into it tomorrow." Unfortunately, she had a lot of experience with people coming after her financially for various reasons once they recognized her. The woman standing outside their car didn't have a back injury, at least not from the crash, but Tess had no doubt she would milk the accident for all it was worth. "We have other things to worry about right now." She nodded toward the front of the Pathfinder. "Maybe try and start the car?" Seeing the condition of the hood made Tess nervous. Although Drew's vehicle was bigger than the woman's red Honda, the Pathfinder's engine had stalled when they collided. If their ride turned out to not be drivable, then Bryce's suggestion of walking somewhere would be the only choice they had. Considering how hard it was raining, the reality wasn't appealing.

Drew nodded. "You're right," she said and pressed the ignition button. Nothing happened. No lights on the dash or anything. Frowning, she tried again. Still no response. "Well, that's not good. Maybe we blew a fuse of something from the impact."

"What's wrong with the car?" Ashley asked, leaning from the backseat. "Did the truck crash do something?" The young woman's eyes shifted to look out the windshield. They widened. "Oh, wow. That's not good."

In complete agreement, Tess was about to ask what they could try next when there was an angry knocking on Drew's window again. "Are you ignoring me?" the woman with the red Honda snapped. "Because I'm not simply going to go away." With a sigh, Drew took a notepad and pen from the center console and quickly jotted down her name and phone number.

As she reached for the button to lower the window, she paused. "Shit," she said. "I can't roll down the window with the car not responding," she said. "I'll have to open the door to push the note through." Tess wasn't a fan of opening the door, even if they could get the woman to go away and was about to say so when the familiar rumbling sound started. Both the woman with the wrecked car and Ashley let out a little yelp of panic in the same instant the ground jolted beneath them. Unlike before, the sensation was more of a bounce. *What is happening?* Tess thought before realizing the car's shock absorbers were reacting as if they were driving over a rough road. Being in a vehicle during the shaking was an entirely different sensation.

"Oh God," Ashley moaned. "Please let it stop." Tess hoped for that too, but unlike the other tremors, the earthquake grew louder and had already lasted longer. *Could this be it?* she wondered, facing the reality they were in a horrible spot. *Is it the 'big one' everyone worried about?* They were in downtown LA, in a traffic jam, trapped in a car that wouldn't start. *What else can go wrong?* Then, she heard the rumble grow louder and the sound of something creaking. A loud crack snapped through the air.

Grabbing the car's armrest, her eyes widened. "What is that?" she asked, looking out through the windows while the vehicle continued to shimmy.

"Oh my God," Drew said, grabbing Tess's arm, shock, and awe in her voice. "Look at the freeway."

Looking out the rain-spattered window, Tess let her eyes drift to the blurry image of the freeway ahead of them. Even from where they were, over a block away, she saw pieces of concrete raining down and the onramp they would have taken starting to shake.

---

24

*B*ryce faced a dilemma as the Pathfinder continued to rock on its tires and the cracking noise from the breaking concrete ahead became more pronounced. Unable to see much of anything from behind Drew in the backseat, especially looking out the rain-speckled windshield, she needed to step out of the vehicle. Considering the tall buildings surrounding them, getting out was a bad idea. With the earth rumbling, anything could happen to her—falling debris, another crazy driver, or something entirely unpredictable. But if she didn't, she would have no idea what was happening. There would be no chance of reacting if any of the structures around them started to crack. Making up her mind, Bryce kissed Ashley on the temple. "Stay here," she said to the woman still clutching her arm. "I'm going to get out of the car."

Ashley's head whipped around. "Wait. What are you doing?" Ashley asked, the panicked sound from earlier rushing back into her voice. "That doesn't make any sense."

"I need to see what's happening," she said, slowly

extracting her arm from Ashley's grasp. "I'm sorry but there's no way to assess the threat if we are all in here."

Drew started to open her car door. "I'm getting out too," she said. "Bryce is right. I can't see enough because of the rain."

As Drew opened her car door, Bryce wondered if Tess would protest but instead heard the unclipping of her seatbelt. "I am too," she said. "Something is happening to the freeway."

"We don't all need to get out," Bryce said, but it was too late. Drew was already gone. *Shit*, she thought as she climbed out too. *That did not go as I intended.* As soon as her feet hit the shaking pavement, she nearly fell, only saved by grabbing the Pathfinder's door for support. Not realizing how much more difficult it would be to keep her balance out of the car, she worried one of the others would fall. The last thing they needed was for one of them to break their leg or something worse. Opening her mouth to ask them to please get back inside, she stopped in awe before saying a word. Up ahead, she noticed a catastrophe in the making. With another crack like thunder, the onramp broke away from the freeway and started to sway. *There's no way it's not going to collapse.* She heard people shouting in alarm as they climbed out of their cars to run away from the impending disaster. *Everyone needs to get away from that ramp.*

One vehicle at the very top tried to back up, but there were a dozen cars behind it blocking the way, including the big, black truck that hit Drew's Pathfinder earlier. For some crazy reason, the driver still used his horn and tried to move forward, apparently not realizing the ramp was not connected to the freeway. When he rammed into cars, the situation grew worse as another vehicle was pushed halfway into the gap to hang suspended over a twenty-five-foot drop. Bryce prayed the car was empty and the truck would stop.

Leave your stupid truck, Bryce thought, while the structure continued to sway. *It's too late. Get out and run.* As if hearing her warning, the driver's side door opened, and she watched someone jump out at precisely the moment the shaking stopped.

Like before, there was a moment of silence in the void of the rumbling. People halted their panicked running, and many turned toward the steep onramp that slowly came to a stop. Bryce let out a deep breath she didn't know she had been holding, thankful the structure held. She started to turn to Ashley in the backseat when a horrible sound cracked through the air from the direction of the onramp. Knowing what she was about to see, she still had to stand there, watching in horror as the tons of metal and concrete tipped like a giant dying beast and fell.

WATCHING the onramp move while doing all she could to keep her balance beside the Pathfinder, Drew assessed the situation ahead of her. It seemed likely the structure would fall, so she quickly counted the vehicles in the area. Roughly twenty-seven were in the most immediate danger, but many drivers were smart enough to flee. She watched a woman in a yellow dress fall from the rocking and roll down the ramp. Further up, the black truck that hit her car was creating havoc of its own. There was nothing but chaos until as quickly as it started, the rumbling ceased, and the ground stilled.

Oh, thank God, she thought when the onramp stopped swaying. At least the injuries from people escaping the area would likely be minimal. *Maybe we will get out of this with nothing but some twisted ankles.* She would get her emergency bag from the back and see where she could help. Before she could take a step, the onramp made one last protest and then, as if in slow motion, tipped over. Almost unable to believe her eyes, she watched as chunks of concrete shot into the air on impact, smashing more of the surrounding cars. People started screaming again, and as she hurried to get to the back of her car, a peppering of small pieces of concrete landed on everything.

"I'm going to go help," Bryce said as Drew rushed by her.

"Good," she replied. "Some people may be trapped and need rescuing." Finding Tess already waiting for her at the rear of the vehicle, Drew liked that the woman had predicted what she would do. *It's because of the baby emergency,* she thought. *And from that experience, I know she'll be a level head.*

Popping open the back of the car, she noticed Ashley's pale face looked at them over the seat. "What happened?" Ashley asked in a whisper. "I could hear but not see."

"The onramp collapsed," Tess replied. "And I think some people are injured."

Drew nodded. "That's my concern too," she said. "Stay in the car Ashley." Drew worried a little that the young woman may go into shock. One tragedy after another was taking its toll. "Tess, can you stay here with Ashley, please? Bryce and I are going to go help."

"No." Ashley surprised her by saying, "I'm going too. I know..." The woman hesitated before taking a deep breath. "I know I've been acting scared, but I want to help. I can't just sit here."

Not wanting to take any more time, Drew nodded. "Then let's go," she said, putting the black duffle bag's strap across her body before jogging in the direction of the smashed cars. As the others went with her, in the distance, she heard sirens and wondered what else had collapsed during the earthquake. There were undoubtedly disasters like the one ahead of her all over the city. The hospital emergency departments would be overrun with injured people. Even though they ran annual drills around an earthquake scenario, there were only so many hands to help. A part of her wished she was there, but she forced that idea out of her head. There were injured people who needed her, and they were her priority.

Approaching the worst of the disaster, others were scattered around working to free people trapped in the massive pile of concrete and twisted metal. Bryce started to join them, but Drew put a hand on her arm. "Wait one second," she said, recognizing problems already. No one appeared to be working together. Looking around for anyone who emerged to take charge, there wasn't anyone obvious although people had gathered to watch. As she heard people moaning, some crying, there was no time to waste. "Climb on top of that car. Get the crowd's attention and ask anyone with medical or first aid experience to come to me."

Bryce nodded. "Okay," she said, ready to go but Drew held on to her. "Wait. I need you to tell others to rally to you to start an organized search. Find who's trapped, then try to assess who is hurt the most or in the most immediate danger." She gave the woman a push. "Go."

Watching Bryce vault onto the top of the sedan, Ashley couldn't help but be impressed even in the chaos as the Marine took charge. For a moment after she overheard Drew's instructions, she worried people might ignore her and refuse to help. That proved unwarranted. When Bryce spoke, it wasn't a yell necessarily, but a booming command, and the group stopped talking to listen. As Bryce told them what to do, people reacted as if they had been waiting to help. Immediately, a search team formed while others went to where Drew stood in an open patch of sidewalk. It was a small space, but everything else was jampacked with vehicles jumbled bumper-to-bumper. Soon, a half dozen people stood with Ashley and Tess, waiting for instruction. Although Ashley had no medical or first aid training and her mother didn't either, there must be some way they could help.

Waiting while Drew surveyed the volunteers for skills, Ashley worked to keep her fears in check. Any second, she expected the ground to shake again. *Just breathe,* she told herself. *Everything is going to be okay.* Finally, Drew pointed at Ashley and Tess. "I want you to split up and start going from car to car around the area," she said. "Check in on people. There have been a few fender-benders, and I know some people, once out of their cars, fell, but there might be things we don't expect too. If anyone needs attention, help them get back here."

"And if they can't walk?" Ashley asked while her mother nodded beside her.

"See what you can determine is wrong and then come tell me," Drew said and looked hard at Ashley. "Are you going to be able to do what I'm asking? There's a chance someone could be badly hurt."

Lifting her chin, knowing Drew might doubt her because of how she reacted to things lately, Ashley met her stare. "I won't let you down."

"Good," Drew said with a nod before turning to the others. Ashley didn't wait to hear anymore and waded into the jam of cars and trucks.

A few rows back was a trapped school bus. "I'm going to go check the school bus," she said to her mom still beside her. "What are you thinking?"

Tess pointed in the opposite direction from the school bus. "Starting here and walking down the center lane as far as I need to." Suddenly, she pulled Ashley into a hug. "Thank you for being so brave."

Ashley hugged her back. "You too, Mom," she said. "We're lucky to be okay. I have to help."

With a slight nod, Tess broke away and started toward the first open car window. Ashley did the same in the direction of the bus. The first three cars Ashley stopped at the people were scared but physically fine. In the fourth was an elderly woman with white hair sitting behind the wheel of a baby-blue Cadillac. From the look of the fins along the back, the car wasn't only older than Ashley, but older than her mom. "Hi, I'm Ashley," she said as she approached the window. "Are you okay?"

The woman cranked the window down. "Hello, Ashley. Nice to meet you. I'm Iris. Other than stuck in my car, I'm fine," she said. "I can't even open my door." She lowered her voice. "And I need to pee."

"I can understand that being a problem," Ashley said. "Let me see if I can get you out." Glancing around, she realized the woman was right. Iris was trapped. Cars on both sides of her had stopped too close, blocking her doors. Unfortunately, the other cars looked blocked in themselves. Turning back to Iris, she had an idea. The car windows of the Cadillac were huge. "With my help, do you think you could climb out the window?"

"You know, I thought about that," Iris said. "But was afraid I'd slip and break a hip. Might work if you hang on to me, though." She looked Ashley up and down. "You look pretty strong." Without waiting for confirmation, she grabbed the steering wheel for leverage and started climbing out. "Sorry, but I really need to go."

Moving to take her arm, Ashley helped her get free from the car. "Well, that worked," Ashley said as soon as Iris stood beside her. "Can you make it from here?"

Patting Ashley's arm, Iris was already moving. "Oh, I can make it, dear. I'm a SilverSneaker," she said. "I can walk for miles."

25

*B*ryce stood with the group she had gathered and watched a man in a red shirt who earlier introduced himself as Allen come huffing and puffing back to the circle of four men and two women. She was shocked to see he carried a full-sized yellow crowbar. "You carry that in your truck all the time?" Bryce asked, pleased that they would have the tool to help. So far, they were working with a half dozen heavy-duty carjacks and a few coils of rope.

"Well, yeah," Allen answered with a puzzled frown. "We live in earthquake country. Doesn't everyone have one?"

Unfortunately not, Bryce thought but made a mental note to add a smaller version to her truck's toolkit. *Assuming I have another truck anytime soon.* "Right," Bryce said. "Good thinking." She waved for everyone to step a little closer so she could explain the game plan. "Here's the strategy. We stretch out in a line about six feet apart or two arm lengths. Then, we step in unison, so no inch is left unchecked. And step carefully. Stuff could shift under you in a second."

One of the other women in the group nodded. "And we listen, right?" she asked. "For someone calling for help."

Bryce nodded. "Exactly. Although they might not be able to talk, so listen for crying, moaning, or anything that makes you think a person is nearby."

"And then what?" asked a man in a purple and gold Laker's jersey.

"When someone is located, we see how bad their situation is to determine if they need attention immediately," Bryce continued to explain. "Everyone else stays in place. If we all rush over, something could shift and make the situation worse." She looked hard into each face. "We will have to make some choices, not necessarily easy ones. But we can't be everywhere at once."

"Jesus," a tall, skinny man said under his breath. "I sure don't want to be the one in charge of making those decisions." Bryce wasn't a big fan of that task falling on her shoulders either but stepping into the breach was what a Marine did. She wouldn't back down in the face of a challenge, no matter how difficult.

Not wanting to waste another second, she started pointing to the left and right. "Let's line up," she said. "Go slow and keep together. The last thing we want is to miss someone."

The others nodded and did as she asked. Once everyone was in place, Bryce started them walking. They had only gone a dozen paces when Allen who was two down from her held up his hand. Everyone stopped, waiting. As Bryce watched, the man knelt until his face was almost touching the concrete rubble. Another moment passed, and then the man raised up, waving his hands. "Someone is here," he yelled, then leaned to listen again. "She says her legs are caught but otherwise is okay." The group started to converge.

"Stop!" Bryce warned. "Stay in the line. It could be dangerous, and we need to keep searching." She saw the reluctance on the faces of the others, but they did what she asked. "Allen, please stay there and talk to her. We will keep going until we reach the other side of the pile, and then I'll come back." When the line was back in place again, she started them moving. Only one other trapped survivor was located by the time they reached the far edge of the rubble. *Should there be more?* she wondered as she stepped carefully to the spot of the second person found. When she had watched the onramp swaying when the earthquake hit, a lot of the people abandoned their cars to run to safety. Time would tell. *We will have to wait for emergency personnel to arrive before we start digging to see if there are others.*

Coming to the edge of the gap in the concrete and twisted metal where the second person was trapped, Bryce joined the man in the Laker's jersey on his hands and knees. "The guy's not doing so good," he advised. "He says there's a bar of metal or something on his chest, and he can't breathe very well."

As Ashley neared the school bus, a couple young boys waved through the windows to get her attention. "Hey, lady," one of them called. "I think something might be wrong with Coach." That was when Ashley realized the kids she could see wore baseball jerseys. *A sports team caught in this*, she thought. *And they don't look very old.* When she reached the doors, they opened before she had to knock. A boy who looked no older than twelve worked the lever from the driver's seat.

He grinned at her when she boarded. "Always wanted to do that," he said but sobered quickly. "Good thing you're here."

Not liking the tremble of fear in his voice, Ashley hurried up the steps. "What's up?" she asked from the front of the bus, and a dozen young voices came at her.

"It's Coach," they all said, pointing over seats to a red-faced, overweight man in a T-shirt with a woodpecker mascot logo, sporting a baseball cap and holding a bat. Even in her non-medical opinion, he did not look good. Sweat poured off his face, and the pinched look around his eyes gave away the pain he felt, even though he appeared to be trying to hide it. *He doesn't want to freak out his baseball team*, she thought, feeling respect for the man already. He had to be in a lot of discomfort.

Walking down the row between the seats, Ashley passed the boys all looking between the ages of nine and twelve if she had to guess. They watched her go by with wide eyes, and she noticed one especially young-looking boy crying quietly against the side of the bus. Whatever was wrong with the coach, she needed to keep a positive appearance or there might be more than one boy crying. Coming to the row where the man they called Coach sat, she knelt beside him. "Hi, I'm Ashley," she said. "What's going on?"

Before the coach could answer, the young man sitting beside him, the only other adult she had seen so far, leaned toward her. "I think it's a heart attack," he whispered, and the coach grunted.

"Don't say that. I only ate too many of those stupid chili dogs with extra onions," he said. "Give me a Pepcid, and I'll be fine." He coughed and then winced as he rubbed his chest. "Let me sit here a minute and catch my breath." Ashley looked him up and down. He might be right, and what he was suffering was indigestion, but he might be wrong too. To be on the safe side, she wanted him to see Drew. The last thing she wanted was for him to get worse there on the bus surrounded by his junior-league baseball team.

Making up her mind, she put a hand on his knee. "Coach, do you think you can walk a little way?" she asked. "I have a friend, a nurse actually, who can help figure out what's going on with you." She smiled. "Get you that Pepcid at least."

He nodded. "I'm sure I can," he said. "But we can't leave the team." Glancing around, Ashley saw a dozen pairs of eyes watching her over the backs of the seats. They looked scared half to death. Having them stay on the bus alone did seem like a bad idea. *Especially if there's another shake,* she thought, feeling her stomach knot with anxiety at the possibility. The thought scared her half to death too. *Please don't let there be more of that.*

Standing, she assessed the options. Someone would have to help the coach walk the distance to the first aid area. Considering he looked like he outweighed Ashley by at least fifty pounds, she knew she couldn't support him. That left the only other adult, which would mean Ashley stayed with the team.

She nodded at the young man. "What's your name?"

"Assistant Coach Ryan. I drive the bus, but Coach lets me help him with the kids too."

"Okay, Assistant Coach Ryan, here's the plan I have in mind."

With the injured woman's arm wrapped across her shoulders, Tess stepped carefully between the cars. "Only a little bit further," she said, coaxing her along. "They've set up a first aid station, and they can take a better look at your ankle."

The woman groaned, limping another step. "Is there a doctor there?"

Furrowing her brow, Tess kept pace with her. "I'm not sure, but there is an amazing nurse in charge," she said. "She's called together—"

"I don't want a nurse," the woman snapped. "I need a doctor."

Hesitating to respond, Tess wasn't even sure what to say at first. "She's an excellent nurse and—"

The woman huffed. "She's still just a nurse."

"I'm not sure I understand—"

"How hard is it to understand?" she said, cutting Tess off a third time. "A doctor is a doctor, and nurse is a nurse. One saves lives, and one takes my blood pressure." Tess had heard enough. It was all she could do to keep her mouth shut at the ridiculous perspective. She saw Drew in action and would put herself in the woman's care over anyone's. The fact she was a nurse made no difference to her.

Tess was impressed by how organized things looked as they approached the cleared spot where people who needed care gathered. Someone had collected blankets and bottles of water donated from other drivers and the surrounding office buildings. Chairs of all types and some tables were brought out too. A triage was clearly in place with those who looked to have minor issues seated along the side of one building. For cases more urgent, she saw Drew had laid out blankets with the mishmash of volunteer medical personnel attending.

Under the circumstances, things were well in hand. "See," Tess said to the woman beside her. "There is nothing to worry about, and they will take care of you."

"We'll see," was all the woman had to say as Tess settled her into a lawn chair. Happy to be free of her, Tess looked for Drew. Her friend talked to a young man with his arm in a makeshift sling. Even though his face was pale and no doubt he was in pain, whatever Drew said to him made him smile. *With relief it looks like,* Tess thought, knowing for a fact something was calming about Drew's presence. *It's all a part of her wonderful bedside manner.* Watching the scene only made the injured woman's comments bother Tess more.

Finishing with the young man, Drew turned, and Tess

was pleased to see the woman's eyes light up when they landed on her. Encouraged, Tess walked closer. "How's it going?" she asked when she closed the gap.

"All things considered, I think we are lucky," she said. "Although Bryce reported they have two people trapped in the rubble."

Tess covered her mouth. "That's horrible," she said, then had another thought. "Have they found anyone..." She couldn't finish.

Drew rubbed Tess's arm. "No," she said. "Thank God. Like I said. Very lucky." She glanced around. "Did you bring someone in?"

Nodding in the direction of the woman with the injured ankle, Tess tried to hide her dislike. "Her," she said. "She can't walk on her ankle because she rolled it running away from the onramp."

Clearly catching her tone, Drew raised an eyebrow. "Is there something more I should know?" she asked, and Tess sighed.

"She doesn't want to see a nurse," she said with a frown. "She insists on a doctor. I tried to tell her that was ridiculous, but..."

Drew nodded. "Don't worry about it," she said. "I've heard it often over the years."

"What?" Tess asked. "Really?"

"Unfortunately, yes," Drew said, starting to move in the direction of the injured woman.

26

Turning when she heard her name called, Tess looked to see Bryce jogging toward her over the pile of broken concrete and other debris from the collapsed onramp. "What's wrong?" Tess asked, feeling a flare of anxiety in her chest to see the Marine needing her attention. *Where's Ashley?* she thought, but then remembered her daughter was headed to the school bus when they last spoke. *But anything could have happened since then.*

Bryce shook her head. "Nothing's wrong necessarily," she said. "I mean, considering everything that's gone wrong. But I need your help with something." The woman came to a stop in front of her. "There are two people trapped. A man and a woman. The guy appears to be worse off, so we are going to get him out first." Tess nodded, following the line of thinking so far but unsure how she could help. Moving concrete would take more strength than she had.

Still, she would do whatever she could. "How can I help?"

"I need you to come to talk to the trapped woman," Bryce explained. "Keep her calm and awake until we can get to her. I thought you would be perfect for that."

Tess wasn't sure if she agreed she would be perfect, but she would do her best. In a time like this, everyone needed to work together. "I was checking on people in cars for Drew, so let me tell her first," she said. "And then show me where the woman is."

Three minutes later, Tess stepped carefully over the broken concrete to follow Bryce to the spot where the woman was trapped. "Hi there," Bryce said as she knelt on the muddy ground near an opening in the rubble. "Linda, I've brought someone with me, and she's going to keep you company while you wait for us. Okay?"

"Okay," Linda replied. To Tess, her voice sounded tired, but not necessarily like she was in pain.

Tess sank onto the ground beside Bryce and peeked under the hunk of concrete angled over the trapped woman. "Hi, Linda," she said. "I'm Tess. Sorry to meet under these conditions, but I'm looking forward to getting to know you better."

Bryce squeezed Tess's shoulder. "Thank you," she said. "Hopefully, we won't need you long. The team is already setting up carjacks to lift the largest slab over the other victim."

"We'll be here," Tess said, appreciating once again the resourcefulness of her daughter's friend. "Be careful." As Bryce left, Tess turned her attention back to Linda and paused. *What do I say to start a conversation with someone trapped under a thousand pounds of broken rock?* she wondered. It was not a normal situation, yet it didn't have to be much different than sitting next to a stranger on a plane. *I'm going to try and make it feel normal if I can.* "Linda, can you hear me okay?"

Linda coughed. "Yes," she said. "Sorry, there's a lot of dust."

Not sure if she should ask if they gave her water yet in

case they couldn't reach her or Linda was too trapped to move, Tess plowed ahead, putting a smile in her voice. "That's okay," she said. "I don't think you need to apologize for anything considering your situation."

Linda gave a little laugh. "No," she said. "I suppose that's true. May I ask you a question? It will sound a little crazy."

"Of course, I don't mind," Tess said, willing to listen to anything Linda had to say, crazy-sounding or otherwise. Anything to keep the woman engaged. "Go ahead and ask."

There was another slight cough. "You wouldn't happen to be Tess as in Tess Landish, movie actress, would you?"

Surprised Linda could recognize her voice so easily, Tess raised her eyebrows. "Wow," she said. "Yes, I am. How did you know?"

"Oh, come on," Linda said. "I think most people would know it was you when they heard your voice and that your name was Tess." Another cough. "I have seen all your movies. And your special New Year's Eve appearance every year during the celebration in New York at Rockefeller Center."

Tess was still surprised. "I suppose so," she said, hearing another little cough and not liking the frequency of them, but she wasn't sure what to do about it. "Well, thank you for being a fan and seeing all my movies."

"Are you kidding?" Linda said. "I can't wait to get out of here and tell everyone I met Tess Landish."

Looking up from the unhappy woman with the sprained ankle she was trying to appease, Drew noticed a guy walking unsteadily between a young man and a boy who looked like he might be thirteen at best. Their progress was slow, and Drew hoped they could get to the first aid area before the injured man stumbled. Deciding that case needed attention more urgently than any other victim, she apologized to her patient. "You'll have to excuse me," she said. "But I need to help someone else for a few minutes."

"Isn't anyone here a doctor?" the woman said with a whine, and Drew shrugged as she turned to leave.

"We have a plastic surgeon."

The woman lifted her chin with a huff. "That will suffice."

Looking amazingly unphased, Drew gave her a nod. "I'll send him over as soon as he's available," she said without another look back. As she approached the three people shuffling their way closer, Drew quickly assessed the scene. The three all wore the same kind of shirt—a red woodpecker in a cap holding a bat, and she guessed they were part of a base-ball team. The heavy-set guy the other two were helping presented sweaty and pale.

"Only a little bit further, Coach," the young man said, coaxing the wobbling man to keep going.

He groaned in response. "I can't catch my breath," he said. "Might need to sit down for a second." As if to underline his situation, he stumbled enough to nearly push the kid off balance.

Alarmed, Drew looked for a temporary place to settle him when someone moved past her.

"Here, let me help him," a man she recognized from her team of volunteers said, moving to slide in to take over the teenager's spot. Like magic, a second helper came to their aid too.

He relieved the exhausted young man. "Let's go, buddy," he said with a glance at Drew. "Where are we going?"

"This way," she replied, stepping out in front. "Take him to that brick building on the left." Moving along faster, but with the coach becoming more flushed, Drew looked at the young man who brought the coach in for help. "Tell me what happened."

"I think he is having a heart attack," the young man said.

"It started after the earthquake. We were on the bus when it hit."

Drew nodded, taking in the information. "A bus from where?"

"We're a baseball team coming down from Seattle, and we got caught in the traffic jam. He's our coach," the young man said. "I'm really worried about him. Can you help?"

Drew nodded, moving faster. "I'll try. Where are the other members of your team?"

"Still on the bus," he answered. "A blonde woman came, told us where to take Coach, and agreed to stay with the boys."

That must be Ashley, she thought, thankful the woman had been able to help. When they reached the brick building, Drew stopped beside an empty office chair. "Sit him down here," she instructed. As soon as he was seated, she knelt in front of the coach and held his wrist. "Hi there. I'm Drew. What's your name?" she asked while looking at her watch.

"He's Coach," said the teenage baseball player who walked over with them. Glancing at him, Drew saw fear in the boy's eyes. "He's going to be okay, right?"

Drew nodded. "Everything will be okay, and we will take good care of him," she said with her most reassuring smile before turning her full attention back to helping the coach. She only hoped she was telling the truth.

MAKING DOUBLY sure the flat head of the tire jack was well in place against the concrete slab, Bryce gave the thumbs up. "We're ready," she said. "Go slow so we can both lift at the same pace."

"You got it, Bryce," Allen said. There was respect in his voice. She guessed it was not only because when he asked if she was military or something, she explained she was a

Marine on leave, but also from her skill in coordinating the effort to free the man caught in the concrete. They had assessed a steel beam pressed down by a six by six hunk of solid cement was pinning him. Fortunately, the part that needed to move rested on other pieces of the irregular jigsaw puzzle that were not on the metal. All it needed was to be lifted high enough to pull the man out. Working together and with the help of the crowbar, they were able to place two jacks at the corners.

This better work, Bryce thought, taking a deep breath to steady her nerves. *Because we're probably only going to get one shot at it.* "Okay, start twisting the wrench on my count to three," she said, and Allen nodded, his hand on the jack handle. "One. Two. Three." At first, the jacks had to find purchase as the weight settled on the load, but slowly, they lifted the slab. "That's it. Easy does it."

"It's working," Allen said. "Thank God."

Bryce agreed. The plan did seem to be going as she envisioned. Not taking her eyes off the jack, she called to the man trapped. "Talk to me, Jerry," she said. "Can you feel any difference in the weight on your chest?"

There was enough of a pause for Bryce to frown, thinking maybe Jerry was unconscious, but then he answered. "Yes," he said, excitement in his voice. "I'm not so pinched." Nodding, Bryce turned the wrench again while Allen did the same. Two others waited on their stomachs at the gap, ready to help pull Jerry free as soon as he wanted to try.

On the next crank, Bryce's corner of the slab suddenly started to crack. It ran down the piece away from her like a snake. *Oh shit*, was all she could think. There was no way the concrete would stay stable much longer. "Faster, Allen," she said, guessing at any second the edge would sheer off. "My side is starting to break." With wide eyes, Allen started cranking harder while she did the same. The slab lifted, but the crack began to widen with it. Bryce guessed they didn't have much time. "It's slipping! Pull him out. Now!" She heard the grunts of her team working behind her and prayed the jacks had lifted the concrete high enough.

"Get me out of here," she heard Jerry yelling, and then there was the sound of the concrete breaking.

"Get away from the jack, Allen," Bryce said while scrabbling backward out of the way. "It's going to fall any second."

"We got him," one of her team yelled at the exact moment the piece split and collapsed onto itself. A puff of rock bits and dust billowed up. "Jesus, that was close."

Standing, Bryce wiped some of the muddy debris from her pants as she climbed over the pile to the group crowded around Jerry. He sat on his butt gulping a bottle of water. There was a bloody cut on his forehead, but otherwise he seemed fine. "Hey, thanks," Jerry said, looking at her. "I owe you."

Bryce smiled when suddenly she felt a hand on her arm and looked to see Tess standing beside her. "I think you need to come to talk to Linda," she said without preamble. "She can't stop coughing."

27

Drew checked the baseball team coach's blood pressure and wished she had more resources, because his condition worried her. Although she couldn't be one hundred percent certain without a blood test, she was betting he had a cardiac event, putting him at a high risk of a full-blown heart attack. Of all the people she had helped so far—a few broken bones, even a concussion—he was her most significant concern. "Should we help him lie down?" one of the men who assisted the man to the first aid area asked. "He's not looking so great."

Even though the coach's face had taken on an ashen hue, and he breathed heavily, Drew shook her head. "No, he needs to stay upright," she answered. "But let's move him so he can be supported sitting against the side of the building." She pointed at a spot on a blanket.

"Got it," the man answered before taking the coach's arm. "Need you to stand up, big guy."

The coach grimaced. "Do I have to?" he asked with a groan. "I'm so tired."

"Just far enough to get to the wall. Then, I'm going to give you some nitroglycerin," Drew said, thankful she still had a supply in her bag of some essential emergency medications from when she was a working nurse.

With a nod, the man let the others help him up. "Anything to help with the pain," he said, standing while the others lifted. As they started to move, Drew heard angry shouting from the direction of the rubble. *Crap*, she thought. *A fight is the last thing we need.*

"Get him sitting," she said. "I'll be right back." Approaching the source of the noise, Drew was disappointed to see two men pushing and shoving each other. *We don't have time for fighting right now*, she thought. One of the men already had blood on his forehead, and the other was in his face.

At any second, someone would throw a punch. "You son of a bitch," the man who had pushed the other said. "You hit my truck." Suddenly, Drew recognized the man with blood on his forehead. He was the one who flipped her off as he passed in the black truck—the jerk who rammed people.

Another man wearing a red shirt stepped forward. "Are you kidding me?" he said. "If I'd known it was you, I might not have helped you get out from under that beam."

"Now wait a minute," the man with the blood on his forehead said. "I was panicked, and I apologize for what happened."

"Do you think saying sorry is going to fix what you did?" the man in his face said. "I can't even drive my truck now."

Drew could empathize with him. She was pretty sure her Pathfinder was totaled. Still, the fight needed to break up before tempers escalated any higher. Stepping forward, she raised her hands in the air to get everyone's attention. "Okay, everybody calm down," she said. "I know tempers are high with all the stress and that what he did upset a lot of us, but right now we have other things to focus on. There are people hurt." She pointed at the man in the red shirt. "Is anyone still trapped in the rubble?"

The man in the red shirt looked chagrined. "Yes, there is a woman stuck," he said. "They sent me to come to get a bottle of water for her."

"Well then get the water and go back to help her. This is ridiculous," Drew said, frustration mounting. "And you." She pointed at the man with blood on his forehead. "I need you to get over to the first aid station and get that cut looked at right now. And then we are going to want your name and insurance information." The man hung his head but started to walk in the direction she pointed.

"You let him off easy," the angry man said.

Drew shook her head at him. "Maybe. There's not much more I can do about it right now," she said. "So break it up, and everybody get back to what they were doing. Until emergency personnel can get here, we are all that's left."

DOWN ON HER hands and knees in the muddy gravel, Bryce used a flashlight to look into the narrow gap under the rubble. The woman Linda was trapped there. What she could see of her face was pale, and Bryce hoped it was only because of dust from the concrete but guessed it wasn't. The fact the woman could not stop coughing was worrisome. "Hey Linda, how are you holding up?" Bryce asked. "We have water on the way, and we will get it in there to you real quick."

"Thank you," Linda said, coughing again. "I could really use a drink. Preferably something stronger than water, but beggars can't be choosers." Bryce couldn't help but grin. She respected the woman's attitude under such circumstances. In Bryce's experience in the Marine Corps, she learned keeping a positive outlook and a sense of humor was a key to survival. Not only because it kept a person in a healthy frame of mind, but it also maintained people's morale around them. Teams worked better together when everyone was getting along.

Allen returned with multiple bottles of water. "I brought extra," he said. "I thought we could all use some." He started handing the bottles around. "And don't worry, there is a lot. It's amazing how many people are stepping up to donate things and help where they can."

Bryce leaned back on her heels and nodded. "Good thinking with the extra water," she said. "And I'm glad to hear people are showing their generosity." She accepted two of the bottles. "Now let's figure out a way to get a couple of these in to Linda."

The task wouldn't be easy. Although wide, the gap between the piece of concrete and the ground couldn't be much more than a foot high. *It will take someone not only slender but brave to crawl in there,* she thought. Although they would only have to go in about four feet to the spot where the bottles could be pushed through an even smaller opening, it would be dark, muddy, and tight. Trying to figure out if she would fit, there was a tap on her shoulder. Looking, she saw Tess standing beside her.

"Someone needs to get in there," she said, taking a deep breath before continuing. "I can do it." Bryce frowned. The woman was beautiful and an incredibly talented actress, but Bryce had never met anyone less selfish. Not only did she put her daughter first always, but she offered to risk her life for a stranger.

"Are you sure?" Bryce asked. "We could go back and see if there's another volunteer."

Tess shook her head. "That would take time," Tess said. "I mean it. I can do what you need to help Linda." Scooting out of the way, Bryce held out her hand to help Tess lower herself to the ground. She laid flat on her stomach, and Allen handed her two bottles of water. "I'm ready to go." Again, Bryce was impressed. Her voice was steady and confident. "But be ready to pull me out the minute I say go. I don't want to spend an extra second in there if I don't have to."

"We will be waiting for you to say the word," Bryce said, and watching with admiration, she saw Tess start what they called a low crawl in the Marine Corps. With her hands occupied with water bottles, she used her elbows and knees to move flat along the ground. Bryce knew it must hurt like hell, considering all the rubble in the mud underneath her. As Tess disappeared inside, Bryce laid on her stomach to watch the progress and prayed the woman would keep calm as the walls closed in.

WHILE BRYCE SHINED the flashlight into the hole, Tess crawled along under the concrete slab inch by inch. "How are you doing, Linda?" Tess asked as much to distract herself as to see how Linda felt. "I'm bringing you some water."

"Tess? Are you really crawling in here?"

"Yes, I sure am," Tess answered, lowering her face closer to the mud as she felt her hair graze the concrete above her. "As luck would have it, I was the only one who would fit. Thank God I'm not claustrophobic."

"I can't believe you're doing this for me," Linda said, the first hint of a tremble in her voice. "I'll never be able to repay you."

Trying to ignore how close the walls were getting around her, Tess forced a laugh. "Just make sure you keep coming to my movies."

"How's it going in there?" Tess heard Bryce yell into the hole.

As another piece of broken concrete dug into her side, Tess held back a grunt of pain. "Walk in the park," Tess answered. "Reminds me of the time I was in that horror movie. Maybe you saw it, Linda?" She wanted to keep her talking as much for her morale as for the other woman's.

"Oh my, God," Linda replied. "Are you talking about the one where you're trapped in a coffin? But that is so morbid right now."

Tess had to agree, considering the circumstances. She hadn't thought that through and hoped it wasn't a self-fulfilling prophecy or something absurd. *And I am not going to think about what might happen if there is another tremor or anything shifts,* she thought, forcing herself to keep crawling. Finally, she reached her side of the narrow gap between her and Linda. In the bit of light coming from Bryce, Tess saw Linda's face pressed up against the hole, watching her crawl closer. "I have a little something for you," Tess said. "How about a drink of water?"

"You have no idea how good that sounds," Linda said. "I never thought I'd be so excited to have a drink of water."

Carefully, Tess pushed one bottle and then the other through the opening. "Do you have them?" she asked.

She heard Linda cough and then the snap of the water bottle top opening. "I have them," she said, and then there was a gulp of the woman taking a drink. *Mission accomplished,* Tess thought, preparing to start her way back out. "Tess?"

"Yes?"

"Can you hold my hand for a minute?" Linda asked, and even though every second Tess spent in the hole made her heart race faster, she reached through the small gap and felt Linda's fingers on hers. "I only wanted to touch someone. You know, just in case."

"You're going to be okay," Tess reassured her. "My friend Bryce has a plan."

"Does she?" Linda asked, and Tess nodded.

"It's a jigsaw puzzle above you, but they can work

together as a team, and one by one take the pieces off. You'll be free in a matter of no time."

Tess felt Linda squeeze her fingers and then let go. "Thank you, Tess," she whispered. "Now get out of here."

Not needing any more encouragement, Tess started to push back. "See you soon," Tess said and then turned her head enough to yell into the gap. "Help me out." She heard Bryce echo the words to the others a moment before gentle hands took hold of her ankles.

"Take it slow, guys," Bryce said, and inch by inch, Tess moved backward through the mud until she was finally free of the opening. Once she was sitting and able to take a deep breath of the fresh air, she realized what she had done. *Crawled under tons of rubble*, she thought, amazed. Bryce knelt beside her, handing her a bottle of water. "That was incredible, Tess. You would make a great Marine."

For Tess, that was the best compliment in the world.

28

"And then you ran into the storage building?" one of the boys on the bus asked. All the team listened with rapt attention, their eyes wide.

Ashley nodded. "That's right. Bryce rammed the gates, and then we went inside," she said. "Just in time. We were very lucky to be in there when the water went past."

All of them were quiet for a moment. "So, your friend," started a boy in the last row. "She lost her truck? Wow, that sucks."

Ashley blinked, pausing for a second. She found it interesting that with all the things that happened in her story, although she didn't get into all the details, the boy focused most on a lost truck. *I guess that's what boys think about when they're turning twelve*, she thought. *At least I haven't scared them.* It all started when one boy had asked if she had heard about the tsunami, and she hadn't thought twice about saying she was almost caught in it. As soon as Ashley said the words, she had second thoughts about giving the details, but they wouldn't let it go. "Yes," she answered. "Bryce lost her truck."

"Your friend is a girl?" asked another boy sitting across the aisle from her.

Feeling proud to say the words, Ashley smiled. "Yes," she replied. "She's a girl, and she's a Marine."

"Whoa," a few of the boys said. "Marines are cool."

From her limited experience, Ashley had to agree. Bryce was cool in her book. "My dad was in the Army," chimed in another boy in the seat behind her. "He served in Afghanistan."

Ashley looked at him. "And is your dad still there?"

The boy shook his head. "No, he's home, and mom's really happy."

Ashley smiled. "I'm sure she is," she said, thinking for a minute about the decision that Bryce needed to make about what she was going to do with her future. They hadn't talked in detail about it yet, but she knew the time was quickly approaching as the end of the week neared. She wasn't sure how she felt about everything. They hardly knew each other, that was true, but Ashley was already feeling very attached to Bryce, and she didn't know what it would mean if she left to go back to the military. *Could I be a military girlfriend?* she wondered, not even sure what that would look like in the future. *And how long would that last?*

Before she could wonder about the scenario any further, the first boy asked her another question. She wasn't sure she heard him right, so she asked him to repeat it. "I said, are you a lesbian?" he repeated, nothing but curiosity on his face.

Ashley raised her eyebrows not sure she was ready to go down that path when luckily the second boy jumped in. "Lesbians are cool. My moms are lesbians." He said it so matter-of-factly it was hard for Ashley not to laugh. It was nice to know that Marines and lesbians were considered cool by twelve-year-old kids in today's society.

There was a loud knock on the front door of the bus followed by, "Hello. Please let us in."

Ashley moved quickly to the front of the bus and saw the faces of four anxious adults. "Oh, thank God," one of the women said. "At least an adult is here." Ashley pulled the lever, and the door opened. The four adults rushed onboard.

"Mom," yelled one of the boys.

"Dad," yelled another. The parents rushed down the aisle and hugged their children.

After a moment, one of the men with his arms around his son looked at Ashley. "Where's Coach and Assistant Coach Ryan?"

"I think Coach had a heart attack," chimed in the boy in the back row.

The parents all looked at each other. "What?" asked one of the moms. "Where are they?"

Ashley held her hands out to calm the situation. "We don't know what happened, but he wasn't feeling well so the assistant coach took him to see the nurse at the first aid station. And they asked me to stay here with the team."

One of the fathers ran his hand through his hair. "This is madness," he said. "When the bus didn't make it onto the freeway, we got separated. Then, there was the earthquake…" He shook his head.

The other father took over. "And with the traffic jam, it took us hours to circle back."

A mother let out a sob as she squeezed her son tight. "I'm so glad we found you," she said. "I'll try to text the other parents. We have been searching everywhere."

"Well, I'm glad you're here," Ashley said. "The team is fine. But if you don't mind staying with them, I will go find my own mom and my friends.

"Her girlfriend's a Marine," one of the boys chimed in.

"And she's a lesbian," said another. Ashley rolled her eyes

but was happy to see the parents didn't even blink at the comments.

Stepping carefully over the damp rubble from the collapsed onramp, Tess followed Bryce and the others as they carried Linda to the first aid area. She could not be more relieved that everything had turned out okay, and they were able to rescue the woman. Although Tess had faith that Bryce could coordinate the men and women to work together to unstack the concrete blocks covering Linda, in the back of her mind, she continued to worry there might be another shake. As they neared the triage station, Tess saw Ashley weaving through the parked cars as she came toward her.

"Mom," Ashley said, running up and throwing her arms around her in a giant hug.

Tess hugged her back, not realizing how anxious she had been about where her daughter was and how she was doing. She was so focused on saving Linda. "I'm okay, sweetheart," Tess said in the woman's ear. "Everyone is fine."

Pulling back, Ashley looked down. They were both covered with mud from Tess's shirt and pants. "Why are you covered in mud?"

Tess let out a little laugh. "It's kind of a long story," she said. "Once we get out of here, and I have both a shower and a glass of wine in my hand, I'll tell you all about it."

Out of the corner of her eye, she saw Drew coming to meet Linda and the others. "Bring her over here," Drew said, leading the way. "On the blanket, please, I want to do a quick examination."

Linda looked around. "Tess?" she asked, a note of distress in her voice.

Tess moved closer as they sat Linda on the blanket. "What do you need?" she asked. "More water? Anything?"

"I know it sounds weird," Linda said with a weak smile. "But I was wondering if you could stay with me a little longer. You have been my lifeline through everything if that makes sense."

Somehow, Tess got it. They had a connection for a few hours. "Absolutely," Tess said and then turned to Ashley beside her. "Linda, I would like you to meet my daughter, Ashley."

Linda's eyes widened. "Oh my God," she said. "You look like each other. Although I would guess you were sisters."

Tess let out a laugh. "I appreciate that."

"Well, it's very nice to meet you, Ashley. Did you know your mother is a hero?" Linda said, her eyes shining with gratitude. "Did she tell you what she did?" Tess wasn't sure she was ready for Ashley to hear about her heroics yet, but Linda kept going. "She crawled on her stomach in the mud under tons of concrete to bring me water when I couldn't stop coughing." Tess saw Ashley's eyes go wide as she turned to stare at her mother. Tess saw emotions run through them —both pride and fear.

Tess pulled her into a side hug. "Everything turned out fine," she said. "There's nothing to worry about."

Ashley shook her head. "Well, that explains the mud," she said with a shaky laugh. Tess smiled but then stopped when she heard people shouting and assumed the worst. She almost expected the ground to shake any second. Instead, she made out the words and was happy to hear them.

"Get in your cars. A lane is finally clear," people were yelling. "And let's get out of here." It sounded like an excellent plan to Tess. She was ready to go home.

As the day grew dark, at last things winded down, and help had arrived. After all the stress of the afternoon, Drew was exhausted. Although only one case had truly worried her, the baseball team's coach, several minor injuries had required medical attention. Still, when the ambulances finally made it to them, the coach was first to go. "We can't thank you enough," the paramedic said as he finished loading the last ambulance. "There were a lot of places where people weren't so lucky to have an experienced ER nurse on the scene."

Drew shook her head. "I only did what I was trained to do," she said. "And honestly, now I'm exhausted."

"We have it from here," the paramedic said, closing the door to the back of the vehicle. "I suggest you head home and get some rest. We don't want to see you end up in the emergency department tonight."

"Going home is exactly what I plan to do," Drew said and watched as the ambulance went on its way before returning to where Tess and Ashley waited. Noticing Bryce wasn't around, she furrowed her brow. "I'm ready to go. Where is Bryce?"

Tess put a hand on Drew's arm and gave her a small smile. Even exhausted, Drew couldn't help but be warm from the woman's touch. "Well, that's kind of a surprise," Tess said, and Drew noticed Ashley beamed beside her. *They are up to something*, she thought, not sure if she was in the mood for any surprises. "Let's go to the Pathfinder and see if Bryce was successful."

Growing more curious, with her emergency bag slung over her shoulder, Drew followed the two women to her vehicle. The load was significantly lighter, and she hoped she remembered to restock all her supplies. *Just in case*, she thought, but hoping there would be no reason to need it for a long time. When they reached the Pathfinder, she noticed the crumpled hood was open, and someone was under it looking at the engine. As she approached, the man in the red shirt she noticed earlier during the altercation with the truck driver stepped back. When he saw her, he grinned. "Okay Bryce," he said. "Give it a go." Bryce sat in the driver's seat, and Drew guessed she pushed the button for the ignition to see if the vehicle would start. Amazingly it came to life, and the engine started.

"How in the world...?" Drew asked as Bryce joined them.

The man cleaned his hands on a rag he pulled from his back pocket. "Only a blown battery fuse, ma'am," he said. "Sometimes that happens with these cars when there's an impact in the front of your vehicle." He shook his head. "You're lucky the airbags didn't deploy."

Drew blinked and hardly knew what to say. "Thank you."

With a shrug, the man turned back to the vehicle. "Bryce, you want to give me a hand getting the hood closed? She's ready to go." Drew watched as the two worked together to slam it hard enough to stay it in place. "That should get you home."

Bryce shook his hand. "Thanks for all your help, Allen," she said. "Glad I learned you're a mechanic."

"It was the least I can do considering how much you helped everyone," Allen said, then gave them a mock salute and started to leave. "Drive home safe."

Drew, still amazed, walked to the back of the Pathfinder to put her emergency bag away. "Which of you snagged my keys from my bag when I wasn't looking?"

Tess shrugged but looked very pleased with herself. "It was a team effort," she answered. "Bryce suggested it when she learned Allen was a mechanic. And you deserved a nice surprise."

29

*W*ith night descending upon them, Drew hadn't anticipated how dark it would be with the power out in major parts of the city. Progress was slow as they navigated from neighborhood to neighborhood trying to get through to Beverly Hills. Considering how crumpled the front of the Pathfinder was after the collision, they were lucky one of her headlights worked. Barely. The cover was cracked, so the light shined in a strange pattern, but the bulb itself was intact and provided some help. Thankfully, the rain finally stopped, and the skies cleared enough to provide a little light. Still, all she could do was go slow and hope the GPS would get them home eventually. At the moment though, the tracking device wasn't much help, and they constantly had to turn around. There was no way for the thing to know if a road was temporarily blocked by a fallen streetlight, wrecked cars abandoned in the street, or even some crumbled buildings spilled into the road. At least with the four-wheel-drive they could go over the places where the road had buckled from the quake.

Coming to yet another snarl of cars, she rolled to a stop

and let out a long, frustrated breath. The one headlight didn't illuminate much, but it was enough for her to know they couldn't easily get around with things like they were. "If any of those cars are unlocked, maybe I can roll them out of the way enough to go through?" Bryce asked, and Drew nodded.

"We need to try something," she said. "I am beginning to feel like a rat in a maze."

She heard Bryce open her door. "Wait, I'll come with you," Ashley said, and Drew wondered if she was going with her girlfriend because she wanted to help or because she didn't want them separated. Since they got back in the car, Ashley hadn't stopped holding onto Bryce. It was as if she reverted to her old fears once the adrenaline wore off.

"Be careful," Tess yelled after them as the door slammed. The woman reached for Drew's hand as soon as they were gone. She intertwined their fingers and rested their hands against Drew's thigh. The tingle of heat the touch sent through her surprised Drew. Considering how exhausted she was, she would have thought nothing could make her heart race again tonight, especially in a good way. *I'm wrong*, she thought, giving Tess's hand a light squeeze. *And I think I like it.* "You are a hero, you know."

Drew raised her eyebrows, caught off guard by the comment. "I'm not, and I was only doing what I needed to in an emergency," she said. "Anyone with my training would have."

Tess leaned closer. "I don't agree with that," she said. "Keeping everyone calm during the disaster is more than training. How you acted was amazing, and I'm proud to know you." She brought her lips to Drew's ear. "And I want to know you even more."

The heat Drew felt a moment before when their hands touched was nothing compared to the flame that roared to life in her at the sensual words. On instinct, she turned her head, and their mouths were nearly touching. *It would be so easy to kiss her,* she thought, remembering what it felt like, craving the touch, and then the backdoor opened. She jerked back and let go of Tess's hand. Nervousness suddenly twisted her stomach even though only Ashley and Bryce were climbing inside. Tess insisted the younger people didn't care that Drew and Tess were attracted to each other. Drew believed her as it was apparent Ashley was all for it, but still, her instinct was to hide. *I wonder how long it will take me to get over that.* She sighed. *Or if I ever will.*

"I think we can get by on the left now," Bryce said, clicking on her seatbelt. "You'll have to go up onto the sidewalk and maybe skim the building, but I figured you wouldn't care, you know…"

Thankful for the distraction from her confusing thoughts, Drew snorted a laugh. "Because my car's already a wreck," she said. "Fair enough." She put the car in drive and followed the flickering light from the one dim headlight in the hope of finding them a way home.

GLAD THEY WERE MOVING AGAIN, Ashley looked out the window and watched the buildings go by. Even though it was hard to see much in the dark, it seemed the worse part of the damage had happened further south, near the middle of the city where they had been trapped. *Beverly Hills should be fine,* she thought, feeling her chest loosen a bit. *Everything is going to be okay.* She snuggled closer to Bryce. "How are you doing?" her girlfriend murmured, and Ashley paused to think. *How am I doing?* Fatigue, stress, and the absence of all the adrenaline that poured through her veins earlier left her feeling like her body weighed a thousand pounds. All she wanted to do was go somewhere safe, take a shower, and sleep.

She squeezed Bryce's arm. "I'm okay," she said, not wanting to let her know how rundown she felt. Admitting her discomfort would make her feel guilty. Everyone was as exhausted, if not more than she was. Like Drew for example. The nurse took charge after the earthquake and kept everyone organized. Things would have been an even bigger disaster without her. And then there was her mom. *She crawled in the mud under slabs of concrete.* The thought of what could have happened made Ashley's heart race. *But everyone is here in the car, safe, and we are on the way home.*

The Pathfinder slowed to a crawl again. "More cars?" Bryce asked, and Ashley was ready to help push so they could get through. Anything to keep them moving.

"No," Drew said, her voice carrying a wary tone. "People are standing in the street."

Both Ashley and Bryce moved to the center of the backseat to lean forward in the gap to look out the windshield. She saw why Drew sounded funny. Four people stood in the middle of the street. There was no way to tell in the dark if they were men or women, but from their sizes, she guessed men. A small flare of orange made her think they were smoking something. As Drew approached, they didn't bother to move but instead turned to watch her driving closer.

"What are they doing?" Tess asked, and Ashley knew her mom well enough to sense both frustration and concern in her voice.

Drew shook her head. "I'm not sure, but I don't like it," she said. "Should I honk?"

"No," Bryce answered. "But don't stop either. Even if you have to bump them to make them move."

Ashley saw Drew grimace at the suggestion. "Let's hope it doesn't come to that," she said only a moment before the tallest of the strangers held up a hand like a traffic cop. Standing square in front of them, he wanted her to stop.

The car started to brake, and Ashley realized Drew didn't know what to do. "Do not stop," Bryce said again, steel in her voice. "Drive a little faster, and he will move at the last minute, I promise."

"But what if they need help?" Tess asked. "It could be entirely innocent."

Bryce shook her head. "It doesn't feel like that," she said. "My instinct is telling me to make a run for it." As if only to prove her right, when it was apparent Drew wasn't stopping, the stranger dropped his hand and instead pulled a gun. Bryce grabbed Ashley by the shoulders and pushed her toward the floor. "Hit the gas, Drew! And everybody get down."

Ashley felt the car surge forward. There was yelling outside the car and finally a gunshot. The back window shattered, and Ashley yelped. Then, the vehicle turned a corner, and they were speeding away. *If things are this dangerous here,* she thought. *What are they like in south or east LA?* She imagined there would be looters all over taking advantage of the fact that the cell phones were not working, and the police were busy. Although she had witnessed a part of the disaster that brought out the best in people, she wasn't naïve enough to think that was the case everywhere. *What will LA be like in the morning?*

PEEKING over the backseat to make sure they weren't being chased, Bryce was relieved to see no one behind them. "Is everyone okay?" she asked, helping Ashley back onto the seat.

"Yes, I am," Tess answered, sitting upright again. "Drew?"

Bryce saw Drew nod. "That was insane," the woman said. "What were they hoping to achieve? It's not like my car is worth stealing."

"It's hard to know," Bryce said, wondering where the bullet ended up and traced her eyes along the roof of the Pathfinder. "Some people like to make mischief in the wake of chaos. I've seen it on missions in the Marine Corps, and the reaction never makes any sense to me." There was a small hole above Tess's head, and Bryce didn't like to think about how bad the attack could have been. She only hoped their luck would hold out.

"Hey," Tess said, interrupting Bryce's thoughts. "Is that Wilshire Boulevard?" Bryce looked over Tess's shoulder to see the major artery through West Los Angeles ahead of them. Cars moved back and forth at a somewhat normal rate, and the street would take them straight to Beverly Hills.

Drew laughed. "It is," she said, sounding surprised. "I am not sure how we ended up here, but it looks like it's open."

Ashley sighed. "We can be home in ten minutes," she said, and Bryce reached to take the woman's hand and squeezed it. The day was incredibly hard on Ashley, on all of them, and getting to Tess's house would go a long way to making them feel better. As Drew turned onto the street and started moving with traffic, Bryce leaned back in her seat and felt her shoulders relax. They headed in the right direction at last. Looking out her window, she noticed a glow in the sky. Furrowing her brow, she tried to figure out why there was so much light. She glanced at her watch. It was too early for the sun to be coming up, yet the glow was strangely similar. And then she realized what she saw, and dread filled her—the glow of fire. *Oh, please not that,* she thought, aware that a considerable risk from earthquakes was gas leaks from ruptured lines. If there was any spark and the gas caught fire, the results could be devastating, *especially in the close-packed communities of Los Angeles.*

It didn't take long for her fears to be realized as they came to a fire department roadblock. They were making people detour around the area. When Drew drove up next to the tired-looking fireman, she rolled down her window. "Can we get through to Sunset Boulevard?" she asked as Tess leaned across Drew to look out the window at the fireman.

"I'm Tess Landish, and I live at 92727, and I want to go home."

"I'm sorry, ma'am," the fireman said. His face was blacked by soot with streaks from sweat running through it. Bryce felt sympathy for him and his team. The day had to have been hell for all the emergency responders. "But we've had to close down access to that part of the city. The gas main that feeds Beverly Hills ruptured from the earthquake earlier today and caught fire."

"Oh, God," Tess whispered, and Bryce guessed what she thought. The house might be in the fire zone, and everything they owned might be in ashes before morning.

"So, what do we do?" Ashley asked as Drew followed the other cars north away from the danger.

"We can go to my place in Malibu," Drew said. "It's up in the hills above the city, and we will be safe there."

---

30

*A*s they followed the line of cars along the detour circling Beverly Hills, Tess tried to be patient. They had been driving for hours, meeting with one obstacle after another. *Hell, we were even shot at,* she thought with a shake of her head—*what a crazy, crazy day.* Traveling through one of the nicer neighborhoods of Los Angeles, she was amazed at the lack of damage to the buildings. Expensive cars sat in driveways completely untouched. Porch lights were on, and streetlamps glowed as if nothing had happened there. Earthquakes were the most discriminating things. Downtown Los Angeles could be in shambles while Pacific Palisades looked like nothing had ever happened. *Let's hope that Drew's house in Malibu is like these and untouched.* She was grateful they had a place to go.

"Thank you for letting us come stay with you," Tess said, touching Drew's leg. "That's very generous. We could have tried to find a hotel."

Drew glanced at Tess's fingers on her thigh, and Tess saw her swallow hard but not pull away. "Those would have filled up by now with displaced people," she said. "And of course, you can come to stay with me. It's only two big bedrooms, but I have a sectional sofa too."

"Turn right in one hundred feet," the GPS blurted, having been silent for the last few minutes while it tried to find where they were on the map. As Drew put on her blinker to turn with the line of traffic, there was suddenly an explosion to Tess's right. Jumping from the noise, she looked on with horror as one of the beautiful houses burst into flames.

"Oh my God," she heard Ashley say from the backseat. "I can't believe I saw that happen."

"Gas explosion," Bryce said, and Tess heard her unclipping her seatbelt. Looking over her shoulder into the backseat, she saw Bryce was already reaching for the door handle. "That's one of the biggest dangers after an earthquake. They likely felt a shake here, but so minor they didn't worry. A gas pipe must have broken loose. Even though everything can look normal like these houses there is still danger. Something must've sparked it." Then, she was out of the car.

Ashley grabbed for her but was too slow. "Bryce, where are you going?" Ashley asked, but Bryce was already gone, running around the back of the car and toward the house. Tess had no idea what the Marine intended to do, but she realized early on that it was Bryce's instinct to help if she could. *That's who she is,* Tess thought. Admiring her courage, she was afraid for her too.

As cars stopped in front of them, Drew pulled to the curb. "I'm going to go see if there's anyone who needs help," she said. "Stay in the car." Tess felt helpless as she watched the fire trying to spread as cinders from the exploded house floated through the air and landed on the rooftops of other houses nearby. Only the recent rains were slowing it down. The part of the neighborhood they stopped in was packed close together, so the fire could spread quickly if it caught, especially if there was more gas leaking. *It could be a nightmare*, Tess thought. *And quickly.*

Not sure what to do or how she could help, she watched through the window as a woman carrying a small child came running out the front door of the house that was on fire. Her pajamas looked singed, and the child pressed her face into the woman's neck, no doubt crying although Tess couldn't hear it. *I can't only sit here,* she thought, opening her door to get out too.

"Mom," Ashley said. "Why are you getting out?"

Before Tess could answer, the mother turned and shouted, "Where's Britney? She was right behind me. Please, somebody help. She's in the house."

Tess heard Ashley scream Bryce's name, but it was too late. The Marine was already sprinting toward the front door.

BRYCE HEARD Ashley calling her name as she raced across the yard, but she couldn't stop. Even though she ran toward danger, it was not only from her training but in her nature. A child was in trouble, and Bryce would do all she could to save her. Knowing every second counted, she ran as fast as she ever had, hoping there would be enough time. If the child was in the house there might be a chance to get to her before flames blocked the doorways. As Bryce reached the porch, she took a deep breath and burst through the open front door into a cloud of smoke and flickering orange light. Glancing around to assess where she was, she realized she was in the house's great room and through the smoke could see flames already climbing the walls.

The kitchen area of the space roared, and Bryce guessed the broken gas line came from that part of the house. In minutes, the fire would spread to the rest of the building.

Racing against time, Bryce started to search. Smoke billowed from the furniture but thankfully it had not yet burst into flames. "Britney," she yelled, hoping the child hadn't fled further into the house. "Where are you?" She stopped to listen but only heard the crackling of flames and the creaking of timbers as the house shuddered from the aftereffects of the explosion. The fire continued to weaken the already damaged structure.

When she didn't hear anything else, she tried again. "Britney, you have to tell me where you are." That time when she listened, she heard crying and moved in the direction of the sound. The child had to be in the same room because the sound was close. *Where is she?* she thought, peering as best she could through the smoke, and then she had a realization. If the child were frightened, she would be hiding. "Britney, where are you hiding? We need to get out of here."

"I'm scared," came a sobbing voice, and Bryce homed in on the direction where the child hid. She saw the couch, and instinct made her rush to it. Fighting the smoke trying to choke her, she pulled the couch further away from the wall and saw Britney's trembling figure. She clutched a doll to her chest and looked up at Bryce with tear-stained cheeks but seemed otherwise unharmed. "I dropped my dolly." Her lips trembled. "And then mommy was gone."

"It's okay," Bryce said, ignoring the sound of crackling that seemed to be getting louder all around her. "We're going to go find her outside." Knowing there wasn't a moment to lose, she grabbed the child around the waist and lifted her to hold against her chest. The movement was rough, and Britney let out a cry of surprise, but Bryce knew they had seconds to get out of the house before the thing started to collapse. Luckily, Britney didn't squirm in Bryce's grasp as they crossed the room, and she was almost to the door when she heard a snapping and instinctively looked up. The ceiling was ready to come down, and as she watched, the support beam that held the heavy light fixture sagged. The moment it started to fall, her foot caught on the edge of the large area rug that covered most of the floor, tripping her. Starting to tumble, she pushed Britney toward the front door. "Run to your mommy."

As she fell, thankfully the child kept her feet and did as Bryce told her, disappearing into the smoke and toward the light that led outside. Slamming hard onto her knees, Bryce didn't have time to get up and started to crawl. *I won't be fast enough,* she thought, and as pieces of the ceiling began to drop, her last thought was of Ashley. There was one final loud crack, and Bryce felt something strike her head a moment before everything went black.

SCREAMING Bryce's name at the top of her lungs, Ashley could not stop her from going into the house. The woman would try to save the child, and it was as simple as that. Struggling to get free of her seatbelt, she watched out the passenger window as Bryce raced across the lawn. With a dozen steps, she shot through the front door and disappeared. In a panic, Ashley left the car, running to stand by Drew trying to calm the hysterical mother.

"My baby," the mom chanted. "My baby."

A group started to form as the calamity grew with the fire finding purchase as it jumped from house to house, and people spilled out of them. Tess came to stand with Ashley, putting an arm around her waist. She knew it was for comfort because her mother was as worried as she was about Bryce inside the burning building.

"Why did she have to be the one?" Ashley murmured, but her mom didn't answer. *Is it because she's a Marine?* Ashley thought, but a part of her didn't think that was it. Something about Bryce made her believe she was the type of person who would always want to help people in trouble. *And that was why she became a Marine.*

After a moment, the little girl came stumbling through the front doorway clutching a doll and crying. "Britney!" the mom yelled, racing across the yard to grab her into her arms while crying hysterically. *Where is Bryce?* Ashley thought, her heart jumping into her throat. She took a step forward, staring at the doorway. *Where is Bryce and why isn't she coming out?* Sensing in her heart something was horribly wrong, she reacted on instinct to help someone who mattered to her. Even as her mother tried to stop her, Ashley ran toward the burning building. Bryce was inside, and she was the one who needed saving for once. Her mom screaming her name behind her was the last thing she heard before plunging through the front door into the smoke. Immediately, she started to choke and cough. Flames were everywhere, and the heat pressed against her almost like a physical force.

"Bryce," she yelled, almost tripping over her unconscious body as she moved deeper into the room. The woman lay sprawled face first and not moving. A blackened beam lay across her back but luckily wasn't burning, and Ashley kicked it out of the way before reaching for Bryce. She shook her shoulder.

"Bryce. Wake up. You need to wake up."

When she didn't respond, Ashley didn't know what to do. The room was in flames and smoke choked her. If she didn't hurry, they would run out of time. Knowing she couldn't carry her, Ashley grabbed Bryce by the arm and dragged her toward the front door. The woman's dead weight was hard to move, but she pulled with all her strength.

"Wake up, Bryce. Please wake up."

They only had seconds to get out of the house—she could feel it. Like a living beast, the fire moved closer and at any moment would engulf them. Her only choice was to let go. *No,* she thought, shaking her head. *I'm not leaving without her.* With another heave, she moved Bryce to the doorjamb the same moment pieces of the ceiling started to fall. *I can do it. I can do it.* Another big pull with everything she had should be enough, and then she felt someone beside her. Her mom was grabbing Bryce's other arm. Then, she saw Drew was there, pulling all of them backward. As a group, they all stumbled away from the burning house, falling in a pile in the yard as the building collapsed and sent a burst of cinders and smoke into the night sky.

31

*W*hen the Pathfinder's headlights splashed over the front of her house in Malibu, Drew took a long, deep breath of relief.

"We made it," Tess said in a way that it wasn't a question but a matter-of-fact statement. Almost as if she were putting a final stamp on their unbelievable journey.

"Yes," Drew said, steering to the edge of the driveway and pulling the vehicle up to the front French doors. "We made it." From what she could see, her house was untouched by any of the disasters. Thinking about Tess's house in Beverly Hills, she hoped that it had survived the fires unscathed. *Right now, I can be her refuge,* she thought. *For as long as she needs to stay.* Even though her home wasn't huge, there were two bedrooms each with bathrooms attached. *Somehow, the four of us will make it work.*

She looked in the rearview mirror and saw Ashley lift her head from Bryce's shoulder. The two were soot-stained and smelled like smoke but were otherwise okay. Other than some small patches of first-degree burns to Bryce's forearms and lower back, they were uninjured. After the emergency personnel arrived and examined Bryce and Ashley, the two were cleared to go home under Drew's supervision. "I don't think I've ever been more relieved to arrive somewhere," Ashley said, and Drew had to agree. The last twenty-four hours were the most terrifying she had ever experienced. One catastrophe after another. *Now we've made it here, and we are due a break*, she thought. *And a long one at that.*

As everyone climbed out, Bryce held out a hand to make them wait. "Drew, can I do a walk thru to smell for rotten eggs?" she asked, and Drew paused.

After what happened in Pacific Palisades, checking for leaking gas made sense. "I'll do it," she said. "Wait here, and I'll be right back." A few minutes later she let the others in the front door. "Everything is fine. Please come in." As the three passed her to walk inside, her stomach rumbled in a loud protest. In the chaos of everything, she hadn't realized it, but she was starving. Their lunch together downtown felt like a lifetime ago.

Bryce smiled. "I heard that," she said. "And if you're hungry we are on the same page. I need to eat something."

Turning toward the kitchen, Drew wracked her brain to think of what she even had to eat in the house. "I usually do frozen dinners, and I'm not much of a cook," she said, looking at the others.

Smiling, Tess held up her hands. "Not my strength either," she said, and Ashley chimed in.

"I'm only good at making coffee."

Drew shrugged. "Well, then it is instant mac and cheese," she said with a smile, and Bryce perked up.

"As long as there is plenty of it, I'm in," she said. "Lead me to the kitchen."

Drew surprised herself by laughing. It felt good after everything they went through. "I'll show you," she said, but Tess shook her head.

"I'm sorry, but I need a shower before I do anything else," she said. "Food, and hopefully lots of wine, will have to wait."

Ashley nodded. "Me too. I don't think I can survive another minute without a shower."

"No problem," Drew said, pointing toward the hallway. "Bedrooms and bathrooms are at the end of the hall, and there should be towels in them so use whatever you need."

Tess stepped forward, pulling Drew into a hug, and whispered in her ear. "Thank you."

Then she was off down the hall with her daughter as Drew led Bryce to the kitchen. "Help yourself to whatever is in the fridge," she said. "And I will take a beer." Not only was she parched, but nothing sounded better than a beer right then. *I don't care if it is only five o'clock in the morning*, she thought. She needed something a little stronger than water.

As Bryce rummaged through the options, Drew started a pot of water boiling and was happy to see there was leftover French bread. Garlic bread and instant macaroni and cheese sounded like heaven. "Here you go," Bryce said, putting the beer on the counter beside her. "I snagged one too."

"Perfect," Drew said, opening the bottle with a twist, and she held it up so she and Bryce could tap them together. "I'm glad to know you, Bryce."

Bryce nodded. "Same," she said, and they both took a long swallow.

WITH STEAMING-HOT shower water running over her body, Tess rinsed the minty-smelling shampoo from her hair. As the suds ran down the drain, Tess felt some of the stress of her day wash away. Not everything, but enough she felt she could breathe normally again, and her heart didn't race from all the adrenaline. *And to think everything started with a kiss*, she remembered. Her talk with Drew in her trailer about the scene the author didn't want. That felt like a lifetime ago. So much insanity happened since the kiss it was almost unfathomable that she lived through it. Yet the events were all very real.

First, the earthquake shook downtown and made the world start to collapse around them. *And my crawling under the concrete to help Linda*, she thought. *Who I hope is okay now and back with her family.* Frowning, she wished she had asked for her phone number. It would feel good to check on her. *Maybe there is a way to find out her information since she went to the hospital.* Especially if Drew could help her. She would find out after her world settled a little more. And then there was the fire and watching her daughter run into the burning house. She thought her heart would stop. Even though she loved her daughter more than anything on Earth, she never imagined she could be so crazy brave, yet she pulled on Bryce as the flames threatened. In some strange way, while they lay on the grass and the house collapsed, Tess was never prouder of her daughter. She was a hero too.

Suddenly, she heard a light knock on the bathroom door. "Hello?" Drew said, and Tess smiled. *I wonder if she's coming to join me*, she thought and then gave a little laugh. Her shy friend, who she hoped would someday be something more, would be the last person to surprise her in the shower. *With people in the house especially.*

"I'm still in the shower," Tess replied loud enough to be heard over the water. "Is everything all right?"

"I brought you a change of clothes," Drew answered clearly behind the closed door. "Everything is fine, but I didn't think you wanted to put on the muddy clothes from today."

Clean clothes sounded like total bliss. "Thank you so much," Tess said. "You are very generous."

Drew laughed. "You might not think so when you see that it's baggy sweatpants and a USC Trojans hoodie."

Tess didn't think there was anything she wouldn't wear under the circumstances. "I'll take it," she said and then heard the door open and close in the blink of an eye. *Yes, she is still very nervous indeed*, Tess thought with a smile. Turning off the water, she stepped out onto the fluffy bathmat to grab a towel. The mirror was foggy, but a quick swipe with her hand and she saw her reflection. Naked. No makeup, wet hair, and a few monster bruises forming on her forearms and knees from the crawl along the ground. Otherwise, she was fine. *Unbelievable. After everything, how can that possibly be?* With a shake of her head, Tess dressed quickly in the too short sweats and red and gold hoodie. She suddenly couldn't wait to join the others. Not because she was suddenly starving, but to be near them all again. To be able to lay eyes on her daughter and friends and know everyone was together. That they were safe.

Tess RETURNED with wet hair and a smile on her face. "That was the best shower of my life," she said, and Drew could not stop looking at how beautiful the woman was. Something about having no makeup and wearing Drew's baggie sweatshirt and sweatpants made her look vulnerable.

"My turn," Bryce said around a mouthful of mac and cheese. She took a drink, finishing her beer, and swallowed. "Drew, that was fantastic. Don't put it away. I'll be back for seconds a minute after I get clean." As she left, Tess and Drew were alone, and the room was suddenly quiet.

Dropping her eyes before Tess noticed she was staring, Drew busied herself putting Bryce's dishes in the sink. "Ready for some food?" she asked, with her back to Tess. For some reason, she suddenly felt emotional toward the woman.

I think a better word is attracted, she thought and didn't know what to do about it. *It's all so crazy.*

As if sensing her confusing thoughts, Tess came to stand near her, leaning her hip against the counter. "I am hungry, but what I really want is wine," she answered with a bit of a laugh. When Drew didn't immediately respond, she felt Tess touch her arm. "Are you okay?"

That is a great question, Drew thought. *After all that has happened, why am I feeling so good? Simply because I am near her? How can I possibly be happy after the last twenty-four hours?* Yet, she was and turned to Tess. The woman searched her face. "Today was hard," Drew answered. "For you as much as anyone."

Tess nodded. "Yes, it was," she said. "And I know it's not over. There is clean-up required, and I don't know what has happened to my home." She took another step closer until they were nearly chest to chest. "But right here, right now, I'm grateful to be alive. Grateful that everyone is safe, and honestly, all I want to focus on is you."

Swallowing hard, feeling a million emotions, Drew had things she wanted to say on her tongue, but the words would not come out. As an author nothing could be more frustrating. Clearly sensing her struggle, Tess touched her cheek with her fingertips, making warmth spread through Drew's body. Not the passion she had felt at times before, but tenderness. Nothing Tess could have done would have felt more intimate. The longing to put her arms around the woman made Drew ache. *But I'm not sure I'm ready*, she thought and stepped away, changing the subject. "Do you want me to turn on the news? Maybe find out more on those fires in Beverly Hills." She started toward the living room.

"Drew, don't," Tess said, her voice soft but enough to make Drew stop. She looked at her. "I don't want to watch the news. I don't want to think about any of it. Not right now." Undeterred by Drew's constant running away, Tess closed the distance between them again. "What I want is to go out on your deck and watch the sky lighten as a new day comes. Do you?"

Turning to look, Drew noticed the clouds from the last few days had disappeared completely. The night's stars had faded, and the sky changed to morning. Drew bit her lip and stopped to listen to her heart for once. Tess mattered to her and made her feel special. No one else had ever done that. "Yes, I want to," she finally whispered, answering Tess as well as her own thoughts. Drawing on a different kind of bravery, Drew took Tess's hand and pulled her closer. "And I also want to try with you. Can you be patient while I figure myself out?"

"I can," Tess murmured as their eyes met. "For as long as you need."

Drew read nothing but warmth and sincerity in Tess's eyes. "Thank you," she said before leaning in to kiss her.

32

The only thing that made Ashley turn off the water in the steaming hot shower was the fact she didn't want to use all the hot water before Bryce and Drew had a chance. *But that doesn't mean I won't be taking a second one*, she thought. Ashley wasn't sure how long it would take to get the smell of smoke out of her long hair, but at least she felt clean. While she was in the shower, Drew had been nice enough to knock on the bathroom door to tell her she laid out shorts and t-shirts for her and Bryce. As she wrapped herself in a towel, she thought about Drew. The woman was remarkable for a lot of reasons. The way she could take control of a situation and somehow make things work out was genuinely incredible. But the thing about Drew she liked the most was how she looked at her mom. *And how my mom looks at her.*

Although her mom dated off and on while Ashley was growing up, there was never anyone serious and definitely not a woman. Tess simply hadn't seemed interested in the celebrity dating scene, and when she did venture out, nothing ever came of it but a few photos for the paparazzi. There were times growing up when Ashley worried about her mom's lack of a partner. She wanted her mother to be happy, but then she would chalk up their relationship troubles as something in their DNA. Ashley's ability to find a good fit was no better. *Until a week ago*, she thought. Out of nowhere Bryce and Drew had come into their lives. *And at precisely the right time*.

As she slipped out of the bathroom and saw the clothing on the bed, there was a light knock on the door. "Hello?" Ashley asked, picking up the blue T-shirt.

"It's me," Bryce said. "Is it okay if I come in?"

Ashley slipped the shirt over her head. "One second, hold on." Usually, she wouldn't be shy about running around naked in front of Bryce, but she wanted to be respectful in Drew's home. She pulled on the shorts. "Okay, you can come in." The clothes were baggy, but they were soft and clean. Under the circumstances, they felt wonderful.

Stepping inside the room, Bryce smiled, clearly enjoying her outfit. "Looks like you loved that shower," Bryce said. "How are you feeling?"

"Hungry and thirsty," Ashley replied, returning the smile. Stepping forward, she pecked Bryce on the lips. "I'm off to find nourishment. Did you save me any mac and cheese?"

Bryce nodded. "Plenty," she said. "Although I plan to go back for seconds soon. Beer is in the fridge too."

With a moan of pleasure, Ashley turned to go. "Then you hop in the shower while I go check out the kitchen."

"Music to my ears," Bryce said, already heading toward the bathroom.

Walking down the hall to the kitchen, Ashley paused when she saw her mom standing with Drew out on the deck. They had their arms around each other as they stared at the water. She stopped and appreciated the scene. Romantic and tender and more than what she could ever hope for when it came to her mom.

. . .

STRIPPING TO HER UNDERWEAR, Bryce was about to turn on the shower water when she heard her cell phone ringing. It was in the pocket of her jeans in a pile on the floor. She was slightly shocked that the thing wasn't dead after all that had happened. Pulling it free, she looked at the screen and saw her company commander from the Marine Corps calling her. *He must be worried about me after hearing about the earthquake*, she thought. *I need to answer.*

Walking out of the bathroom to sit on the edge of the bed, Bryce answered. "Good morning, sir."

"Corporal Cooper," the man said, relief in his voice. "I've been trying to get a call to connect for hours. All kinds of things are coming over the wire about an earthquake in Los Angeles, and the accounts of devastation are staggering. Are you still in the area?"

"Yes, sir," Bryce said. "I'm still here, and the reports are correct. It is quite the disaster."

"Does that mean you were near some of the damage?" Captain Roberts asked.

"I was, sir," Bryce answered. "It's been a very long day." *And that's an understatement*, Bryce thought. "I'm in a safe place for the moment, but I don't know how long I'll be here." She didn't elaborate, and there was a pause on the line. Bryce waited to hear what the man was going to say.

Captain Roberts cleared his throat. "Corporal, we want you back. I know you've been through a very long few months with the passing of your father and these catastrophes in Southern California. But the Marine Corps needs you."

Bryce nodded even though he couldn't see her. She had a huge decision to make, and she couldn't put it off much longer. "I promise to call you within the next forty-eight hours, sir," Bryce answered. "And let you know what I'm going to do."

Again, there was a long pause, and Bryce guessed he didn't like what she told him. Then he sighed. "You're a good Marine, Corporal, but you have to follow your own path," Captain Roberts said. "If you want to talk things over, call me anytime. You need to know you have a family here."

Bryce felt a lump form in her throat at the man's kind words. "Thank you, sir," Bryce answered.

"I look forward to hearing back from you," the captain said and hung up. In complete frustration, Bryce flopped back onto the bed and put her forearm over her eyes to block out the world. *What am I going to do?* she thought. She was at the most significant crossroads of her life. Coming back to see Ashley had turned out to be a wonderful decision. Even though they had been through a lot, the events only made Bryce like her more. She felt a great connection and knew they had a future if she wanted one. *But then there is the Marine Corps.* The decision seemed impossible.

As she lay there, she suddenly thought about her father and wondered what advice he would give her. She heard his voice in her head, and a sad smile crossed her face. "You always wanted to be a Marine, Bryce," he would have said. The words were valid. With time, she believed she could love Ashley, but the honor of serving her country was something she wasn't sure she could walk away from right now.

SNEAKING a plate full of macaroni and cheese, Ashley was about to return to the bedroom when she heard the patio door open. "We see you," her mom called. "Don't rush off."

Pausing in the kitchen, she waited for them to come around the corner. "Are you sure? Ashley asked with a smile. "I don't want to interrupt anything again." The two women walked into the kitchen, and Drew had a hint of a blush at the comment, but Ashley was glad to see her smiling too.

"We were only enjoying the morning air," Tess said with a wink. "Where is Bryce?"

Ashley nodded toward the hall. "Hit the shower."

"That sounds like a perfect thing to be doing," Drew said. "I'm heading that way myself."

"It's a life-altering experience after everything," Ashley said as Drew left the room. Once she was gone, Ashley hugged her mom. They held each other for a full minute, not saying a word, and when Ashley finally stepped back, they both had tears in her eyes. "I love you, Mom. I couldn't have made it through today without you."

Tess took Ashley's face in her hands and kissed her forehead. "The same for me," she said. "I love you so much. And now, you know what? I think we should share a bottle of wine."

Ashley raised her eyebrows. "I see nothing wrong with that," she said. "Because honestly, I could not tell you what time it is if I couldn't see it's light outside." She groaned. "It feels like I've been awake forever."

"We sort of have," Tess said, going to the refrigerator and fishing out a bottle of white wine. "Help me find some glasses." Ashley opened a cupboard with a pathetic number of non-perishables inside before moving to the next one and finding what she looked for. Taking down two glasses, Tess opened the bottle and poured them a healthy share. Picking her glass up, Ashley sat at the kitchen table and appraised her mother. Even though it had been an unbelievably hard twenty-four hours, she looked happy.

It must have to do with Drew, Ashley thought as she took a sip. "So, do you want to talk about Drew?" Ashley asked, and Tess playfully narrowed her eyes.

"Maybe," she answered. "What do you want to talk about?"

Ashley looked at the ceiling, trying to find the words. "Just that the two of you seem to be... I'm not sure. She's very shy about stuff."

Tess nodded. "She is," she replied. "But I'm willing to be patient."

"Good. I think she's worth it. She seems pretty wonderful."

"I agree," Tess said, taking a sip of her wine before tilting her head and giving her daughter an appraising look. "Now, how about we talk about Bryce?"

Ashley raised an eyebrow. "What do you want to talk about?"

"She is a remarkable young woman," Tess said. "And honestly, I don't know if we would all be here in one piece without her."

Ashley smiled, a warmth grew inside her as she thought about Bryce and all she did for everyone. "Yes, she is my heroic Marine," Ashley said.

Tess raised an eyebrow. "That leads me to another question," she said. "Is she still a Marine? Won't she have to go back?"

Ashley looked at her wine glass while considering the question. "I'm not sure," she answered. "But maybe it's time I asked. Right now." Standing, she kissed her mom on the cheek before disappearing down the hall to the bedroom. The door was ajar, so she slipped inside only to see Bryce still sitting on the bed in her sports bra and boxers. She was holding her cell phone in her hand. "What's wrong?" Ashley sat beside her on the bed.

Bryce shook her head. "Nothing is really wrong," Bryce replied. "But I need to tell you some things."

Ashley was not sure she liked the sound of her comment but wanted to hear Bryce out. "Okay, I'm listening."

Bryce set the phone beside her on the bed and then turned to face Ashley. She took her hands, meeting her eye. "Actually," she started. "I haven't told you, but ever since I met you in college years ago, I have thought about you probably every day. And most especially when times in my life were hard."

"Bryce…" Ashley started, but Bryce shook her head.

"Let me continue," she said. "I'm crazy about you, and you are the only reason I came back to Los Angeles." Bryce hesitated but then seemed to gather her courage. "And when I realized there could be something between us, I felt like I won the lottery."

Ashley nodded slowly. "I feel like that too," she said. "Why are you telling me all this right now?"

Bryce looked down at their joined hands. "I got a call from my company commander," she said. "He'd been trying to call me for hours, but the lines were down. Ashley, they want me to come back to the Marine Corps."

"Look at me, Bryce," Ashley said, squeezing her hands. "Are you telling me that I'm going to be a long-distance girlfriend?" She smiled. "Because I'm okay with that if it's what you want."

Slowly, Bryce lifted her head. "You're sure?" she asked, and Ashley nodded.

"I want you in my life, Bryce," she said. "Whatever that looks like."

Pulling her closer, Bryce kissed her gently on the mouth. "I want that too," she murmured. "Whatever that looks like."

EPILOGUE

*O*ne year later.

Sitting at the makeup table under the bright lights, Ashley carefully applied her makeup. She wanted to look extra special tonight because it was an important evening. Tonight, Ashley was her mother's guest at the Academy Awards. "I'm so excited I can barely keep my hand still," Ashley said, looking into the mirror while holding her mascara brush.

She heard Bryce laugh over Facetime on the cell phone propped on the shelf. "Don't poke your eye out," she said as Ashley worked on one lid.

"Are you giving me makeup advice, Bryce?" she asked, leaning back in her chair to appraise herself in the mirror.

"Absolutely not, Bryce said. "I think you look great without it."

Ashley turned toward the camera on the phone. "Oh really?" Ashley said, giving the woman her most dazzling smile.

She watched Bryce's eyebrows shoot up. "Whoa," Bryce said. "You are a knockout."

Tilting her head, Ashley appreciated the comment but

couldn't help teasing her girlfriend. "Now you like me better with makeup?" Ashley asked. Bryce held up her hands and leaned away from the camera, not saying another word. She was smart enough to leave that question alone. Ashley laughed. "I'm teasing you." Fluffing her hair in the mirror, Ashley turned her head back and forth to see every angle. The likeness to her mother was uncanny. *The red carpet will go crazy over it, I'm sure,* she thought. *Can't be helped.*

"I'm only glad I could change around my duty schedule so I can watch the ceremony," Bryce said. "Only took two six-packs to find a volunteer."

"Thank you for doing that," Ashley said. "I know that must've been a little bit more difficult than you're saying." Ashley didn't quite understand what Bryce did in Japan where she was stationed, but she missed her every day. *At least we have technology in our favor,* she thought. Most days they could Facetime, sometimes multiple times a day. Other days, Bryce was unavailable for a week or so, and she wondered what she did, but they could never talk about it. *All part of being a Marine's girlfriend.*

"How is Drew holding up?" Bryce asked, interrupting Ashley's thoughts.

She looked at Bryce. "Drew is a little overwhelmed," Ashley admitted. "At least my mom was nominated once before so she had some idea what to expect, but awards season is a lot to handle."

Bryce nodded. "Drew doesn't like to be in the spotlight," she said. "Unless she's in her role as a nurse and then she takes charge. It's amazing how she can be so incredibly confident in an emergency but so shy the rest of the time."

Ashley sighed. "True. Well, at least she's working things through with mom. They have never seemed happier."

"Any chance they are going to move in with each other sometime soon?"

"I hope so," Ashley said. "But it won't be until they're willing to come out about the relationship. Mom says she doesn't care what happens, but Drew is worried about Mom's career." There was the sound of someone speaking to Bryce off camera. "I got to go, babe," Bryce said. "I'll be watching."

As camera flashes went off all around them, Tess held Ashley's arm while they stood posing on the red carpet outside of the Dolby Theater in Hollywood. Award season had been exciting but crazy. *Maybe crazier than last time*, Tess thought. *It seems like after the earthquake and all the reconstruction, people have a renewed energy for life.* That included anything to do with entertainment. Thankfully, Ashley was a trooper and accompanied her to the many events. And although she loved being there with Ashley, she missed Drew and wanted to be holding onto her arm instead. They had come a long way over the last year. Drew was relaxed around Tess, and they spent most nights together. Plus, she was also no longer shy when Ashley came to dinner, and Tess would show affection. *But we still have a long way to go.* Even though Tess didn't care who found out about them and didn't think it would have much of an effect on her career, Drew was concerned. Not for herself but for Tess. She didn't want to be the one who kept Tess from getting future roles. Once again, Tess reminded herself to be patient and let Drew take the lead. *It will all happen when she is ready.*

"So why aren't you in the movies, Ashley?" the reporter interviewing them before the live cameras asked, bringing Tess back to the moment. "You and your mother are both so beautiful and look so much alike. Agents must beg you to consider it."

"Thank you," Ashley said, giving her a megawatt smile

that truly did make her look like Tess. "But I'm not interested in the entertainment business. That's my mom's area of expertise."

The reporter pursed her lips. "Then what do you do?" she asked.

Incredibly proud of her daughter, Tess squeezed Ashley's arm and answered for her. "She is rebuilding on the Venice Beach boardwalk. Not only her original coffee shop but Ashley is helping the entire effort to rebuild and revitalize the location."

"Wow," the reporter said. "That's a big task."

Watching her, Tess saw the excitement in Ashley's eyes over the project. "I could not be more energized about the new development," Ashley said. "Landish Coffee will be back in business by the end of next month, and I hope people will be excited to come to the grand opening."

"We will have to visit," the reporter said, turning back to Tess. "So, how much impact do you think saving the life of State Senator Chamberlain had on your nomination?" Tess shook her head. When she and Linda had been chatting while the woman lay buried under the concrete, she never mentioned her last name or explained who she was. It wasn't until later when there were headlines in the newspaper about the heroics of Tess Landish that she even knew.

The news started a flurry of interviews where Tess recounted the actions of that day. "First, I didn't save her life. Others did that. As for the impact on my nomination, I'm not sure," Tess answered. "But Linda and I are very close friends now, and that makes me happy." Just then, a black limousine pulled up, and Tess watched Drew step out. She looked fantastic in her cream Armani suit, taking Tess's breath away.

Working hard not to stare but apparently not well enough, the reporter waved in Drew's direction. "You must be excited for your friend. What was it like working with her on this amazing film?"

Tess smiled. "It was life changing."

SITTING NEXT to Ashley in the auditorium's audience, Drew worked hard to keep her hands from tapping on the armrests. She was never more nervous than at that moment, and she wished she could be closer to Tess. Holding her hand for reassurance would make all the difference. Yet Drew insisted they let Ashley sit between them. *If I was beside her, it would be impossible not to reach for her*, Drew thought. *And I can't do that to her career*, especially since the movie swept the awards, including the best actress for Tess. When Drew saw the woman up on stage tearfully accepting her award, Drew thought her heart would burst with pride. It was hard to believe that talented, beautiful, and loving woman wanted her, but she learned to accept it over the last year.

Finally, the next award coming up was Best Writing, Adapted Screenplay. It was the one she was nominated for tonight. Although everyone from the cast and crew sent her notes and reassured her that she would win, Drew could not quite believe it. Everything about the book had seemed like a dream, and eventually she had to wake up. *And it could start with tonight,* she thought as she sat and watched the two actors on the stage read off the names of the writers nominated. Drew held her breath, and for a moment, she heard nothing, and then Ashley was grabbing her with excitement. Only then did it register they had said her name. Rising from her seat, she felt Ashley hug her, and then she was in the arms of Tess. The place she loved to be, and every instinct wanted her to kiss her, but Drew kept her reserve and pulled away.

Tears were running down Tess's cheeks. "I'm so proud of

you," she mouthed over the applause. Then as if by magic, Drew found herself walking up the stairs to the microphone. Amazed that she didn't stumble, she looked over the audience under the bright lights, finally realizing everything wasn't a dream and her life was real.

Clearing her throat, she began to speak. "When I started my book over ten years ago, I never imagined it would be published, let alone made into a movie that people wanted to watch. That part I could not have done alone, and I want to thank…" She listed the names of those who helped make the movie, and then she paused, her heart racing. Taking a deep breath, she looked at Tess. The woman covered her mouth with her hands and looked back. She started to nod, and Drew smiled. "And most of all, I would like to thank Tess Landish. Not only because she made my character come to life but because she supported me through all of this—as my girlfriend. Tess, thank you so much for being patient. I love you."

THE END

ABOUT THE AUTHOR

Bestselling author KC Luck writes action adventure, contemporary romance, and lesbian fiction. Writing is her passion, and nothing energizes her more than creating new characters facing trials and tribulations in a complex plot. Whether it is apocalypse, horror, or a little naughty, with every story, KC tries to add her own unique twist. She has written over a dozen books (which include *The Darkness Series* and *Everybody Needs a Hero*) and multiple short stories across many genres. KC is active in the LGBTQ+ community and is the founder of the collective iReadIndies.

KC Luck is always thrilled to hear from her readers at kc.luck.author@gmail.com

THANK YOU!

Enjoy this book?
You can make a big difference

Honest reviews of my books help bring them to the attention of other readers. If you've enjoyed this story, I would be incredibly grateful if you could spend a couple minutes leaving a review (it can be as short as you like) on the book's Amazon and Goodreads pages.

ALSO BY KC LUCK

Rescue Her Heart

Save Her Heart

Welcome to Ruby's

Back to Ruby's

Darkness Falls

Darkness Remains

Darkness United

Wind Dancer

Darkness San Francisco

The Lesbian Billionaires Club

The Lesbian Billionaires Seduction

The Lesbian Billionaires Last Hope

Venandi

What the Heart Sees

Everybody Needs a Hero

Can't Fight Love

IREADINDIES

iReadIndies

This author is part of iReadIndies, a collective of self-published independent authors of sapphic literature. Please visit our website at iReadIndies.com for more information and to find links to the books published by our authors.